Please renew or return items by the date shown on your receipt

www.hertfordshire.gov.uk/libraries

Renewals and enquiries: 0300 123 4049

Textphone for hearing or 0300 123 4041
speech impaired users:

L32 11.16

D0259861

Dear Reader,

In many myths of the American first peoples, the Coyote is 'Trickster'. Coyotes are wily and resourceful ... I've always liked to watch them. Their eyes are beautiful and clever. Their feet pick their way delicately. Their fur, in the winter especially, is thick and gorgeously multi-toned.

Since the first European settlers, coyotes have been relentlessly hunted. They still are. In many US states, it is legal to kill coyotes any time of year ... and hunters can use any method they'd like. Coyotes are trapped, shot, lured, poisoned, and snared. They have been persecuted for over 200 years.

Yet, in spite of all that, they've actually expanded their territory and increased their population.

There are more coyotes now than when the Pilgrims first landed on the continent.

I just love knowing that.

I hope you enjoy this story. I also hope that you take some of that coyote spirit for yourself. Remember: What is beautiful and wild in you can never be stopped.

Mimi Thebo

For my family

OXFORD
UNIVERSITY PRESS

Great Clarendon Street, Oxford OX2 6DP
Oxford University Press is a department of the University of Oxford.
It furthers the University's objective of excellence in research, scholarship,
and education by publishing worldwide. Oxford is a registered trade mark
of Oxford University Press in the UK and in certain other countries

British Library Cataloguing in Publication Data

Data available

ISBN: 978-0-19-275943-6

3 5 7 9 10 8 6 4 2

Printed in Great Britain

Paper used in the production of this book is a natural,
recyclable product made from wood grown in sustainable forests.
The manufacturing process conforms to the environmental
regulations of the country of origin.

Coyote Summer

MIMI THEBO

OXFORD
UNIVERSITY PRESS

CHAPTER ONE

Halfway down the M4 motorway, Mum turned off her phone.

She hadn't really spoken to me since she'd arrived at my school that morning, and she certainly hadn't listened to me. Stefan was driving us in the big, black car. It whispered along the damp tarmac. I could hear myself breathe.

Mum only turned off her phone for two reasons: to play with me or to lecture me. I knew she wasn't starting a round of car bingo.

Outside my window were soft green hills. Sheep. A rook flying out of a hedgerow. A low grey sky. The pointy bit of a church and then the rest of it, with low grey houses huddled around it. England, basically.

I turned to look at Mum, who had folded her arms. Her blue eyes were bright and hard and not as light as they'd been in the headmaster's office. She was chewing on her bottom lip.

'It wasn't my fault,' I tried to explain again, but she put up one manicured hand. She kind of flips it up and bows her head a little at the same time. There was no point in talking once Mum had put her hand up like that. All over the world, the entire oil industry knew not to talk to my mother once she'd put her hand up like that. Even the Russians don't bother any more.

I stopped trying to explain.

Nobody had listened. The headmaster hadn't, which is why I'd been expelled. And getting expelled is why Mum and the company driver came to get me in the middle of term. And Mum and Stefan coming to get me was why I was going to get the lecture.

I hated Mum's lectures. They always started the same way, '*When I was a girl in Kansas...*'

Mum finally spoke to me. 'When I was a girl in Kansas,' she said.

I sighed. It just came out. And she shot me a look that could have melted the glass in the window.

'When I was a girl in Kansas,' Mum said again, very firmly, 'One of us sisters was hand-raising a runt pig.'

I had to turn and look out the window again, quickly, because I nearly giggled. It was 'runt pig'. Mum gets very American in times of stress, but that phrase was too much.

Mum continued, 'If you raised a runt pig by hand, they would usually live, and then you could sell them. You could get quite a lot of money for a grown hog, back then, and the rest of the family would have given her half that money for herself.'

Despite myself, and despite the whole 'runt pig' thing, I was getting interested. I knew better, because this was a lecture about back on the family farm in Kansas, and something horrible would happen soon, but I couldn't help getting interested.

'But,' Mum said. 'The sister was busy with schoolwork and other things and kept forgetting to feed the baby pig

2

and clean out its little pen. The other sisters reminded her a few times, but then Mom told them to stop.'

She looked at me, and I looked back.

'The piglet died,' she said. 'And the sister learned that her actions had consequences.'

Oh, God. Poor baby piglet. That really *was* horrible. Probably the most horrible one I'd heard so far.

I could barely remember my grandmother. My aunties had visited more, but I kind of remembered them as interchangeable large, tanned women with big voices. Together, they'd let a defenceless baby pig die, just to teach one of them a lesson. Hideous.

The lectures were always hideous. One sister was always messing up. The rest were giving her tough love to help her straighten out. I was surprised they'd all *survived* their childhoods, let alone become so successful. I'd heard the story a hundred times: when Grandpa died and Grandma was left on the farm with four girls—two of them still in primary school, she'd come home from the funeral, cut off her long hair and started farming the land herself. Sometimes I thought all the sisters had done so well just so they could keep their hair.

None of them had become as successful as Mum, of course.

She'd been looking out her window and gulping a bit. The lectures about Kansas and her family always left her emotional. I looked out, too, just to see where we were—at the turning for Slough. We were nearly at Heathrow. Soon we'd be home in London.

It felt weird not being in school. I couldn't quite believe I wouldn't be going back. I could imagine the faces of all my friends, could picture Sophia in class, chewing on her pen top to help her think, Izzy filing her nails under the desk while keeping an 'I'm so interested' look on her face. Hurtling down the M4, I kept smoothing my uniform skirt over my knees and thinking, 'this is the last time I'll do this,' and trying to feel sad.

But really, I couldn't wait to be home, to be back in our London townhouse. Four floors of luxury. My games. The telly room. My Jacuzzi. Marta's cakes. Bliss. No more six a.m. wake-ups. No more getting told off for every little thing.

The Slough exit went by and Mum finally got control of herself and said, 'You have to learn that your actions have consequences, too.' Her big blue eyes were shaded and still. 'We both do,' she added. 'Because if you could hurt someone as badly as Archie is hurt—'

I wasn't having that. 'I *didn't* hurt him! It wasn't *my* fault! He *slipped*!' Why wasn't anyone hearing me?

Mum's eyes darkened more and narrowed. 'And whose idea was it to climb out on the roof in the first place? And who dared Archie to do it, shaming him, and telling him that he would never, and I quote, "grow a pair and start shaving until he could stop being such a wussy girly freak?"'

That would be mine and me. Maybe, I suddenly thought, maybe it had been a bit my fault. I slumped down. A hard, hot thing landed in my chest. Shame.

'Both his legs are broken in two places. He's going into surgery right now, because they think he ruptured his *spleen*. Judith was on the phone to me in the middle of the night, crying, because he *hadn't regained consciousness*. Thank God he has, now. Thank God he will probably be okay. Thank God he doesn't have a brain injury. *That boy could have **died**, Jules.*'

Sweet little Archie.

It was like getting hit, hard, somewhere right in the middle of me. I suddenly realized why none of my friends had answered my texts. Why I'd been expelled. Why Mum had chewed a layer of skin off her bottom lip and had turned off her phone to lecture me, right in the middle of a big negotiation. Stefan's eyes caught mine, briefly, in the rear view mirror and then kind of slid away. So he'd already known, too.

Everyone would blame me. I closed my eyes, just to avoid Mum's and Stefan's, but when I did, I saw last night: Archie's white, panicked face and his fingers, scrabbling at the wet roof tiles. I snapped my eyes back open again.

We were turning into Heathrow. Why were we turning into Heathrow?

'As I was saying,' Mum said, 'if you could do something like that, then it's not just you who has failed, it's me, too.'

This was a huge deal. My mother doesn't fail at *anything*.

She said, 'I've really enjoyed being your mother. I know we don't have a great deal of time together, but I've tried to make what time we have count. I did a lot of research before I sent you to that particular school, just like I did before I hired Gloria, or sent you to Skerne, or...' she kind of trailed off.

Mum. She'd outsourced my childhood.

'...maybe I should have spent more time with you,' she said softly.

You think? I nearly said it out loud. But what was the use? I'd said it before, loads of times. I just looked at her.

She sighed again. And then she took my hand. Hers was cool and soft and mine felt hot and sticky. She undid her belt and slid over and cuddled me. When you've really messed up, and you get a cuddle, it means so much, you know? It means that although you're an idiot, you can still be loved. I held onto her and tried not to sniffle.

She held me tight and said, 'Ever since you didn't make it into the Royal Ballet School...'

Seriously? I thought. *Must* we? I pulled away. 'When are you going to give it a rest, Mum? It's not about that. *Nothing* is about that.'

So I didn't get into *ballet school*. Most people who try out for it *don't* get into the Royal Ballet School. The ratio is ridiculous. I didn't even really *want* to go.

Everybody keeps talking about *ballet school*. It's been over a year, it doesn't matter to me *at all* and just I wish they'd shut up about it.

Mum didn't slide back to her side. She sat in the middle and twisted her ring. Finally, she looked up. She said, 'Look, Jules. We have to face it. You've been different since you failed the audition.'

You *failed*. That's a nice thing to keep hearing from your mother. You *failed*, I *failed*, you *failed more*. I looked out the window, wishing I could jump through the glass and run away, right across the roads and onto the airstrips. I would run and run across the whole of Heathrow Airport and through the fences at the other end, and keep going. I'd never, ever stop.

'I don't know what to do with you any more.' Mum had never known what to do with me. That's why she'd outsourced my childhood. I'd been a surprise, a mistake, an inconvenience all my life.

'So, I'm sending you where I *know* you'll get what you need. I'm sending you home to Kansas.'

'*WHAT?*'

I shouted before I thought. I was so horrified that I— it just…God, I wished I hadn't shouted. Shouting at my mother was so *stupid*.

Shouting at my mother always shut her face down, hard. I looked and it was already like that. Her fine eyebrows were drawn together tight and she had that crease between her eyes, deep, deep.

'No,' I begged. 'Please, no,' although I knew, from looking at her face, that it was already too late.

'You've never even *been* there,' Mum said, in a hard, bright, cheerful voice. She had disappeared behind her professional shell. Nothing got through that shell.

Stefan pulled up outside Terminal 3, jumped out and opened my door. He and Mum seemed to be moving much faster than I was…I nearly fell onto the pavement.

As I scrambled to stand, he briskly loaded my cases onto a trolley. Mum handed a folder to a vaguely familiar blonde girl in a smart suit and thanked her.

'Bethany will explain and help you pack,' Mum said.

'Mum, no!' She hugged me again and I held onto her. She felt good to me again. She felt amazing. Warm and soft and firm at the same time. She smelled wonderful.

I begged again. 'Don't do this. Please.'

People were looking. I must have been louder than I thought. Oh, and I had started to sniffle, too.

My mother pushed me away from her, gently, but firmly. She cupped my cheek in her hand for a moment. Her blue eyes were nearly navy with emotion and I knew how upset I'd made her. I hated that—I hated that she was making me go, I hated that I had to leave her, I hated that I'd made her upset and I hated that she'd called me a failure. I hated everything about that moment.

And then that moment was gone. I was just standing there, watching the car roll smoothly away. Mum didn't even look back.

By the time Bethany had taken me to the private lounge, my head felt like it, too, was full of low grey cloud. There was a buzzing in my ears and I felt a long way away from my body.

I was very obedient in this state. I handed over my blazer and my phone. I put on a t-shirt and jeans and socks and trainers and Bethany passed me a cardigan.

My tablet, my computer, my Bluetooth speaker and my school kit went into our monogrammed cases with my blazer and school shoes—it was easy to see they would all be going home without me. A big plastic rolling case I'd never seen before got packed with pants and bras and jeans and t-shirts and bikinis and shorts and jumpers and the waterproof jacket I would normally only wear at Skerne Lodge or if we were going walking. Some cotton summer dresses I'd never seen and didn't much like went into that case with new sandals, in a soft brown suede that matched the cashmere cardigan I'd been handed.

The whole time, Bethany kept up a running monologue. I'd once told Mum she was nice...so now she was apparently in charge of my life.

She dropped a word that made my inner clouds clear. Abruptly, I had a working brain. 'What was that?' I asked. 'Economy class?'

Bethany pushed in my sponge bag and zipped up my new case and then turned. 'Your Auntie Margaret said that she'd have you on one condition...that she be completely in charge of you. Including paying your expenses.'

Margaret was the one who'd taken over running the family farm. I could vaguely remember her—dark hair.

Bethany grimaced. 'I think you're going to have a bit of a lifestyle change.'

Someone came to collect all the monogrammed cases and I got to watch a stranger roll my entire life away.

We crossed the terminal to enter an enormous queue. Bethany took the money and cards out of my purse and put in twenty dollars. She looked critically at the big handbag I'd used for my books at school. 'That's ridiculously expensive,' she said. 'It's going to stand out a mile, but there's nothing we can do about it, now.'

She took out her phone and started answering emails.

I had literally nothing to do because *I had no phone*. I looked in my bag and there was nothing in there but a pack of tissues, my make-up bag and a hairbrush. Oh, and the purse that contained a whole twenty dollars. I wished I had the grey cloud back inside my head again.

I had literally nothing.

I rolled my case along by infinitesimal bits—the guy in front of me was so slow—and tried to understand how this had happened.

Last night, I had been at school. We'd had risotto for dinner and a nice salad. We'd gone to the Common Room to study and Mr Blake had gone to get his marking. I'd opened the window and climbed out on the roof. I'd done it before. I'd gotten all the way to the next window and had ditched study time and the teacher hadn't even noticed…

And now my entire life was gone.

I didn't, I suddenly realised, even have *pictures* of my friends or Mum, or any of my life. I didn't have any way of getting in touch with anyone. It was like I had never existed.

That thought made me feel cold right through my body, like I was actually standing in a snowfield in just a t-shirt and jeans. My hot, shamed heart turned into a block of ice and I got goosebumps down my arms.

I pulled on my cardigan, but it wasn't even *my* cardigan. It was a cardigan I'd never even seen before.

'Here,' Bethany said. We were right at the front of the queue and she gave me my ticketing information and my American passport. I usually used my British one. I flipped it open.

Julia Evelyn Percy. There was my birthday. There was the way I'd looked when I was twelve. Black hair, brown skin, brown eyes. Even though I had been told not to smile, I looked a lot happier in the photograph than I did now.

I had eight greasy and uncomfortable hours in the air, then my cousin Vicky helped me get from JFK to La Guardia in New York. She lectured me the whole way across New York City.

I knew Vicky better than I knew her mum or my other aunts… or anyone else in my family. She'd had a year of study abroad in England and had practically lived with us.

I must have looked as sad as I felt, because she took a break from telling me how stupid I was to tell me not to worry. 'Mom is never unfair,' she said. 'She's tough, but if you do right by her, she'll do right by you.'

I had no idea how to 'do right by' anybody, and this must have showed on my face, because Vicky rolled her big brown eyes and started ticking things off on her manicured fingers. 'Don't lie, like you do when Marta asks you where the cake went.'

I started to protest, but Vicky talked over me. 'Don't cheat, like you do in basketball.'

I couldn't argue with that one. Vicky was wearing a smart black dress. Her hair was straight and shining and her bare brown legs ended in nice court shoes. When she'd been at our house, she'd lived in flannel pyjama bottoms and sweatshirts and had usually shoved her hair into a frizzy ponytail. I really *had* cheated playing basketball. She was so good that she could beat me wearing flip-flops.

'Don't be lazy. Your mother might let you sleep until noon, but mine won't.'

Don't waste money. Don't say you'll do something and not do it. Don't talk back. Don't be sarcastic. Don't try to hide things.

Working backwards from Vicky's list, it was pretty clear my cousin thought I was a lazy, cheating, lying, sarcastic sneak who was spoilt rotten. The year she was with us, I'd made her spicy tomato drinks when she was hung over. I wished now I'd just let her suffer.

I was almost glad to get my next 'Unaccompanied Minor' lanyard and say goodbye, even though the sign they hung from my neck was huge with little planes in primary colours.

Vicky gave me a nasty plastic flip-up phone, hugged me tightly and told me that she loved me.

Why? I wanted to ask. And how could you possibly, if I'm so horrible?

The second plane was even more crowded and greasy. One my right was a window. On my left was an old man reading every word of a big broadsheet newspaper. There was no in-flight entertainment, and I soon discovered that my new phone had nothing...no games, no apps *at all*.

After the excitement of choosing my soft drink and opening my pretzels faded, I felt my eyes pulling shut.

And saw Archie's little face, white with terror, sliding over the wet roof tiles.

I snapped my eyes open again. Both legs broken in two places. In surgery...no, he'd be out by now. That cold and hot heavy thing in my chest hurt again.

I was so tired. My eyes pulled shut.

Archie's face, so white. He didn't scream. His fingernails clicked on the tiles as he tried desperately to hold on. The night was black with clouds. No moon, no stars, just the security light over the edge of the roof and Archie, sliding, sliding.

I felt hot and sweaty under my arms. I felt sick in my stomach and I hurt in that place where I sometimes felt cold and sometimes felt hot. I looked out the window, but I couldn't really see anything. There wasn't anything to see.

I must have slept somehow. I woke up to the whole plane shaking and the engines roaring and had a panicky moment before I realized it was only our landing. It was an old plane and bounced a little, coming down.

The tannoy told us we could switch on our phones, but I hadn't actually switched mine off. Just then, it made a horrendously loud pinging noise. A text from my aunt. I was meant to get my luggage and wait outside.

CHAPTER TWO

I'd been travelling for over 24 hours. I smelled and my hair was coming out of its plait. My whole body felt like it had been squished together in a ball. There were only six or seven of us waiting for checked baggage. Everyone else only had carry-on.

Americans have absolutely no problem stretching their bodies in public. One of my fellow passengers was doing Achilles tendon stretches against a wall. Another one was doing that yoga stretch where you take one arm across your body and pull to release tension in your shoulders.

And something about that, and being sweaty and tired in a crowded little glass box made me think of my old ballet studio.

I quit ballet when...when I didn't get into ballet school. When I'd told my teacher, she'd smiled in her really irritating way and said, 'You'll miss it, you know.'

Well. I hadn't. Not at all. They'd kind of forced me to dance in the school musical and I'd hated every second of it, even though everyone told me how brilliantly I'd done. Except for that, I hadn't thought about dancing at all.

So I had no idea why, all of a sudden, I wanted to do a ballet class.

But I did. I wanted to sweat. I wanted to stretch. I wanted, so badly, to put one foot up on a barre and reach, reach, reach until it hurt.

And that was so typical of me, it wasn't even funny. All that time, living fifteen minutes from some of the greatest ballet studios in the world, and I couldn't be bothered. And now, when my feet had just touched the ground in Kansas, I suddenly *wanted* to take a ballet class.

You know those films where the hero is secretly a trained killer and there's a password that flips him from ordinary person into super? It was like that. Before my toes touched Kansas, I was not interested in dance anymore. Once my toes touched Kansas, I missed it like mad. Someone had whispered in my ear, or sent a message right into my brain and had flipped me back into being a dancer.

It had only been about an hour's sleep, but it was the first I'd had in three days, and somehow, I felt...better. I'd dreamed...something. It had seemed important. I tried to remember what it was about, as I wheeled outside to wait for Auntie Margaret.

The terminal was dwarfed by the huge sky. It was like an enormous blue bowl had been turned upside down over us. Tiny wisps of white cloud rode impossibly high. All the colours were Disney-bright. Neon grass. Crayon sky. A tomato-red car passing by. I fumbled in my bag for sunglasses, but they didn't do much to change the intensity of the light.

I stripped off my cardigan. The warm light sank into the skin on my arms, as if it was claiming me.

Under the huge sky, people walking around looked insignificant. I felt exposed, like anyone could see everything about me in the merciless sun and crystal-clear air. I can't even tell you how many countries I've been to… and a lot of them have been hot. But this felt different, somehow. Something about the sky… I couldn't stop looking at it, even though it hurt my eyes.

I didn't recognize Auntie Margaret, at first. And then I did, and took my case over to her pick-up truck. I waited, I guess for her to get out and hug me and tell me how much I'd grown. Finally, I understood that none of that was going to happen.

She rolled down the window.

I said, 'Hello, Aunt Margaret.'

She said, 'Well. You got here.'

We looked at each other some more. All the sisters look exactly alike and completely different, at the same time. Mum was dark blonde and blue-eyed, but Margaret's hair was so dark that her blue eyes were startling. Mum is… elegant is what the magazines always say, when she's in the society page. Margaret was wearing a checked shirt and her hair was up in the same any-old-way ponytail that Vicky used to wear.

Right before she told me to do it, I realized I should put my case in the back. I hate that. In shops, when you are just about to put your card in the machine and they tell you to put your card in the machine? That just kills me. But that wasn't a problem any longer, I thought, as I wheeled to the back. I didn't have any cards, now.

The new case was big and heavy and I was tired and

I knew I'd better not bang the black wheels all over the silver paintwork of the truck. I was really struggling when Auntie Margaret muttered something under her breath and got out of the truck.

I thought she was going to lift it over the side for me, so I put my case back down.

What she actually did was touch something that lowered the tailgate. I waited, and she looked at me for a minute and then I realized she was waiting for me to lift my case in, so I did.

Auntie Margaret looked at it standing in the back of the truck and looked at me. I had no idea what was wrong. I said, 'What?'

She did that muttering thing again and this time I could hear her say 'Lord, have mercy.' Then she laid my case down flat and tucked it around the bump in the truck bed where the back wheels went, so it wouldn't, I could totally see *now*, roll around and bang into the truck a million times on the drive back to the farm.

I was about to say thank you, but she was already back in the truck, waiting. So instead, I tried to figure out how to put the tailgate back up by myself. I touched about fifteen different bits of black plastic, but I couldn't find the right thing.

She watched me in the rear view window for a little while. Then she got out and pushed the button again and it went back up. We both got into the truck. She looked at me, shook her head, turned up the radio, and pulled out into the sparse traffic.

I'd been to New York several times and Mum had taken me to Disney World in Florida and to Miami on a huge girly shopping trip and spa retreat, just the two of us. We'd been to L.A. and San Francisco, where my Auntie Jan has her school, and then we'd been to Puerto Vallarta in Mexico and skiing at Banff in Canada, if they count.

But I'd never been to the middle bits before. Mum had talked about going and had planned several trips, but we'd never made it.

Now I could see why. There was literally nothing in Kansas.

The country music radio station was horrible. The ads (for help with your problem feet and something you put on your house called 'siding') were just as horrible as the music. Auntie Margaret was driving down a huge motorway and there were no cars, no buildings, no one walking around... just grass and trees and that huge sky.

I was relieved when we saw a cluster of buildings. The emptiness hadn't looked like humans could live there. I'd imagined opening the truck door and being choked by the atmosphere.

Three or four buildings turned into a housing estate and then another one and then, suddenly, we were on the edges of the city... suburbia.

It looked like every American film you've ever seen. Big, new-looking wooden houses as simple as building blocks. So much tarmac and so many traffic islands—huge roads and enormous car parks. The trees looked small, like shrubs. But they weren't. They were normal-sized. It was the scale of everything else. There was so much land that they kind of wasted it.

We made a series of swerves and turns on complicated slip roads and then, suddenly, we were back in nothing again. Auntie Margaret switched off the radio and glanced over at me.

'You're welcome,' she said. 'I've been waiting a half an hour now for you to thank me for picking you up at the airport.'

'Sorry,' I said.

We drove another couple of minutes. 'Oh,' I said. 'Thank you.'

'You're welcome,' she repeated.

The land flattened out more and the buildings got even less frequent. There were these shiny mushroom-shaped metal things every so often.

'What are those?' I asked.

'What?'

I pointed at a white one with a railing. It had District 7 painted on the side. 'That's a water tower,' Margaret said. There was a kindness in her voice that hadn't been there before. 'Haven't you ever seen a water tower?' she asked.

I shook my head, no.

'Sorry,' she said. 'No, really. I'm sorry.' I looked over at her and she reached and patted my knee. 'You remind me so much of your mama. I forget you don't know anything.

You don't know how to put a load in a pick-up truck. You don't know that driving for half a day costs a farmer money because of wasted time. You don't even know what a water tower is!'

She shook her head as if it was the saddest thing she'd ever heard. Really, I'd been quite happy not knowing anything about water towers. I didn't actually want to know about them now. But I knew not to say anything, because being sarcastic would not be 'doing right by' Auntie Margaret.

'You are so much like your mother,' she said. 'It's easy to think you're Lisa Ann.'

My mother's name is Annalise, but evidently she'd been born Lisa Ann, because all my aunties call her that. It's hard to believe, but not as hard to believe as the idea that I look like my mother.

I don't know who my father was, and Mum says she won't tell me until I'm eighteen, so I'm not to bother asking. But I know one thing... he was darker-skinned than my mother and my aunties. I am light brown and go dark brown in about one second of sunlight. That sun on my arms at the airport? They'd be a different colour by morning. My eyes are dark brown and my hair is dark and thick and poker-straight. I have my mother's face shape, but my cheekbones are higher and my nose is fatter.

I cleared my throat because it felt stiff from not talking. I said, 'I didn't think I looked that much like Mum.'

Auntie Margaret smiled. She said, 'That English accent

just kills me.' And then, 'No. You don't look that much like Lisa Ann. But you sure as heck act like her.'

We drove for a few more miles. Now I could see that water towers popped up on the horizon when there was a town on the way. Margaret fiddled with the radio, but didn't turn it on. If I hadn't known so much about her, I would have thought she was nervous.

'Does she talk about us?' she asked. Her voice was hesitant. 'Does she...tell you anything about when we were kids?'

I nodded, suddenly so homesick for my mum that it would have been worth hearing one of her lectures just to be back in England. It seemed a million miles and a hundred years away from our conversation in the back of the Mercedes. I had to clear my throat again, this time because it felt like tears were going down the back of it.

'Yeah,' I said. 'The day I left, she told me about the runt pig.'

'Oh, God,' Margaret said and sighed. 'She let that poor thing die. It was horrible. And Mama would *not* let any of us save it.' Margaret covered her mouth and stared at the highway as if she could still see the dead piglet.

Then she uncovered it. 'Lisa Ann always had to learn everything the hard way,' she said. 'She never could be told.'

I've seen Mum say the same thing in business news interviews. 'I always had to learn the hard way,' she'd say. 'The biggest change I've ever made in my life is learning to listen to what other people have to say.'

Aunt Margaret laughed softly. 'Did she ever tell you

about the time she let the bull go? Or the time she tipped the hay in the ditch?' she laughed a little harder. 'Or what about the one where she went walking in a brown sweater during hunting season and got a seat full of buckshot?'

I nodded. I'd heard all these stories, but they were always, 'One of us sisters.'

'Wait,' I said, as it suddenly clicked. 'Were *all* those stories about *Mum*?'

Margaret nodded, laughing so hard now that she couldn't answer, bubbling over with it.

'The cake without the milk?'

'Lisa Ann,' Margaret said, snorting.

'The homemade dogsled that ended in a broken leg?'

'Lisa Ann!' Margaret wailed.

'Practising casting for trout from a bedroom and breaking the living-room window?'

Margaret's face was red. She was laughing so hard she could barely breathe. She couldn't answer me any more. She just nodded her head, yes.

That hard, hot and then hard, cold thing in my chest kind of melted and eased. All that 'you failed' stuff... W*ell, you failed, too, Mum*, I thought, *over and over*...

'She always said, "one of us sisters",' I told Margaret.

'Well,' she said, catching her breath and wiping her eyes. 'Wouldn't you?'

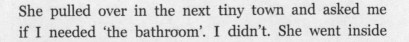

She pulled over in the next tiny town and asked me if I needed 'the bathroom'. I didn't. She went inside something called a 'Tasty Queen' and came out with two absolutely enormous cold drinks.

'Here,' she said, handing me one. It was a coke, ice cold. I don't usually like them that much, but it tasted good. I thanked her and she smiled.

'You're welcome,' she said. 'And I'm sorry again about being a jerk earlier.'

We drove along in silence for a little while, and then she switched the radio back on. She kept saying, 'one of us sisters' to herself and giggling. She turned to me at one point and said, 'Can't wait to tell Karen and Jan,' and giggled some more.

It was funny, I guess, that Mum had never said it was her doing all those things wrong and getting all that punishment. But it was also kind of sad. She must still be ashamed of herself, after all those years, after all she'd accomplished in life. All those failures must still bother her. Because she didn't tell me—she'd hidden that all the stories had been about her. And some of the punishments had been pretty grim. It was a hard way to grow up.

I looked at Auntie Margaret and hoped I wouldn't have to finish growing up that same, grim way.

CHAPTER THREE

We went through a big town called Fort Scott. It had a Walmart and other actual shops. It had a little twee Main Street that looked like Disneyland and an actual old fort. It was obviously a big tourist draw around here... but so was the world's largest ball of twine.

'You'll come back here tomorrow,' Auntie Margaret said. The town seemed to end very suddenly. There were flat buildings in big tarmac car parks and flat buildings in big tarmac car parks and flat buildings in big tarmac car parks. And then there was absolutely nothing again.

Auntie Margaret turned left, the first turn she'd made in literally hours.

I looked out the window at miles and miles of nothing, as far as the eye could see. Fields. The occasional barn or house, or both. It was kind of pretty and it was kind of totally terrible, at the same time. Talking about Mum with Auntie Margaret had made me uncertain about what I felt, too. My insides and the outside—I didn't know if they were okay or not okay. I didn't know if everything was absolutely fine or a hideous disaster. Both could go either way.

Suddenly, the truck slowed to a stop. It wasn't like there was any traffic. My aunt could stop the truck whenever she felt like it. But I wondered why she felt like it right there in the middle of nowhere, and turned to see her looking at me again.

'Julia.'

Her rough hand came to rest on my shoulder. It felt warm, right through my shirt. 'I love you,' she said, totally without embarrassment. Only Americans can do that. Mum can't even do it any more, she's been in England too long. Or maybe that's why she moved there in the first place.

'I love you enough to take you in and raise you like one of my own.' Her soft blue eyes were staring right into mine. 'And that's because I love your mama, too. I always did.' Her face was open. It was so weird how she looked just like Mum and nothing like Mum at all. 'But—'

She looked past me. 'Well!' she said. I turned around to see.

It was a wolf, only not a wolf because there are no wolves in Kansas. I knew that much, so I knew it had to be the animal my Mum called a coyote.

It had thick golden fur and elegant long legs. It was trotting along through grass in a field where cattle were grazing. A huge rabbit hung dead in its jaws. Its big pointed ears rode high on its head and its ruff was fluffy.

'Just like he owned the place and paid the taxes,' Margaret exclaimed.

As if it could hear her, the coyote looked at us for a moment, looked right into my eyes, like my aunt had just moments before, only its eyes were golden and wild. Then it turned its back and trotted over a little ridge in the field and was gone.

'He's beautiful.' I exhaled the words, only then realizing I'd been holding my breath.

'You think?' My aunt put the truck in gear again. 'Well, you'll probably see a lot of them.'

The house was small. There were three bedrooms upstairs and one downstairs and a bathroom up and a shower room down. The dining-room was about as wide as a railway carriage and had patio doors on the other end, leading onto a deck. The patio doors were open.

I left my suitcase by the front door and walked through the house and out the other side onto a wooden deck. I had to slide a flimsy mesh door out of my way to get through. 'Close the screen door,' Auntie Margaret called, 'Or we'll have every bug in the county.' I slid the mesh door shut behind me.

The bright red metal barn had solar panels on top of it. Tractors were parked just beyond the deck. Under the tree was a rope swing and under that, hens clucked and scratched.

It smelled kind of dusty and dirty, but it also smelled green. The sun was still warm. A big man in brown dungarees came around the corner of the barn and opened the door to the chicken house. Some of them went right in, others kept scratching around. He started trying to chase them in.

After watching for a while, I went over. 'Can I help?' I asked. He straightened his back and looked down at me. He was huge—tall and muscled, but also carrying a bit of a belly. He took a minute to look me over, like he was deciding whether or not I was up to the job.

'Sure,' he finally said.

You'd think it would be easy, herding chickens into a hen house. I've done it before at some of my friends' country houses and it *was* easy. But a lot of these chickens just didn't want to go. You'd get behind them and walk with your arms spread out, but one or two would always flutter off to the side. After a few runs, I looked at my Uncle Ethan... at least I *thought* he must be my Uncle Ethan... and I said, 'I don't think they want to go. Can't we just leave them out?'

He made a grunting sound that might have been a laugh. 'Coyotes will get them. Or foxes.' He stood up straight and pointed. 'Had to bury that fence six foot deep,' he said. 'Four foot wasn't doing it.'

We went back to herding chickens and in about five million years, they were all in the coop.

I straightened my own back and looked around at what I could see of the actual farm part of the farm. It was... peaceful, I guess. It also smelled of poo.

I couldn't believe how quickly the light had faded in the time we'd been herding chickens. Then I heard something... I thought at first it was the kind of white noise you get when your phone is too close to your laptop, but it wasn't. It got louder and louder.

My uncle was watching me with an amused look on his face. 'Cicadas,' he said. And then explained. 'Insects.' He measured out about two thirds of the length of his thumb. 'About yay big.'

28

That was *enormous*. 'Ew,' I said. 'Do they fly?'

He nodded and then laughed when I looked around me. Loud giant flying bugs. Lovely.

'Dinner!'

Ethan took me over to the mud door sink and we washed our hands and came into the kitchen that way. Nobody had to tell me to shut the screen door against insects.

My suitcase was still right where I'd left it.

There were mashed potatoes and baby squash in a cream sauce with pork chops. I wasn't stupid and I ate it without complaint, even though it was probably full of butter, as well as cream.

I didn't eat any of the bread, though it looked homemade. I wasn't asked if I wanted a glass of their wine...that looked homemade, too.

Afterwards, I stood up and offered to take in the plates to the kitchen, which I thought was very nice of me. I stacked them by the sink and came back to where my aunt and uncle softly chatted. 'That was delicious,' I said. 'Do you mind showing me my room, now? I'd like to have a bath, if that's okay.'

Auntie Margaret just pointed to my chair.

I had a bad feeling as I sat down. This was, I thought, where the absolutely terrible bit was going to start.

Uncle Ethan reached in his bib overall pocket for his pen. A bit of paper appeared and he wrote down, 'Dinner. $5,' and showed it to me.

'I'm glad you liked your dinner,' Aunt Margaret said.

'I hope you like all your meals. Dinner is five dollars, breakfast and lunch are three dollars each.'

What? Who charges houseguests? And anyway, I didn't have my cards. 'I don't have any money,' I said, and Margaret kind of nodded.

'So you start off five dollars in the hole. I was going to charge you for your plane ticket and the gas and my time for the ride here, but Ethan thought that was going too far. If you decide to pay us back, that's fine, but you don't have to. With the airmiles your mom gave us, the total is two hundred and eighty-eight dollars.'

The narrow dining-room seemed to close in on me. The buttermilk paint on the walls kind of pulsed and swirled. My head hurt...But my aunt and uncle were acting like what they said was perfectly reasonable.

They were going to bill me for looking after me. And Mum probably knew that when she'd sent me.

'You'll be paid minimum wage,' Margaret said. 'In fact, we're going to round it up to eight dollars an hour. So, if you only want your meals, you can work for just an hour and a half a day.'

'Or you can do more,' Ethan said. 'And get more money.'

'You won't *just* work,' Margaret said with a smile. 'You'd go crazy just working on the farm.'

Well, thank goodness for that, I thought. There was a cinema in Fort Scott. And Kansas City was only an hour or two away.

Then she went on. 'I've also signed you up for softball league.'

Softball. That was like rounders. I didn't mind doing sport, but that was stupid sport.

'Of course, you'll go to church on Sunday,' Ethan said. There was no way I was going to church, I thought.

'They hold an under-age disco every two weeks in the summer.'

I couldn't hold it in any longer. It kind of bubbled up out of me. I said, 'Wow. What a great summer. The disco sounds *particularly* good,' in my most sarcastic voice and Margaret looked at me. Her soft blue eyes had suddenly gone hard and bright.

'You'll work, young lady. And you'll go to church,' she said. 'And you'll play ball. And when your uncle tells you something nice he's thought of *for you*, you'll say, "Thank you, Uncle Ethan."'

'Or?' I asked. 'Or what? What more can you all *do* to me? You've dragged me here to the middle of *nowhere* and cut off all my communication with the outside world.' I threw my arms up into the air, 'I'm dirty. I'm tired. Do you call this *parenting*?'

Aunt Margaret looked amused. She said, 'You, Missy, are a special case. You've had everything handed to you on a plate, all your life. And now, just because you didn't get into ballet school—'

I felt myself get hot. 'This is *not about ballet school*,' I shouted.

She acted like she hadn't heard me. '—your grades have gone down the pan and you keep getting into trouble. Last summer, you led five thirteen-year-old girls to sneak out of their houses and meet you *at midnight* to try and get into *a West End night club*. On your fancy-dancy school's away week, you snuck into the boy's dorm and *spent the night in there*. And then you thought it was really funny to hide from all your teachers on a trip to another school for that field hockey you all play. They had to get *the police*. Your mom just about *lost her mind*. She called me and she was *crying*.'

Her words hit like bullets, right in that spot that had cracked open in my mother's car. I put my head down on the table, and covered it with my arms. It was too much. It was all too, too much. I couldn't take any more. I'd completely break apart.

'Now you've nearly *killed a boy*, leading him out onto the school roof, and you've got yourself *expelled from school*. Your mom sent you here because *no other decent school would have you*.'

It hurt. It hurt so badly that thought I might vomit.

'Look at me.'

I raised my head up and rested it on my hands. If I rolled my eyes up, I could see Auntie Margaret and Uncle Ethan. But Uncle Ethan gave me an infinitesimal headshake and so I sat up, properly, even though my middle actually, physically hurt where the cracked bit was.

Margaret's eyes had gone soft and kind-looking again. Her mouth was curled up into a little smile and her shoulders were loose and relaxed. 'Listen,' she said. 'It would be easier for me not to bother with all this. It would be easier for Ethan not to keep track of your balance sheet. We're not doing this *at* you. We're doing it *for* you. You can't keep going in the direction you're going in.'

I knew that already, I thought. I didn't have to come here to learn that. I didn't have to be broken with words.

But evidently, everybody else thought I did.

Aunt Margaret nodded towards the stairs. 'Yours is the white one, just past the bathroom,' she said. 'Holler if you need anything.'

She went to go and clean up the kitchen and I staggered to my feet. I stood there for a moment and watched her move around. Uncle Ethan had gone back outside with the insects and I was there, just myself. Just alone and totally destroyed. Just completely terrible, after all.

With a pang of homesickness so bad it made my throat close, I thought about Marta back home, how we'd leave the kitchen in a tip every night and how it would be all gleaming and smell of lemons in the morning.

I didn't think that Margaret's kitchen would ever gleam or smell of lemons. There was a tangle of barbed wire in the fruit bowl and a big stack of papers stapled together on the corner of the counter.

I took a deep breath, forcing my throat to open again and shoving the homesickness down it. I started to haul my case up the stairs.

If I'd learned anything at all in fourteen years, it's that you have to stay positive. You have to stay positive and have a plan. You have to do *something* to make things better for yourself. Even if it doesn't seem to make any sense to anyone else.

When things look dark, you have to find any little bit of something inside yourself and think about that, concentrate on that.

The smell of lemons reminded me of Tuscany.

We always try and rent this certain villa in Tuscany for August. Mum stays with me the whole month and only works a few hours a day. We swim every morning. We go to galleries and shows and take long drives to the sea. There's a lemon grove nearby and we go to yoga classes there.

I knew we had the villa booked and paid for. It was part of my Christmas present.

It was May. That meant I really only had to survive the farm for three months. If I could make everyone think I'd completely changed, that they'd totally sorted me out, by August I could be doing yoga in the lemon grove.

I could have my life back.

All I had to do was bite my tongue and do what I was told and make everyone think they had fixed me. I'd nearly been obedient at school. And I could be even better at it here. It was only three months. Surely I could do three months.

While I waited for my bath, I tried a little bit of yoga. I was so stiff it was hard to stretch. In fact, I couldn't really do *any* of the stretches I used to be able to do. I extended my leg in a développé—a kind of slow ballet kick—and saw myself frowning in the bathroom mirror. My leg didn't come up anywhere near as high as it used to come up.

I could hear my ballet teacher's voice in my head. *'You never stretch. You never practise. You'll never succeed if you don't stop being so lazy.'*

When I'd quit ballet, I'd quit because I couldn't be bothered to keep trying to get better. I didn't think I'd ever actually get *worse*. But I had. I'd actually got worse.

Keeping positive wasn't easy. It was like eating a big ball of despair. But at last, I got it down.

CHAPTER FOUR

My room was painted white, just like Auntie Margaret had said. There was an old dark brown chest of drawers and a big old dark brown wardrobe. There was a proper armchair in pale green stripes and a handmade quilt, patched in pale flower patterns, on the metal-framed double bed. There was also a fluffy white rug on the wide white floorboards.

The bed was wide, and soft, and squeaked in a kind of comforting way. I was afraid to close my eyes, afraid I'd see Archie's white face again, hear his hands scrabbling at the wet roof tiles. But I finally closed them. And I didn't.

My room didn't have proper curtains or blinds...just some muslin trimmed with old lace at the window. It might have stopped anyone looking in, but it certainly didn't keep any light out.

I woke up so early that I could hear Uncle Ethan putting on water for coffee. In the country, it's never completely quiet—the chickens were complaining, wanting out. There were cows somewhere, and sheep. There were tons of birds, twittering away like mad. But it was country quiet—no cars, no music, no footsteps, no talking. It gave me that 'humans can't survive here' feeling again and made me homesick.

That hurt place in my middle actually ached when I thought about home.

Before I'd thought about it, I was down on the fluffy rug, stretching. Stretching when my muscles were warm and soft and pliable from bed, just like my dance teachers had always urged me to do. Up from my ribcage and down, over my legs. Grab my feet and pull, pull.

I could feel tension being released from the base of my spine. Goodbye, economy seats, I thought. And now, legs wide... I reached up and over, over and... ow! I had lost *so much* extension. I used to be able to get my chest right down on the floor. Horrified, I jumped up and lowered myself into splits.

I'd never been able to do Russian splits, the crossways ones, but I could always do ordinary splits. Only now, I couldn't do *any* splits *at all*. And it hurt, God, it hurt *so badly* to even *try*.

I'd been able to do the splits since I was seven years old. I got up and marched to the bathroom to brush my teeth. Right, I told myself in the mirror. You've got three months. Russian splits in three months. You are *not* allowed to be a failure.

As soon as Auntie Margaret had swallowed her coffee, she was calling to me up the stairs.

I got a fresh t-shirt and jeans out of the case and some new socks for my trainers. I brushed my hair, put on some light make-up and called that dressed. Good enough for Kansas, anyway.

Going down the stairs, I could still feel the pull in my

legs and thighs. I thought I might have pushed myself a bit too hard.

Uncle Ethan was flipping pancakes. Auntie Margaret looked up. 'What took you so long?' she asked. 'I could hear you moving around.'

I don't know why, but I really didn't want to tell Auntie Margaret I'd been doing ballet stretches. So I just shrugged. I said, 'You know what it's like. Finding things in suitcases.'

'Didn't you unpack?' she asked, just as I realised I should have unpacked.

Uncle Ethan turned his attention away from the stove for a moment and a little muscle popped by his lip that could have been meant for a smile.

'I'll do it right after breakfast,' I promised.

'You mean after you've cleaned up the kitchen,' my aunt amended.

I told myself sternly not to roll my eyes and I think I managed not to. But she gave me an amused look anyway. 'While you're up there, bring down your passport,' she said. 'We've got to be in town by eight thirty.'

I nodded. I was only half listening at this point because I was looking at a huge sheet of tracing paper that had been hung up on the dining-room wall. It was held up by little clips and the clips went on nails, so that you could lift it off and on easily.

I looked because it had my name on it.

Auntie Margaret saw me notice and blushed a little. 'Oh,' she said. 'I'm doing some research into our genealogy. I was cleaning out the attic and found a whole bunch of papers and photographs, so I subscribed to one of those ancestry services.'

At the stove, Ethan shook his head slightly and I could tell that he wasn't all that keen on her project.

She pointed to my name and said, 'Here's you,' and then went up a row, 'and here's your mom and me and Jan and Karen.' Then she pointed up a lot higher. I found out more about your great-great-grandmother last night. Evelyn Porter was a telephone operator in Kansas City, in the 1920s. She was a flapper. Wait a second, I've got a picture.'

She went into the living-room and rummaged for a moment in a big metal box, bringing out a little card wallet. 'Here she is at her cousin's wedding.'

I looked down because I was told to, but then I looked closer because it was actually a bit interesting. There were all these girls in huge puffy up-dos and ankle-length dresses, and then there was one in a really tight little hat with a floppy flower on the side of it, a short skirt and what might have even been a bit of eye make-up. Even with the hat, you could tell she'd cut her hair short. She didn't just look a bit different from the other girls, she looked like a time traveller who hadn't got the memo on native fashions.

'She had her own money,' Auntie Margaret said. 'So she bought her own clothes. Look—the other girls are still wearing corsets!'

'And here's *her* wedding,' Auntie Margaret pointed again. A long bit of lace pinned tightly to her head. Her hair looked like it had been painted on. She was bolder with the make-up now she was getting married... lipstick marked out the curve of her lips and her eyes were heavy with liner and mascara. Her dress was short and sheer and you could tell all the other girls were desperate to try and look as cool as she was. She would still be an amazing bride today, nearly a hundred years later.

'She won a Charleston contest,' Auntie Margaret said. 'I could see the headline, but I'm having trouble finding the article online. If I do, I'll print it out for you.'

'Yeah,' I said. 'Okay.' I suddenly realized it had been stupid to show any interest at all. I was going to get updates on genealogy all summer.

Ethan turned around and the way he looked at me was so funny, I had to turn away. 'Breakfast,' he said.

When I went up to unpack and get my passport, I put all my things into drawers. There were no leotards. No ballet shoes or character shoes. No tights. No hairpins, no bun nets.

There had always been dance things in my drawers at school... Mum had packed them with me, even after I quit dance. There had been dance things in my drawers since I was two years old. I hadn't thought about it at Heathrow, but now it felt strangely *wrong*, as if I'd made a terrible mistake not taking practice shoes and leotards with me to the farm. I tried to shake it off, but I kept thinking about it, even when I was hurrying back down the stairs.

There was no morning mist or coolness in the air outside. At seven o'clock, the sun was already hard-bright and hot. I cleaned the kitchen the best I could, but had to be shown how twice how to properly load a dishwasher. It was easier doing the pans by hand, in the big old enamelled sink. Three months, I'd kept telling myself, three months. I tried to look interested and keen to do a good job. I thought the sooner that I looked like I'd learned something, the sooner I could leave.

So what I don't have any dance things? I thought, as I went outside and walked with Margaret to the front of the garage. If I kept on wanting to do a class, Mum would be completely overjoyed to organize it for me when I got home. But I'd probably just forget about it again...

Margaret went off to do something with a fence and I was on my own for a moment. Again, I got the feeling someone was watching me and I looked around, but of course there was nothing there *at all*, just the huge sky and animals and things.

Still, the feeling was so intense that it nearly made me shiver, even in the heat of the sun. It wasn't just that it felt like someone was watching me. It was that it felt like something was watching me and could *see* me, like that cracked place had cracked me open and *things* were getting in.

Then Auntie Margaret came back and I was okay again.

Ethan had disappeared early with a trailer at the back of the silver truck, so we took the shiny little SUV into town.

I looked for the coyote, but there was nothing in the field where we turned onto 69 Highway but cows and the big tree. Up above, though, huge birds circled. I mentioned them to Margaret and she told me, 'Buzzards. Carrion eaters. Probably after whatever the coyote left of that jackrabbit. Buzzards like to make sure what they're going for won't hurt them before they land.'

She sighed. 'I don't like that coyote so close to our place. We need a new dog.'

It made sense. Living out of town, you'd want a dog for protection.

'Old Shep did just about everything with Ethan. It broke his heart when we lost him last month. But it's time.'

I couldn't tell the buildings apart. The post office looked almost exactly like the 'drugstore', which was what Margaret called the pharmacy. We didn't go anywhere on the twee Main Street, but stuck mainly to the flat building and tarmac part of town.

'This is my niece, Julia,' she kept saying to everyone. I couldn't see why they would care, but they all said, 'Welcome,' and asked me how I liked it so far. I'd say something that I didn't really mean, like that it was lovely countryside and then they'd all get excited about my accent and we'd go off to the next errand. I couldn't believe everything was open at eight a.m.

Just before eight thirty, Aunt Margaret pulled up to

yet another breeze-block one-storey building in a huge car park. A queue of kids about my age stretched along the side. Everyone was holding a piece of paper and a brown paper bag.

Margaret fished in her folder for a piece of paper with a cheque attached and made sure I had my passport. Then she nodded towards the queue. 'Off you go,' she said. 'Oh, and here's your lunch,' she said, handing me a brown paper bag. 'See you tonight.'

I had no idea what I was doing. I took the paper and the lunch and settled my sunglasses on my nose before I got out of the car. I tried to look like I didn't care that everyone in that long queue was staring at me.

A pale boy with red curly hair nodded at me as I took my place at the end of the queue and leaned against the wall just like everybody else. My heart was pounding with nerves, and my head was reeling. I hoped it didn't show, but I really had *no idea* what I was meant to be doing. The feeling like something was in the sky, watching me, came back and I nearly choked with anxiety.

I looked at my piece of paper and could hardly focus on the words. Drivers' Educational Training, One Week Intensive. What? *Drivers'* training? I was *fourteen years old.*

The ginger boy looked at me and said, 'How old are you?' Like he'd read my mind.

Ordinarily, I would have blanked him or said something sarky, but I was so kind of...broken that I answered. 'Fourteen,' I said.

He nodded. 'Farm kid?' he asked.

I started to say no, but then realised that yes, I was a farm kid, and nodded dumbly.

'Me, too,' he said. 'What high school do you go to? I go to Frontenac.'

'I...' I tried to pull myself together. 'Sorry,' I said. 'I only got here yesterday, and I'm not sure what I'll be doing for school.'

'Where are you from?'

'I'm British.'

His brown eyes kind of blinked at me for a moment. I knew what he was going to say. I was used to it. 'You don't *look* British. You look kind of...' he put his head on one side, 'Indian.' He blushed. 'I mean, Native American... First Peoples.'

Well. I hadn't heard that one before. I'd heard 'Asian', 'Indian', 'Pakistani' and 'Mediterranean'. I'd even heard 'Mexican', which had made all the Mexicans around me laugh, because evidently I look nothing like a Mexican.

I did what I always do. I shrugged. I said, 'My mother's American, but I was born in London. We're dual nationals.'

'And you only got here yesterday?'

I nodded. 'I flew into Kansas City.'

The girl in front of him had been kind of listening and now she leaned around him. 'Wow,' she said. 'You sure *sound* British.' She stuck out her hand. 'Hi,' she said. 'I'm Whitney.' She looked as American as her name. Dazzling teeth, shiny brown hair, blue jean shorts.

The ginger boy said, 'Freddie. I'm Freddie.'

'Jules.'

We stood there for a moment.

'I turn fifteen on Friday,' Whitney said. 'I'll be getting my restricted license on the very first day I can use it!' She kind of bounced with excitement. I met Freddie's eye. Neither of us had anything to add to that.

Just then, the door opened and the first boy went inside, stayed for a few moments, and came back out again. He walked around the corner and disappeared. Then the second boy went in. As the queue snaked along, I learned from Freddie and Whitney that with a farm license I'd be able to run errands for the farm, drive myself to work if I had a job, drive myself to sport practices and even to school—if I stayed long enough.

It was just the end of May, but their school had already broken up. They started back in the middle of August.

'Let me see your address,' Whitney finally said, snatching my bit of paper and looking at it. 'You'll go to Fort Scott High. That's where I go.'

She thought for a moment. 'Hey, are you Margaret Buchwald's niece? She used to be Margaret Percy?'

I nodded. 'Oh!' she said. 'Then you're on my softball team, too. Margaret said you wouldn't start until next week, I guess that's so you can drive to practice.'

Whitney knew more about me than I did. She seemed to think she knew pretty much everything about everything.

CHAPTER FIVE

When I went in the door, somebody took my bit of paper and photocopied my passport. I went along the other side of the building and walked in the only other door into a hallway. It's not hard to find a room full of teenagers. I just went towards the noise.

Whitney had saved me a seat. Soon I was introduced to a Chastity, two Madisons and a boy named Brad who seemed to think he was devastatingly handsome. To be fair, he actually *was* rather beautiful, with dark blond hair and big blue eyes and tanned skin.

I looked around for Freddie's white skin and red curly hair, but he was on the other side of the room, with people who weren't quite as Americans-on-television-looking as the Whitney bunch.

Brad said hello to other very shiny-looking American boys and they settled around me, learning my name.

By Freddie a girl with a pink stripe in her hair looked over and smiled. She looked nice. She even looked interesting. But Whitney and Brad and the Madisons were obviously the popular kids.

At nursery, it had been Courtney and Louis who were the popular kids. They had the best birthday parties and the richest mums and dads and the prettiest nannies (although I thought Gloria was prettier). At my primary school, it was Ruby and Tallulah and Olivia and we didn't bother with the boys. At my last school, it was Sophia and Max and Archie and Izzy.

And me. I've always been in the cool crowd. So I didn't even really think about moving. I just did what I always do and went along with everyone else. But just for a moment, Freddie said something that made the pink-haired girl laugh, and I wanted to know what it was, what he'd said. And I wondered what we looked like, all us shiny people with perfect teeth and nice clothes... from the outside.

Over the next week, I chased chickens, washed, dried and folded laundry, learned to turn off the electric fence so I could feed and water the sheep, took the scraps to the pigs, and cleaned the kitchen about a million times. I was still jet lagged and sometimes got sleepy. But I also learned to drive.

It was amazing. I had quick reaction times and figured out all the pedals and gear selector stuff. All those years walking around London evidently made me good at seeing potential problems in the videos they played us. I was excellent at driver's training. Before lunch on Friday, I had a driver's license.

Friday afternoon, Margaret picked me up and then slid over and let me drive her car back to the farm. I didn't even get lost. I indicated, turned, glanced very briefly at the coyote field—no coyote—and got us back safely.

Ethan was out front, wiping his hands on a rag. An old blue pick-up truck was in front of the garage. It looked smaller than the silver one, but had a cream coloured top over the back part, the 'bed'. I hadn't seen it before, and it didn't really fit in with their other stuff, but it was kind of cute, in a totally worn-out way.

Uncle Ethan waved me over with a tiny movement of his head and Margaret followed close behind me.

'Here,' he said. He threw something that glittered in the afternoon sunlight. When I caught it, a key-ring with just one key scratched my hand. I looked at it for a moment. And then I looked at the truck, and then I looked at my Uncle Ethan's face, grinning at me.

Margaret went over and opened up the door. 'Well?' she said.

It was higher than the practice car had been, but when I climbed in, I could reach the pedals okay. 'The shifter is on the wheel,' Uncle Ethan said. He showed me how everything worked. 'Here's your parking brake. Here's your indicators. Here's the light switch.'

'And here's some money and a coupon,' Aunt Margaret said, handing me an envelope. 'Why don't you go into town and pick the farm up a couple of large pizzas? Make one of them the Pepperoni Pleaser and get what you want on the other one.'

'Oooooooookay,' I said. I'd never driven *alone* before. My hands were shaking and my mouth was dry. 'Do you think I can?'

'Did you get a license?' Ethan asked. I nodded. It was in my back pocket. The picture was horrible. 'Well, then,' he said. 'If anything goes wrong, just give us a call.' My nasty little phone was deep in the front pocket of my jeans. I nodded again.

I found the ignition on the dashboard. I stuck in the key, pushed the brake down and turned over the engine. When I put the automatic transmission into D for Drive, the blue truck tried to surge forwards, but I held it down. It had a louder engine than the practice car. And then I lifted off the brake, and drove, all by myself, down the long drive to the county road.

On the way to Highway 69, I stopped at the coyote field and looked for the coyote. Mainly because I could. Because I didn't have to ask anyone or tell anyone. I rolled down the window and stared. There were little hummocky hills and it was a big field...a pasture, I guess. Cows and calves. They were red with white faces and white bits on their chests and legs and moved slowly around, eating the grass.

Over in the far left corner, just for a moment, I thought I saw something tawny. I put the truck into P for Park and waited. I saw it again, just for a flashing instant and then, just as I was about to give up and pull away, it was a head, peering right back at me.

There were thirty metres between us, but its ears were so expressive, it was like having a conversation. It asked if I was looking at it and I moved my head forward to say, yes, I'm looking at you. It pulled back a little, like it was saying, 'What? What's your problem?' and I shrugged and kept looking. 'No problem,' I was saying. It looked at me a while longer and then it went away.

I smiled to myself as I pulled back the chrome selector

and pushed it into D for Drive again. I was driving myself around for the first time and I'd had a conversation with a coyote. Despite being a broken and expelled failure, my life had its high points.

The pizza place was right on the 'main drag', which was what Margaret called Highway 69 when it went through town. Inside was a long line of the same teenagers who had been in my driving class. 'It's a tradition,' Brad explained to me.

One of the Madisons and Chastity were with him. They'd shyly said, 'Hi,' but had edged around so that they were kind of flanking me.

'Once we get our farms or our restricteds, our parents celebrate by sending us out for pizza.' He must have been right, because nearly everyone was there, clutching the same coupon.

When I looked around, Freddie had come in with the not-so-shiny people he'd hung out with at Drivers' Ed. He waved at me, and I waved back, just as Whitney bustled up.

'God,' she said. 'Parking is so hard. I got here before you did, Madison! It just took *forever.*' She coolly pushed into line before Madison, jumping the queue. Freddie and I were still looking at each other and he rolled his eyes and I rolled mine back.

Whitney was annoying. There was no doubt about it.

I ordered the Pepperoni Pleaser and made about five hundred decisions for my own pizza and got told to come back in half an hour. We waited in the car park so we could 'check out each other's rides'.

Madison had a huge estate car, so ancient it looked like a dinosaur. Brad had his sister's old Beetle... it was lime green and all the other boys laughed at him until he actually blushed. 'It doesn't matter,' he said. 'Wait until you have to pay for your gas. I'll have enough money to treat a special girl to the movies *and* pizza afterwards.'

He looked right at me when he said 'special girl'. And that was... kind of nice and also kind of... really uncomfortable because everyone else looked at me, too.

Thank goodness just then the other Madison pulled up in a big white thing called a Taurus and we all helped her get it parked. Whitney talked about how hard it was to park her big grey Volvo estate. She said was on its fourth generation of learner drivers. Then we started sitting in each other's cars, and it was fun trying to cram into Brad's Beetle after Whitney's tank.

But it was only us and a few of Brad's friends out there. Freddie and the other kids waited inside.

I could see them crammed into a booth together, drinking sodas and laughing.

Out here, the talk had turned to what our 'real' cars would be, when we hit sixteen and got our proper licenses. I wouldn't even have my license in England until I was 17 and wouldn't probably have a car in London at all. There was totally no point in even thinking about it. Unless I was actually going to be stuck here. Forever.

The thought made my mouth go dry and I wished, more than ever, I was sitting inside and drinking soda. Whitney and Brad and a boy named Carter were leaning all over Madison's Taurus, talking about how solid it was. Then they started talking about car crashes.

The stories were gruesome and I got nervous enough. So I went over to the door of my truck and opened it. 'Ta da!' I said. 'These are my wheels.' I sounded sarcastic, even to me.

'What?' Brad said. 'That's a '66 F-100! Suh-weet!'

Some of the boys I hadn't talked to before came over and everyone got excited about my old blue truck. 'The bumper has been re-chromed,' Carter said. 'It's still got the wooden bed!' another one said, looking in the back through the camper thing.

Then a cook shouted out the back door of the pizza place and we all had to go into get our pizzas. And then everyone looked at my pizza, too, because I got a white pizza with spinach and evidently nobody in that town had ever seen one before. It made me kind of smile to myself as I carefully, carefully backed out of my car park space and turned left across Highway 69.

After dinner, I ran the bathwater as hot as I could stand it and stayed in until I felt like I was going to faint. Then I climbed out, towel-dried my hair and brushed it through, so I could start stretching. There was no point messing around. I went straight down into Russian splits, holding myself up by my hands to where it hurt. It was ridiculously high. I could hardly reach the ground.

The back of my bed was almost right for a barre. I could

plié and circle through positions, and open the wardrobe
door mirror to see a bit of my pitifully stubby développés
and arabesques.

For some reason, I thought of the coyote, and the
way it had talked to me with its head...it reminded me
of Uncle Ethan, who could say so many things just with
a little movement of his lip or a tilt of his own head.
Holding onto the back of the bed, I tried it. I tried, 'Are
you looking at me?' and 'What? What's wrong?'.

None of it was right.

'Julia?' Auntie Margaret called from downstairs.
'What are you doing up there? It sounds like a herd of
elephants!'

I shouted down that I was sorry and I'd dropped
something.

It was a good thing I didn't care about ballet, because
I didn't have a place to do it. And I wasn't any good at it,
anyway.

I laid down in the big white bed and wondered if I'd
see Archie's face all night again. I'd been exhausted, but
suddenly, I was afraid to try and sleep.

Auntie Margaret knocked at the door. 'You okay?' she
asked and pushed the door open.

She had a bunch of paper and a pencil in her hand.
'What did you drop?'

I shrugged. 'Nothing,' I said. 'A shoe.'

She came and sat on my bed. 'You sure you're okay?'

she asked again. 'I hear you tossing and turning at night sometimes.' She looked at me. 'We can get you some counselling, if you think you need it. I got a name of a man in Kansas City. We could go.'

I thought about it for a moment, about the broken feeling and the things that tried to get in through the crack. Was I a little...ill? Probably. But I shrugged again.

I didn't want to talk to a counsellor. I didn't even want to talk about talking to a counsellor.

So I changed the subject. 'What are you finding out tonight?' I asked. My throat felt tight, as if I wasn't used to talking.

'Well,' she said, pulling out her ponytail and ruffling up her hair. 'I think I might need a counsellor myself after tonight.' She twisted her hair elastic around in her hands. 'I just found out my dad wasn't even American. And that your mother knew...that's how she got the job in England. She got British citizenship through Dad...'

She showed me a piece of paper that didn't mean anything to me, but had my mother's unmistakable neat, clear, round handwriting all along the margin. 'Dad wasn't Grandpa's son. Grandpa adopted him...I mean, I knew Grandma was from Yorkshire, but...'

She said 'York Shyer' instead of 'York Sure', but it wasn't the right time to correct her.

She showed me an article she'd printed out. It was about a ballroom dancing championship in Blackpool. A man and a woman smiled at the camera with big numbers pinned to their backs. 'That's your *real* great-grandfather and *my* real Grandpa, with my Grandma. He was killed six months after that, in the war.'

Her voice sounded shocked. 'Are you okay?' I asked her.

'I guess,' she said. 'I guess it doesn't change anything... but she could have told me.' I didn't know who the 'she' was. Did she mean her grandmother or my mother?

Auntie Margaret looked at me for a moment and then reached out and pulled the sheet up under my chin and smoothed back my hair. 'It doesn't matter,' she said. She kissed my forehead and left.

I listened to her walk down the stairs. Halfway down, Margaret must have stopped to read the article again, because I went to sleep waiting for her to get all the way to the bottom.

CHAPTER SIX

They hadn't given me a truck just to be nice. I drove it. All the time.

Auntie Margaret had things for me to do. I took tomatoes and eggs to the roadside stand, I went to the bank with cheques and with the money from the roadside stand, I sent Uncle Ethan's honey off at the post office and delivered it to the tourist shops at the fort and on the dinky little high street. I picked up prescriptions at the chemist, got baling wire and cement mix and about a million other things at the seed store or the feed store or the tractor supply store.

I also started going to softball practice and softball games, where I learned I was rubbish at catching and throwing, but fairly good at hitting a softball and running.

And on the way, wherever I was going, I'd visit the coyote.

I used to just slow down and look for him. But one day, I watched Uncle Ethan step through a barbed wire fence. He kind of held it down with his foot and held another strand up with his hand and bent over and went through it. And so, on my way to Walmart to stock up on laundry detergent that was on sale and to drop off some tomatoes and eggs at the roadside stand, I pulled the truck over and stepped into the pasture.

The cows came over and looked at me, but when I didn't have any food and started walking, they went away. One big cow shouted at me…at least that's what it sounded like, but I told her not to be stupid and she snorted and trotted off, two calves at her heels.

It was going to be another warm and sunny day. The sky was already intensely blue and there were only a few wisps of clouds, really high up. Inside the truck, I felt okay, but sometimes, when I was out here, I got that feeling again like something was looking at me. Like something was getting into the crack in my middle and rummaging through all the things I didn't want anybody to know.

I didn't know why I kept on getting that feeling. I stopped and looked for the coyote several times, but I couldn't see him. He wasn't on this side of the ridge, so I went to the top.

It wasn't really a hill. The land looked like green waves and this was just the crest of one of the little waves. When I stood on top, I could see a little farther than I could before, but not much. But what I could see was interesting.

I didn't know if it had been a barn or a house. All that was left was a stone foundation and about half a wooden floor. I scrambled up onto it.

Under my feet, the stone felt uneven and rough, but the floor was still okay. I crept along, ready for it to break underneath me, but even though the boards were weathered and some were broken on the edges, the floor still felt fairly solid. I flexed my knees and bounced a little, but nothing cracked or sagged.

Then I saw him.

He must have been watching me all along, from a bit of brush near a big tree, but now he stood up. He looked ready to... I don't know... maybe run away. Maybe... and I couldn't believe I hadn't thought about this before... run over and fight me. Bite me.

I looked back at him. I don't know what I said to him with my body. Maybe it was just, 'Oh, hi!' or something. But he relaxed. I could see him relax... something about how he carried his neck and shoulders. I found myself wiggling my own shoulders, testing them out, seeing what they looked like and he... he was interested in me, in what I was doing.

This close, his ears looked far too big for his head, and they were so movable, it was no wonder I'd found them expressive. He put them forward and put his head a tiny bit to one side and you could easily tell he was asking, 'What are you doing?'

I shrugged, saying, 'I'm not sure.'

And he gave a big yawn, like, 'Whatever,' and then laid down to watch me. 'Let's see what you've got.'

And I guess it's because I was on a kind of stage and someone was watching me, but I started to dance. I did a bit of my exam piece, a little bit I could do in trainers and jeans, just a couple of attitudes and then a gallop and a jump. The jump was loud when I landed and I was fairly certain he would run away.

But he just... he just watched. And when I stopped, he left. He turned around and trotted off, looking back over his shoulder a few times. He didn't look that impressed.

Something about that made me feel cross. I jumped down off the floor and walked back over the ridge. When the big cow shouted at me, I told her to shut up.

I snagged my t-shirt coming through the barbed wire. It didn't tear or anything, but there was a little hole on my shoulder.

It had been a really cool moment, on the wooden floor with the coyote, but now, I felt all jangled and upset and kind of *hurt*, like I'd been in a bad argument. Like I'd had an audition and had *failed*.

I jumped into the truck, shoved it into Drive and took off…and nearly ran into a truck coming the other way. I hadn't seen it. I hadn't looked. It was just suddenly *there*. I was so stunned, I could hardly push down the brake pedal.

But I did. I pushed down the brake and grabbed the wheel and closed my eyes. I could hear wheels and gravel and skidding and I waited for the collision. But it didn't happen.

Then a big man stuck his head in my window. 'What in the Sam Hill did you think you were doing?' he shouted. 'You didn't look where you were going. You were parked on the *wrong side of the road* anyway.' His face was bright red around a big blond moustache. He looked at me, took a breath and then shouted *again*, 'Good God Almighty! You aren't even wearing your damnation *seatbelt*!'

He was right. I'd forgotten all about it.

He was huge—even bigger than Uncle Ethan, but dressed just like him. I said, 'I…I…I…I'm sorry,' and I couldn't help it, I started to cry.

'Oh, now,' he said. 'Oh, now, don't do that.'

I cried even harder.

'Oh, hell*fire*,' he said. He reached in the truck window and awkwardly patted my back. I was still clutching the steering wheel. He said, 'Get out of the truck.'

I put it in Park and turned off the engine and got out of the truck. The man said, 'You must be the little English girl.'

I nodded and then absolutely *wailed*. I couldn't even see him anymore, because I buried my head in my hands and I could *not* stop crying.

I could hear the man say, 'Dang it! I guess I was kind of hard on you there. Nothing happened. No bumps. No bruises. We're all good.'

I didn't know what was wrong with me. I just couldn't stop. The man reached into the pocket of his overalls and brought out an ironed and neatly-folded navy blue bandana and handed it to me. 'Here,' he said. And something about that, and the way it smelled like Auntie Margaret's laundry made me feel a little better. A little normal.

And I could stop crying.

I wiped my eyes and blew my nose, wondering what all *that* was about. I *never* cry. Sometimes I come close, and sometimes a few tears drop, but I never really lose it like that. I hoped I looked okay.

'All that stuff they teach you in Driver's Ed,' he said, 'about doing your seatbelt and checking your mirrors and signalling?'

I nodded again and then cleared my throat and said, 'Yes?'

'You gotta do that *every* time,' he said. 'You just never know. Things change every second. You have to *concentrate*.'

'Okay.' My voice sounded shaky, even to me.

'And don't park on the wrong side of the road.'

When I told Whitney and Madison B about it at softball practice, they already knew. 'You've got to remember to drive on the right,' Whitney told me seriously. Madison nodded earnestly.

'I wasn't *driving* on the wrong side of the road,' I said. 'I'd just parked on that side to see a coyote.'

It was hot. I was drinking the squash Mrs Hall brought every practice and it tasted good to me. Usually, it tasted like squashed snails or something. It took me a minute to realise that Whitney and Madison were registering disbelief. 'You *what?*' Whitney asked.

I wasn't stupid enough to repeat it, or explain.

'They don't have them in England,' Madison B said. Whitney shot her an evil look and she shrugged. 'Maybe,' she amended.

'You don't have coyotes?' Whitney asked, clearly unbelieving.

I shook my head, no. 'We have foxes,' I said. 'And badgers, and...things. But not coyotes.'

'Well, you're welcome to all of ours,' Whitney laughed.

'Coyotes are pests, Jules. They're *vermin*…it's like pulling over to look at a *rat*.'

But then I remembered that Auntie Margaret had watched him when he had the jackrabbit. Whitney was wrong, then. But I nodded, anyway. I wasn't going to get into it with Whitney Hall.

She put her arm around me and kind of hugged me sideways. 'You need somebody to look after you,' she said warmly. 'It's too bad you can't go swimming with us on Saturday.'

Madison A plunked down on the bench with a cup of squash. She'd heard the last of the conversation. 'Yeah,' she said. 'Your aunt told my mom you were kind of grounded.'

'Yeah,' Madison B said. 'Because of nearly killing that kid at your school.'

'Shut *up*, Madison,' Whitney said. '*God!*'

Madison B winced. 'Sorry,' she whispered.

I had started getting regular updates from my aunt and uncle on Archie's condition. They talked to Mum, even though I wasn't allowed to…yet. Archie was recovering well, but…but he shouldn't have to recover at all, should he? Just for a moment, my mind flashed back to that night; the rain in the air, the dark, wet roof tiles shining in the security lights. Archie's white, white face.

Whitney hugged me again and it actually felt kind of nice because I was afraid I was going to start hurting again in my middle.

'Don't worry about it,' she said. 'We're all going to get cokes later, want to come?'

And I found myself saying yes.

In the booth at the Tasty Queen, Brad sat next to me.

'How's your truck?' he asked. 'I hear you're putting in the miles.'

'Yeah,' I said. I felt like I had to say *something* back, and that's the witty repartee I'd come up with. The boys all practised baseball before our softball practice. His practice uniform had a big dirt streak down the front. That was because, I knew enough about baseball to understand, he had slid along the baseline on his front to try and get to a base before he was tagged out.

Slides were dangerous but they could be effective. We got warned against doing them, all the time. So, what kind of idiot would do a massive great slide like that, just in practice?

I looked up and Brad leaned over me a bit, and his perfect dark blond hair with light blond streaks fell a little over his perfect big blue eyes.

'Maybe we could meet up for lunch some time.' He was just so ... American ... so sure of himself. And he was so sure of *me*, too. Suddenly the coke tasted gloopy and unpleasant on the back of my throat.

I said, 'I've got to use the loo,' and stood up.

Afterwards, I just waved at everyone as I walked across the restaurant to the doors and pointed to where a watch would be, if I wore one. They all waved at me. 'See you on Thursday!' Whitney called. Brad winked at me and smiled, like we'd had some kind of special moment. I was so stunned that I didn't even roll my eyes until I got outside the door.

Great, I thought. That was just great. My new best friend. My new boyfriend. And I didn't actually like either of them. What was wrong with me? How did things like this keep on happening to me? Why did everything *keep happening* when I wasn't doing anything?

I'd only stopped for a coke because I hadn't wanted to argue about stopping for a coke. I wasn't even, technically, supposed to stop off for a coke. My farm license was a little different from their restricted ones. I was supposed to take the most direct route and the only reason I could drive to softball was because it was, for legal purposes, a school programme. And, if I *was* grounded (though nobody had actually said that word to me) I shouldn't be going out for cokes. And, anyway, seriously, Whitney and Brad? Was that my social life now? Why couldn't I just say no, thank you? Why couldn't I just…I don't know…be somebody *else*?

I groaned. It was all such a mess. The metal of my truck was cool—from the breeze and the shade of the tree I'd parked underneath. I laid my head against it and it felt nice.

'Are you okay?'

An older boy with long, poker-straight black hair had walked up behind me. He was holding a huge drink. 'Do you want some cherry limeade?' he asked. 'Cures anything.'

'No,' I said. 'Thank you.'

His truck was parked next to mine, under a tree. It was nearly as old as mine, but not as cute, more beat up and rusty and tired-looking. He put down his tailgate and hopped up to sit on the flap. He took a deep drink of his limeade and said, 'Man. I miss those when I'm gone. It's the first thing I do when I get home for the summer. I come here and sit on my truck and have a cherry limeade.' He flipped his hair back over his shoulder and patted the other side of the tailgate. 'You can come into my office, if you want.'

Something about him made me feel better. I knew it was a bit of a risk to hang out with a total stranger, but I went over and hopped up and sat on his tailgate, too. We could see all the cars coming up and down the strip. My legs dangled in the air and I watched the cars for a minute.

Then I wondered, 'So,' I asked, 'Where do you go? When you're away?'

'School,' he said. 'I'm a boarding school student.'

'I used to do that,' I said.

He looked at me and smiled. 'You talk funny.'

'I'm English. From England?' For a moment, we sized each other up. His skin was brown and his eyes looked nearly black in the twilight.

'You look Cherokee to me. Or maybe Lakota. I'm on the Cherokee tribal roll, but Mom says I'm part Delaware.'

That was two people who'd thought I was Native American. 'Stick your leg out,' he said. I straightened my leg and he slid over to measure it against his own. 'Cherokee, I'll bet,' he said. He stuck out his hand, 'Robbie Slater. We're probably related.'

'I don't think so,' I said. He'd made me smile. 'I'm Jules Percy... I'm staying with Ethan and Margaret Buchwald.'

'And how old are you?'

I shrugged and smiled. 'Fourteen.'

'Uh-huh,' he said. 'And how long have you been driving?'

For the second time that night, I pretended to wear a watch. I squinted at my wrist. 'About a week and a half?' I said.

'Uh-huh,' he said again. 'Right.'

He motioned me off the tailgate and pushed it up with a clang, swinging his hair back over his shoulder. Then he looked at me. 'I work for Ethan Buchwald sometimes. It's getting late. Get in your truck. I'll follow you home.'

Night came on quickly in Kansas, and I kept forgetting that. It was very nearly completely dark when I pulled in the driveway. Margaret and Ethan were on the porch.

'*Where* have you been?' Auntie Margaret didn't even wait for me to shut the truck door before she started.

Then Robbie pulled in behind me and jumped out of his truck. You'd think that would make Auntie Margaret wait to shout at me, but it didn't. 'I must have called your phone twenty times!'

I went to pat my jeans pocket, but of course I was wearing the nasty shorts we used for softball practice and they didn't have any pockets for my nasty little phone. 'I'm sorry,' I said. 'I must have left it in my jeans.'

'You left your phone in your *jeans*?' Auntie Margaret looked big and scary on the porch. She threw up her hands and looked up as if she was asking God to witness what a terrible person I was. 'I thought teenagers were in love with their phones.'

Stupidly, I tried to explain. 'I *was* in love with *my* phone. But it's kind of hard to remember the one you got me.'

Auntie Margaret glared at me. 'If you think,' she said, 'I'm going to buy you some fancy...' she trailed off as if she'd just noticed there was somebody else there. 'Hi, Robbie,' she said.

Uncle Ethan came down the steps and put out his hand. 'Son,' he said.

'Hello, Sir,' Robbie said. 'I...um...saw your niece here having a bit of car trouble.'

Car trouble? I cut him a quick look, but at least I didn't say anything to blow it because he said, 'I think she wasn't used to her lights and ran the battery down? But I gave her a jump and it was fine. I just came along to make sure she made it home.'

'Oh, honey,' Auntie Margaret hugged me. 'You've had *such* a bad day today. I'm sorry for ragging on you. Why don't you come in, Robbie? I just made some sugar cookies.'

It wasn't awkward *at all* sitting around the table with Robbie Slater in my softball kit and eating cookies and drinking tea while Uncle Ethan asked me questions about what had gone wrong with the truck when nothing had actually gone wrong with it and I was lying my head off about something I knew nothing about. Nope. Not at all awkward.

Luckily, Robbie kept saying things like, 'It just wouldn't turn over, would it, Jules,' and 'I don't think the lights came on when you tried the key, did they, Jules?'

I said, 'It was just a nightmare and of course I'd forgotten my phone...'

Robbie looked at me. I was overdoing it. I shut up.

After about four hundred years, I was allowed to go up for my bath. Ethan and Robbie talked outside for a few minutes and then I heard his truck pull away.

I was in bed before I remembered to stretch. I got back out again and, as quietly as I could, gently asked my tendons and muscles to get longer. Please get longer, I thought.

Please.

I didn't know why it suddenly felt so important.

But it did.

CHAPTER SEVEN

The next morning, a new name was inked in on the family tree. Honestly, I'd barely glanced at it, but Margaret decided I was interested.

'That's Harry Dent, the ballroom champion,' she said. 'My biological grandfather and your great-grandfather. I put him in last night. He got killed at Dunkirk. I emailed the Yorkshire Post and they said they could send me a scan of the article, for a fee. I think I'm going to pay it.' She started talking to me about how to send money to England, but I kind of switched off. It was too early to think about complicated bank transactions.

I was glad when Ethan said it was time for breakfast.

I helped Ethan collect stuff from the old junk heap to take into the municipal dump. He was cleaning up some acreage that had been ignored, he thought, since the second world war. It was a big day, I thought, for talking about the second world war.

Uncle Ethan and Aunt Margaret had done well out of farming when a lot of people had gone under—by trying new things and by keeping their quality high. Their beef and pork and lamb all went to restaurants in Kansas City. Some of their hay was sent to a company that extracted the dust and sold it in beautifully-designed pouches for pampered small pets—ten dollars for fifteen ounces. Now they were keeping more and more sheep and selling the wool to fancy knitting shops. But sheep are fairly stupid and they get everywhere...into places that they can't get out of again. If they were going to use that bit of the farm for sheep, they'd have to get rid of the junk first.

We walked through a hay meadow to get to the new sheep pasture. Ethan told me we wouldn't take the truck through it and we wouldn't take the sheep through it, because they'd never come back out...they'd want to eat it all up. He pointed to where the farm track bent around and back, showing me the way we'd drive to it. I asked why we didn't just drive that way to look at the dump, too, and Ethan grunted.

'How many times have you walked through an original Kansas hay meadow?' he asked. 'This one has *never* been ploughed. It's never had any pesticides or herbicides on it. People come out from the ag college every year, just to look at it.'

I hadn't thought about it that way, as something I *got* to do. I'd been thinking of it as something I *had* to do. But now that I stopped and looked around, it was kind of...beautiful. There were flowers everywhere in the grass, and Ethan pointed out some of them as we went— blue wild indigo, rose vervain, spiderwort, purple prairie-clover, milkweed.

'It all used to be like this,' he said. 'The whole prairie. And the buffalo herds grazed it, huge herds with thousands of buffaloes.'

The dump was a kind of hollow bit in the ground where the Percys had been throwing things away for a hundred

70

and fifty years or so. We looked at it all and Ethan and I discussed what we would do to clear it.

Some things were so big, Ethan would have to use the tractor and a trailer. He could winch them in with the tractor and then take some time and haul them off to the dump or the scrap metal people. But some things weren't very big and could fit in my truck. Ethan said we could spread tarps and old blankets to protect the wooden truck bed.

So we went back and got my truck and I drove it the long way around, with Ethan sitting on the tailgate and hopping off and on to do the gates. Then we carried old sinks and bits of pipe and gateposts, a big, heavy ironing board...and a whole suitcase of rotten old sheets that stank horribly when it fell open...and a bunch of other things. I learned which were the metal things to go and sell, and which were the junk things to dump at the municipal dump. There hadn't been a city dump when the Percys had made this hollow into a dump, Ethan said. There hadn't even been a rubbish...a *trash* collection.

The last thing he put into my truck was a big standing mirror, cracked right down the middle.

'Hope you don't believe in bad luck,' he said.

'I think I already had my share,' I answered, and he huffed a little laugh.

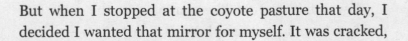

But when I stopped at the coyote pasture that day, I decided I wanted that mirror for myself. It was cracked, but it was big. If I put it up on the platform, I'd be able to see myself dance, and suddenly, that seemed terribly important.

I lay the mirror on the ground. I pushed the top half of the mirror under the bottom strand of barbed wire, climbed through myself, and then pulled the bottom half through. The big red cow ran over and gave me a load of grief and I put it upright to face her. 'Look,' I said. 'See what you get like?' and she shied away, as if the sight of herself was terribly frightening.

I giggled all the way down to the platform. I put the mirror just off the edge of the wooden bit, on two big flat stones and then got down and found two loose rocks to wedge it into place. I had to roll them along, they were too big and heavy to lift.

I tried all the corners of the platform and could see myself from all but one, the top right. Now, I thought, all I need is a barre.

And two minutes later, I'd taken out the huge ironing board and was sliding it under the barbed wire and dragging it across the pasture. It wasn't like it was stealing… it wouldn't have fetched much at the metal recycling place. I didn't feel bad about doing it.

The grumpy old cow looked up from grazing and glared at me. She seemed to have convinced all the other cows that I was dangerous… they were huddled in the corner by the water trough.

They didn't seem to like coming over the ridge that much, so once I was there, I didn't have to deal with her.

I put the ironing board up and down notches, trying to get it the right height. I was going to have to stop wearing jeans, I realized. It was hard to get my leg onto the ironing board to see if it was the right height and that *wasn't* because my extension was so bad. It was because my jeans were tight. I leant down to feel the boards and they were soft but gritty. I'd have to bring a brush, too...a *broom*.

When I stood up again, I could feel the coyote watching my back. In my mirror, he was framed standing up in the tall grass, observing me carefully. He looked like a painting, or a poster you'd buy for your wall, or a postcard you'd send to a friend. In the tall green grass, with the big tree in the background, he looked like he came from another time—maybe the times that Ethan was talking about, before the Europeans came and broke up the prairie. He was like a symbol—of wildness, I guess, or freedom.

And he'd come back to see me dance.

I couldn't do much in jeans and trainers. I could pirouette. I could jump and plié, a bit, and do some attitudes. I did some locking and popping, too, and then laughed. When I laughed, my coyote flinched, as if I was shouting. Then his ears settled down a little and he did the yawn he always did when he was trying to look not all that bothered.

When I was outside on my own, I still felt kind of... watched. But when I was with my coyote and really was being watched, I didn't feel poked and prodded by the sky. I felt safe.

It was getting late, and I had the tomatoes and eggs to deliver to the roadside stand, so I jumped down off the platform, and he startled and trotted away into the brush by the tree.

I had this mad thought that I would be able to impress him the next day, when I wore something that would let me actually move.

When I got home from my last trip to town, Robbie was just coming in from the barn. He looked like he'd been working all day, but it hadn't been for us. His hair was in a long ponytail under a feed cap and his old shirt and jeans were streaked with soil a slightly different colour to the soil we had on our farm.

'You want to stay to dinner?' Auntie Margaret called from the porch, but he shook his head.

'Mom's expecting me,' he said. And then he said, 'But can I come back later?' and turned to me. 'Would you like to get a cherry limeade?'

I started to say, 'I'm grounded,' but Auntie Margaret beat me to it. 'She's grounded,' she said. There was a little edge of satisfaction in her voice that I didn't think was necessary. But Uncle Ethan came around the corner, wiping his hands. He said, 'I think it would be all right.'

Auntie Margaret looked at him and he got really interested in drying his hands on the towel. But he said, to Robbie, 'That'd be okay, I reckon.'

He reached into his pocket and took out an envelope

full of cash. 'This is your pay,' he said, handing it to me with the scrap of paper. Everything was itemized on there, even my petrol and the cost of my softball uniform. And I'd still made seventy-eight dollars and twenty cents. I took out twenty and gave it to Auntie Margaret. 'Here,' I said. 'It might take me a while, but I'll pay you back for the flight and everything.'

She looked at Robbie and blushed bright red. 'Don't be silly,' she said. 'I was just joking.'

But I offered it to her again at dinner. That time, she took it. She said, 'Thanks, Jules. That'll come in handy.' I was carrying the plates through and saw that there were more inked-in spots on the family tree. Margaret saw me noticing and blushed again.

'It got so hot today,' she said. 'That I took a break. I'd looked up those two last night, but I found more about them today.'

She pointed. 'This one is another dancer. She was Harry Dent's mother, you know, the ballroom guy. Hang on. I'll show you her picture.'

I didn't hang on, because I wanted to be ready for when Robbie picked me up and I was super aware that I was sweaty and my hair was dusty. I took all the dishes in and started loading the dishwasher, while my aunt poked around in the big metal box she kept by the sofa.

Even when she said, 'Here,' I didn't show the slightest bit of interest. She actually had to bring the photo into the kitchen and shove it under my nose. 'I think she looks like Lisa Ann.'

My mother's not that big on top...or anywhere, I thought, but I could see what Margaret meant. She had Mum's face shape and colouring...at least it looked like she did from the faded sepia photograph. She was wearing what looked to be silver sandals, sequins and not a whole lot else, except for tights, and feathers on her head. She did, however, look kind of cool.

'That's Rosemary Pickering,' Margaret said. 'She married a man named Dent...he worked in a department store. They had fifteen children. Fifteen!' It was hard to imagine that tiny waist carrying one baby, let alone fifteen.

'She was a musical hall dancer,' Margaret continued. 'She started touring when she was only seven years old.' She showed me another photo, this one of a group of girls in sailor suits in back of a sign that read 'Little Bluebells'. She pointed out the same face near the end of the row.

'These were taken only six months apart,' she said. 'Just think, she went from this...' I looked again. The sailor suits were kind of designed to make the girls look like babies. They had big sashes high up on their chests. Now that I looked, you could see that my ancestor's sash was actually kind of squishing down her breasts, to make her look younger.

'...to this,' Margaret held out the grown up one again, 'in six months, when she was fifteen years old.' She rubbed at her eyes with the back of one hand and I could see she was nearly crying, even though I didn't know why. 'Your mom did that,' she said. 'Lisa Ann. When she was seventeen. She just completely changed, nearly overnight, and told us all to call her Annalise.'

I looked at the photo again and my aunt slid her arm around me and put her head against mine, so we could look at it together for a moment. Then I went back to washing dishes.

That night at Tasty Queen, when Robbie Slater and I went in and got our cherry limeades, Chastity was there with her parents. Her whole family had different shades of red hair and were all pale and freckled. They looked sweet sitting there together.

I gave her a little wave and she half-smiled back. She was already on her phone, texting Whitney about me and Robbie, I'd bet a hundred pounds.

Robbie flopped down his tailgate and we hopped up and sat, one on either end, watching the traffic. He was right. It was restful and nice. The pop music the place played was far enough away that it sounded kind of good. The night was warm. I liked the way my feet dangled, like the muscles in my legs could get longer, just by hanging there.

'Sorry to hear about your trouble back home,' he finally said. I felt my back stiffen.

'What did you hear?' I asked. I tried not to sound cross, but I'm not sure I succeeded. I sounded a little cross to me. I looked over at him to see if he'd noticed. He had a smile on the corner of his mouth, and kept looking out at the traffic.

'Well, Mr Buchwald's not exactly Chatty Kathy,' he said. 'He just told me you'd been getting into trouble since you didn't get into ballet school.'

'God!' I said, 'It's *not*...' I'd been about to say, *It's not about ballet school*. I'd said that a hundred times. To teachers. To Mum. To friends. But now, I suddenly couldn't say it again. Not here. Not to him.

I took a big drink of my cherry limeade. It was so cold that it gave you headaches if you had a big drink and I got one and had to wait a minute for the pain to clear, holding onto my head.

Robbie laughed. 'You got to take these bad boys easy,' he said. 'They'll get you if you slug em' back.'

He waited a minute. 'Anyway. You were saying that it wasn't... wasn't what?'

This time when I looked at him, he was looking back. His face was lovely—high cheekbones and a strong chin, but it looked like his nose had been broken at some point. That didn't make him any less good-looking though. And I had never seen a boy with hair that long before. It made him look... I don't know... kind of special.

'Robbie Slater?' A woman had walked up to us and I hadn't even noticed. She was tall and strong-looking and about my mum's age.

Robbie hopped down from the tailgate and put down his drink. 'Yes, ma'am?' he said.

'I'm Nancy Salter, from over by Gardiner?' Robbie kind of nodded at that, as if to say he knew. 'We're going to try and hay three times this year and thought we'd cut next week. Could you come and help out? We'll have to use the conditioner.'

'Yes, Mrs Salter,' Robbie said. 'I can't come Monday, because I'm working at the Walker place. But I'm free from Tuesday to Friday.' He reached into his back pocket and gave her a business card. 'This has my cell number.'

They shook hands and Robbie hopped back up after she left. It really *was* his office.

'*Anyway*,' he said. 'You were saying.'

We got interrupted by Robbie's clients another three times that night. And we had to have another round of cherry limeades and use the 'bathroom', too. But even with all that, it seemed the most natural thing in the world to tell Robbie Slater the truth about not getting into ballet school.

I told him about how my teachers had told me to stretch and how I hardly ever did. I told him about how my mum kept arranging special classes for me until I refused to go. I told him about Becky D'Angelo and how we'd danced together since we were four and that *she* got in and that I hadn't spoken to her since. I told him that I'd thought my mother only seemed to care about me when I was dancing and that after I'd quit I'd felt so unhappy and angry at everything that yes, I probably did do some stupid stuff. In fact, I knew I'd done some stupid stuff.

Then Robbie's cell buzzed and he hopped down off the tailgate, saying, 'That was Mr Buchwald. It's time to get you home.'

Just outside of town, he got another text and he said, 'Sorry. I've got to stop and write back.' He pulled over. The moon was up, only a crescent, but it looked incredibly big in the enormous sky. There were all those stars you get in the countryside, only more, because there was more room up there. And sitting there, doing nothing in the quiet of the night, waiting, that feeling of something pushing at me came back again, harder than ever, as if the night sky held more of the something than the day sky ever could. It nearly felt physical, as if busy little hands were clawing at the cracked place in my chest.

I thought to myself, 'I'm going to lose it. I'm going to crack up completely. And I'm going to do it in Robbie Slater's truck.'

But just then I heard a howl. Then there were more and then more until it was like a crescendo of howling that trailed off into yips and barks. I'd never heard anything like it before, but I knew it was coyotes. And the moment they started to howl, the somethings went away from my cracked bit and I lost that feeling of somebody prying into my secrets.

Robbie finished his text and signalled to pull back out. 'Sounds like a big pack,' he said. His eyes shot over to me in the dash light. 'You okay?'

'I thought coyotes lived alone.'

He glanced over at me and smiled. 'No way. They live in packs of twenty or so. If you see one alone, it's been kicked out.'

We drove another five or six miles and then turned off the highway. I wondered if that was my coyote's old pack. I wondered if he'd heard them from where he was in the cow pasture. We had a lot in common, I thought. Just that day I'd seen him as a symbol of wildness and freedom, when, really, he was lonely... and maybe a little lost.

'Oh, by the way,' Robbie said. 'If you want a better phone, I can get you one second hand. I've got a cousin that unlocks them from the network. They go from about thirty dollars.'

I said yes. Anybody would have said yes.

It was strange not having a bath before I went to bed, but I'd already had a shower and it seemed silly to have a bath, too. Besides, I was tired in that lovely way you get when you've tired out your body and you've sort of satisfied your mind, too. Hanging out with Robbie felt like that—satisfying. I propped my head on my hands and looked out the window. I thought I'd think about the whole day for a while. But I fell asleep like that.

I woke up in the middle of the night with a stiff neck and rolled off my numb hands.

CHAPTER EIGHT

The next morning, I got out of bed quietly and started to stretch. It was so early that the chickens had just begun to grumble... early enough that the house didn't smell of coffee. I measured my Russian split—still had about thirty centimetres to go—and then, for the first time, tried ordinary splits. I went right down into them.

A 'whoop!' of delight came up into my throat but I caught it before it passed my lips, covering my mouth with my hands and smothering it. I tried it with the other leg lead and I could do it that way, too.

Ordinarily, I would have just thought, 'Yes!' and then stopped stretching. But I didn't do that. I went through all the stretches again, even harder. And I noticed that and I noticed myself noticing.

I'd never really noticed anything about myself before. I suppose totally messing up my life and getting sent away had made me start. Actually, I thought, as I leaned over my right leg, grabbed my foot in both hands and started to pull, everything Mum hoped would happen by sending me here had already happened.

I'd learned to work. I'd learned to be more respectful... although I doubted I'd ever be able to Sir and Ma'am people like Robbie... and I'd started paying attention to my life. *And* I paid attention to other people. I missed Mum—didn't just miss her house and her attention, but missed the way she tucked her hair behind her ear when she was thinking, wondered how her negotiations had gone. I thought about Archie all the time. I'd even remembered Becky D'Angelo, my old dance friend. I'd completely cut her out of my life when I didn't get into the Royal Ballet School. I'd stopped answering her texts and following her and...I wondered how she was.

All of those people. Just...gone out of my life. Or maybe they had *been* my life, but I hadn't noticed. Maybe I had existed on their edges, maybe they'd kind of formed what *I* was by what *they* were. Maybe I was forming in a new way because of the people in my life now...maybe my edges were differently shaped because of what Ethan and Margaret and Robbie and even Whitney were.

And in that case, what *was* I, really? Who was *I*? Who actually was I if I could change so completely, so quickly?

I had been thinking so deeply that I had dressed in jeans and a t-shirt, like an idiot. I got undressed again, found a couple of strappy vests and put on one of those and a pair of sweatshorts instead. I swirled my hair up into a messy bun...my hands seemed to remember how to do it without me.

Now I started thinking about money. I didn't know how much a broom was going to be. I'd asked Robbie to get me a forty-dollar smartphone. I could use the SIM card from the one I had—we'd looked at it. I wouldn't have any data, but I could use the farm's WiFi, of course...and he said there was free WiFi at a few places in town. I'd given Auntie Margaret twenty dollars. I'd have to buy Robbie a couple of limeades back, and that would be about eight. I had ten dollars left to buy a broom.

I didn't think it was going to be enough.

But I didn't want to just take one of the farm's, either. I noticed that, too. I really *was* changing, I thought.

Over breakfast, I asked Uncle Ethan if he was going to cut three hay crops this year. Auntie Margaret had been pouring tea and she nearly spilt it, staring at me. Then she put the pot down and started to laugh.

'Oh,' she said, wiping her eyes. 'I'm sorry, Julia. I just couldn't help it.' She imitated my accent, 'Oh, Uncle Ethan. Are you planning to cut hay thrice this year?'

Ethan's mouth twitched up on both corners, but he asked, 'Who's cutting three hay crops?'

'Mrs Salter.'

Margaret sniffed. 'Their hay is sudan grass—quick-growing,' Margaret said. 'Cheap and nasty, and if you're not careful it can be full of prussic acid.' She had a bite of pancake and then asked, 'Is Robbie helping them to get it in?'

I nodded.

'Hmm,' she said. 'Well, he's got to make money when he can, now that he's left the family to go to that school.'

I loaded up for another dump visit that morning and Uncle Ethan checked under the tarps and blankets. 'We don't want to wreck that truck bed,' he said. He went into the barn and came out with a big bright blue plastic broom.

'After you dump the stuff,' he said, 'take out the tarps and give it a good sweep.'

He looked critically at my bare legs. 'Don't get yourself scratched up, running around in shorts,' he said. 'And be careful, too. It's getting hot and the snakes will be out.'

'Snakes?' I didn't like the sound of that.

He nodded solemnly. 'Denim won't stop a rattler's fangs,' he said. 'But sometimes they'll just hit denim and not hit your leg. It's happened to me.' He lifted the leg of his overalls and said, 'I wear these boots. Mister Rattler would have a tough time chomping through them.'

When I took off my leather gloves to drive, I noticed my hands shook a little. Rattlesnake weather? Brilliant.

Auntie Margaret looked worried, too, when I pulled up and went inside the house for her list of errands. 'Julia,' she said, 'this is really helping. All your driving around.'

It was one of the first compliments she gave me. I said, 'Good.' And then, 'I'm glad,' because she seemed to want more.

'I heard about the wrong side of the road. And I know you all sometimes park on the other side from where you drive. But we don't do that here.' She still looked worried.

I said, 'I'll never forget that, after getting shouted at.'

'Mr Hanson called and apologized. He also said you hadn't looked where you were going *at all*.' I remembered that horrible moment, holding the wheel and waiting for the inevitable crash.

I said, 'I think I learned my lesson.'

'Good. Because...' She passed her hand over her forehead and muttered to herself and then said, 'Do you think you could drive all the way down to Pittsburg today? It's about twenty minutes down Highway 69.'

The radio in the truck was rubbish. I'd be listening to Country or nothing. But really, once I started to drive one mile down Highway 69, I might as well drive twenty. I said as much.

She wanted me to go to the Walmart there. They had some curtains that they didn't carry at the Fort Scott one. She gave me money for the curtains and extra money for my lunch, because I wouldn't be back in time. Whenever they did this, they always gave me seven dollars, but they only charged me the normal three.

I said something about that and Margaret blushed again. 'You'd never get anything for three dollars,' she said. 'You'd starve. And a packed lunch will get all nasty, riding around in the truck.'

I also got my usual envelope with all the directions and maps on it and the stock number for the curtains.

I pulled up on the other side of the road from the coyote pasture and got the broom out of the back of the truck. The broom made it easier to prise apart the barbed wire and slip into the pasture and I thought my leather work gloves would make it even easier and I'd have to remember them the next time.

My mirror was still standing, and so was my barre. I was worried that they'd have blown over the breeze the night before, but they still felt steady. I brushed and brushed the old floor, but when I took off my trainers, it still felt rough and gritty underfoot. I'd danced without shoes a hundred times in the studio, when I'd forgotten them, but dancing barefoot on the platform felt...it didn't feel right. I didn't actually get a splinter, but I couldn't stop worrying that I would. I wanted to do the splits in front of my mirror, but the idea of sliding that far, that fast on that surface...just...no.

I was going to need ballet shoes to really do much here. Maybe I'd ask Mum to send mine, once I was allowed to speak to her...in August. The thought of not having any ballet shoes until August made me feel...kind of destroyed.

I braced myself, looking around, for that feeling of being watched, prised apart, preyed on...but then I just started moving into my morning workout. My body did it without me.

And that's the thing about dance. It doesn't really matter how you feel in your morning workout. You don't need to feel happy or determined...or even really ready. You just do it. The good feeling about it comes *after* you do it. I did my barre exercises on the ironing board and it was so big and old and heavy that it worked perfectly well. And I started to feel like I could flick those things in the sky away, if I had to.

I was running through positions and doing a few pliés when the coyote came out of the shadow of the cottonwood tree and trotted up, calm as you please, to lay in the grass about ten metres away. I bowed to him and then did one of the complicated bows that we call a reverence. He twitched his big fluffy ears in a kind of a laugh, and turned his head away for a moment, as if to say, 'Stop, you idiot.'

I looked in the mirror and practised turning my head away that way. Then I went over to the edge of the platform and did it back at him. He looked insulted and got up and turned his whole body, so that he lay in a circle with his head at a right angle to me. He was still watching, though, from the corner of his eye. And his huge pointed ears still looked interested.

I flung myself into a pirouette of disgust. Then I did the head movement and the pirouette of disgust right after it. It was so perfect, it looked so much like him, that it made me laugh. He kind of rolled himself to face me again and I did it for him... I think he was amused, too. He certainly looked interested.

He really was lonely, I realised. Lonely enough that watching me dance made him feel better. I danced a bit of sadness, and loneliness—long diagonal walks with stops for attitudes; low curtsies, big empty circles of arms. I took low, long, trembling steps that swooped down towards the floor as if it was clutching at me, like the trees do when Snow White is lost.

The coyote watched everything, as if he was actually *hungry* for my dancing, as if he *needed* it. For the first time, he watched me like an audience watches a dance.

I probably danced too long. Finally, I jumped up from

a plié and did a very saucy little bow. 'That's our show for today, Mr Coyote,' I said. I tied on my trainers, took my broom and marched off to the truck. The coyote didn't startle at anything I did. He just lay there and watched me go.

The big red cow had completely ignored me today, I realised, as I winnowed my way through the barbed wire. I stuck my tongue out at her, anyway.

So, except for the drive down to Pittsburg, Kansas, it was an ordinary day. The people at the metal buyers and the dump knew me now. I dropped off tomatoes and eggs. The sky behaved itself and didn't turn into anything horrible. The highway wasn't that terrifying and I found the Walmart and the curtains okay.

I cut through the women's clothing on my way back, to see if there was anything interesting, and found myself in sportswear. I kind of looked, you know, at sports bras and leggings, thinking they might work better as a leotard than my shorts and vest and then I turned a corner and... there were ballet shoes. Actual ballet shoes. On little cardboard things on hooks. In the middle of a Walmart. They had my size. And I had enough money to buy them. But not the phone, too. But I didn't care. I *had* to have them.

I was in the truck and headed back up Highway 69 when it started again. It started really hard, that feeling like I was being watched. But it wasn't like it was before.

I didn't feel got at. I felt...like something wanted me to notice it.

I got stuck behind a big truck trying to turn left and I found myself reaching out to hold my dance shoes, still on their little cardboard hanger. And it was like the sky was saying, 'Yes!' to me. Really loudly. My cracked place was...not hurting exactly...stinging. Burning.

And then I started to wonder. I'd needed a place to dance and I'd found one. I'd needed a mirror and a barre and I'd been given them. I'd wanted a broom and I'd been given one of those, too. I'd decided I needed ballet shoes and I'd been sent to find them.

It was like the somethings in the sky wanted me *to dance*.

I'd been going to church with Auntie Margaret and Uncle Ethan. I'd sat and stood and knelt. I'd tried to sing along and to say the right things at the right time. But I didn't really *believe* any of it. I did it because I was meant to do it, because it was a big deal for Margaret and Ethan and because it was one of the ways I was supposed to 'do right'. But it wasn't anything to do with me—not really.

I didn't believe in God. Or any kind of magic. I didn't believe in sky spirits or whatever they were, that was for absolute rock bottom certain. I didn't believe in anything that I was feeling.

I was in that big old truck underneath the huge blue bowl of the sky. My hand and wrists on the giant steering wheel still looked childlike to me. Sometimes I couldn't believe that I was allowed to steer all this metal, to be by myself in this way. Everything was so enormous—the land stretched out all around me, as far as I could see. And I was this little bundle of bone and muscle and brain surviving in the middle of it. That was miracle enough.

I said it, out loud. I said, 'Life is miracle enough.' And then I thought that I might be actually losing it. Really, properly going off the rails.

Someone pipped behind me and I realized the traffic had cleared and I was still sitting in the middle of Highway 69. I put the truck into gear and pulled away, leaving, I hoped, all those crazy thoughts behind me.

When I made the right turn and drove past the coyote pasture, I thought again about spirits in the sky, pushing me to get a broom and ballet shoes. Only now, it made me laugh, because it was so ridiculous.

This place, I decided, was starting to get to me.

CHAPTER NINE

Three hours later, I was at softball practice.

The boys' baseball practice was right before ours and they tended to hang around and watch us. At first, Mrs Hall used to chase them away, but she kind of gave up on that and just let them stay.

During a match...a *game*...we all sat in the dugout—a kind of half-underground shed by first base. But during practice, we just sat on the benches...the *bleachers*...where spectators were meant to sit. Brad and the other boys kept moving down and Whitney and the girls kept moving up. I think we were supposed to be running laps while the other half of the team did a complicated double-play exercise, but instead we lazed on the benches and chatted.

Well, they chatted, anyway. I sat there and imagined looking at my imaginary watch, trying to make the time go quicker. Every once in a while, I'd find that my eyes had drifted over to Brad, not actually looking at *him*, but just resting, kind of, on one of his arms, or his hair, or the way his leg looked in the stretchy practice trousers they wore for baseball. And sometimes, he'd see me looking and he'd smile and then I'd look back at my imaginary watch and wish I could go home.

It pretty much went like that every practice.

That night, Brad said my name. He was looking right at me, with a big smile on his perfect, tanned American face. 'You like coyotes?' he said.

I shrugged. I said, 'I think they're interesting.'

Everyone laughed a little. Whitney rolled her eyes as if she could only just barely tolerate my weirdness. But Brad said, 'I downloaded a video for you,' and motioned to me with his phone.

I climbed up one more row and sat in between him and Carter. They smelled like boys smell when they get hot, and it reminded me of hanging out at school with Max and Archie. It was a horrible smell, don't get me wrong, but it was a *familiar* horrible smell.

So, I probably leaned a little closer to Brad than I ordinarily would have, to watch the video, because the horrible smell was familiar.

He turned his phone sideways and hit play and there was a coyote, filling the screen. Its eyes were darker than my coyote, more greenish, and its ears were tipped with a whitey-grey colour. It had more red in its coat. But it was breathtakingly beautiful.

It was moving across a field of grass, intent on a sound. Brad said, 'Wait a minute,' paused it, and fiddled with the volume on his phone before he hit play again. I could hear a yelping noise.

'That's the lure,' Carter explained. 'It sounds like coyote puppies crying.'

The coyote's face showed concern and worry. He sped up, trotting forwards and looking all around, stopping to sniff, because his nose was better than his eyes or ears to find the puppies.

Then, suddenly, there was a loud popping sound and

the coyote fell over, flat, and a man wearing camouflage stood up in front of the camera and whooped. 'He's a big one!' He shut off a box and the sound stopped, so that must have been the coyote lure. The camera turned and there was a heap of dead coyotes in the back of a red truck. 'That's ten today! What a day!' and then went back onto the man. He picked up the poor coyote's dead head and smiled into the camera.

Margaret had made us burgers that night, cooked outside on the grill. My stomach turned over, and even though I could hear everyone laughing, I pushed through them all blindly to get down the bleacher and over to the fence. I kept seeing that moment when the coyote was hurrying to help the puppies and then boom and then...

I vomited up my dinner into the tall grass by the fence. Thank goodness I had my hair up under my baseball cap, because I didn't have time to do anything else but bend over and...

...it was disgusting.

My sick was disgusting and the video was disgusting and *those people* were even more disgusting and...I was *not* going to cry. I was *not*.

My stomach turned over again. That poor animal...

'Here.' It was Whitney, who had brought me a cup of the horrible squash. I wiped my mouth with the back of my hand and just glared at her.

She motioned with the red plastic cup. 'Come on,' she said. 'It's got electrolytes in it. You'll feel better, right away.'

I was weak and shaky-feeling, so I took it and drank it and once I started to drink it, I drank the whole big cup straight down and pushed my tears down with it. 'Those jerks,' Whitney said. 'I'm really sorry.'

We moved away from my sick and I leaned against a pole in the fencing. 'All the boys here,' Whitney said, 'are into hunting. That was Brad's dad on the video.' She chuckled. 'Brad's dad. Sounds funny,' she giggled, and then composed her face into sympathy again and said, 'Sorry.'

I said, 'Thanks for the drink,' and took off my softball mitt. I swung by the dugout and grabbed the handbag I'd started to carry again from the bench in there.

Mrs Hall called after me, 'Julia? Are you okay?', but I left the others to explain and got into my truck.

I was shaking all over. I had to take some deep breaths to stop myself, had to turn on the radio loud to cover up the sound of that shot echoing in my ears.

When I drove down the main drag, I saw Robbie at Tasty Queen, sitting on the back of his truck and I turned on my signal and pulled over and parked up, kind of on autopilot and then before I knew it, I really was crying, and Robbie Slater was holding me in his strong arms and telling me it was going to be all right.

Half a cherry limeade later, we were still talking about it. 'It's legal,' Robbie kept telling me. 'You can trap their paws or their bodies in big metal clamps with teeth. You can poison them. You can lure them, like you saw. You can shoot them with a bow and arrow. Some people trap them and then use them to train fighting dogs or starve them and torture them until they fight each other. It's not legal to fight with dogs, but there's no law against fighting coyotes.'

I wondered if my coyote knew any of that, on any kind of level. Did he know how dangerous it was to hang out with me? Did he hang out with me anyway? Or was he just too stupid to stay away from humans?

'That's horrible,' I said.

Robbie nodded slowly. 'Yeah,' he agreed. 'There's just a lot of coyotes. If they were rare or something, they'd be more protected.' He looked off into the distance for a moment. 'Or maybe not,' he said. 'The government isn't always super good at looking after native animals.'

The air felt warm, but it also felt pressured somehow. I looked up at the sky and it looked as if it had lowered.

Robbie pointed up. 'Weather's coming in,' he said.

I started to jump down and he laughed. 'You've got a few more hours,' he told me and waved his limeade at the tree behind us. 'Keep an eye on the cottonwood leaves,' he said. 'When the whole tree looks silvery, you know the rain is about to hit.'

He looked at me sideways. He started to say…but I'll never know what it was, because Brad was suddenly standing there.

'I'm really sorry, Jules,' he said. 'Madison told me you guys don't even have guns over there. I didn't mean to freak you out.'

I hadn't even thought about that aspect of it. Brad had access to guns? And Carter, too, presumably and all those boys. They all had guns. The idea was totally insane.

I don't know what I said. I think I mumbled something about it being all right. I didn't want a big scene with Brad. I didn't want a big scene with *anybody*. I just wanted to get along.

'Come on,' he said, holding out his hand, as if to help me jump down. 'I'll buy you some curly fries.' He smiled at me. 'You can tell me all about how stupid I am. Whitney's just scratched the surface.'

Robbie was looking up at the clouds rolling in, as if he wasn't even there. He wasn't going to interfere. He was leaving it up to me.

I said, 'It's okay, Brad. But I'm good here.'

He looked as if I'd slapped him. 'Oh, come on, Jules,' he said. 'Don't be like that. You know I just wanted you to talk to me.'

He grabbed my hand and tugged, just a little. It didn't hurt or anything, but…but I didn't *want* to go and sit with them. I wanted to stay sitting outside with Robbie, watching the clouds roll in. I pulled my hand away and said, 'I'm not cross with you, Brad. I'm just happy here.'

Brad glanced behind him towards the Tasty Queen windows. 'Don't be like this, Jules,' he said. He looked up at me from where his perfect hair had flopped over his lovely eyes. There was this moment, when I looked at Brad and actually wanted to be with him.

But then Robbie put down his limeade and hopped down from the truck. He didn't say anything. He just looked at Brad.

'Well,' Brad said, backing away. 'I'll see you later, Jules.' He and Robbie exchanged a long, slow glance that seemed to have a lot of history in it.

I watched Brad walk back up into Tasty Queen alone. From the back, in his stripy t-shirt, he looked like a much younger boy. I turned to Robbie, 'It seems like you two know each other,' and Robbie just huffed and looked back at the sky.

Robbie had the same edges of silence that my Uncle Ethan had, places where you just didn't want to put words. I let it go without asking.

I kept looking up at the sky and the cottonwood tree, and, about five minutes later, I drove home. The night was coming in fast again, blacker than any night I'd ever seen in my life. There were no lines on the tarmac and then I was driving on gravel and the light was fading and I could barely see where the turn to our drive was, even with my lights on full beam.

And then I opened the truck door and a wild animal was there, black and shining in the yard light, with rolling eyes and huge, sharp teeth. It jumped at me and barked and then there were two more and I scrambled back into the truck and fumbled for my phone to tell Aunt Margaret...

...who was there, now, saying, 'Calm down, you idiots. Shut up!'

And they were dogs. Three black dogs. They looked kind of cute now that they weren't trying to kill me. I started to open the door and one of them growled and Margaret smacked it across the nose with two fingers. 'I said it was *okay*,' she thundered. 'If I say it's okay, it's *okay*!' They cowered around her and she patted all their heads. They seemed to have about twenty apiece.

I opened the truck door again and had to put one bare leg out to slide down. They all rushed over to me and smelled me and one jumped up and scratched its claws all down my arm. '*Down*,' Margaret bellowed and it cowered down. 'Good,' she said, and it scampered around her, wagging its tail.

She looked up and I could tell she was embarrassed. 'I went by the shelter today,' she said. 'Just to look.'

I couldn't help laughing. They were huge—big, black, shining dogs with big, fat, round feet. My aunt saw me noticing their feet and nodded shamefacedly. 'Yeah,' she said. 'They're just puppies. They're going to get bigger.'

'What are they?'

'God knows.' She rolled her eyes to heaven. 'Labrador and Rottweiler is what the shelter lady said. But it might be Great Dane and Rottweiler.'

'Or horse.' Uncle Ethan was by the mudroom door. 'In,' he said, and all three stopped their prancing around Margaret and filed meekly into the mudroom. 'Bed.' There were now three dog beds in the mudroom and it had a baby gate into the kitchen. The dogs walked sedately to their beds. 'Down.' They immediately laid down and put their heads on their paws.

We went into the kitchen and Ethan looked back. 'Good,' he said and three tails beat softly against the tiles of the mudroom floor. He grunted and turned away.

'He thinks I'm crazy,' Margaret confided. 'But they were going to be gassed. I couldn't choose just *one*.'

Evidently, the rain was heavy. I slept right through it.

I woke up the next morning and did my stretches, but when I started to clatter down the stairs like normal, Uncle Ethan met me at the bottom with his finger to his lips and led me to the new baby gate in the kitchen.

On an old quilt, in the middle of the mudroom floor, my Auntie Margaret lay sound asleep, with all three puppies burrowed around her.

CHAPTER TEN

That morning, I noticed that the farmhouse was... different. I didn't spend a whole lot of time downstairs. I was either outdoors or driving around or falling into my bed half-dead, but even I noticed it that morning. I made the pancakes (I'd watched Ethan enough) and Auntie Margaret hobbled around in her dressing-gown, fat eyed and achey from the night with the puppies.

The kitchen was... properly clean. There were no more piles of paper and no more untidy stacks of... stuff. The fruit bowl had actual fruit in it. It actually did smell of lemons and a little bit of bleach.

The curtains I'd picked up from Walmart looked really nice at the big window in the living-room. All the rugs had been cleaned and the floors shone. All the glass was clear.

I said something about it over breakfast to Uncle Ethan, who had put down his paper to try and be sociable, since Auntie Margaret was in the shower. He said, 'Well, that's you.'

I must have looked blank, because he explained. 'You've been helping out. Margaret gets more done. We've been a bit short-handed since the kids moved away.'

They had started a family right out of high school and had four. Vicky was the youngest. Tony was a heart surgeon in California—we'd had dinner with him when we went to L.A. Paul played the cello and taught music in South Dakota. Ellie was married and they were both in law, again in California (they hadn't had time to come to dinner with us). Tony had three children; I remembered the photos he'd shown us on his phone.

I said, 'Don't any of them want to...' and kind of waved my hand around at the farm. Uncle Ethan did his little lip movement that meant he was smiling and shook his head. 'Well,' he said. 'Tony keeps saying he's going to retire early and bring the kids to live here, but I'm not sure Carleen agrees with that plan.'

I'd seen photographs of Tony's wife on social media— lots of jewellery and teeth and beach holidays.

Auntie Margaret had come out of their bathroom while we were talking. Her hair was wet, but she was dressed. She got another cup of coffee and sat down. 'Yeah,' she said. 'I guess that's our big problem. I mean, we'll keep farming until we can't do it any more, but we're already getting to the point where help is sure nice.'

I thought about it as I cleaned the kitchen and loaded up for the day. I was going to the feed store again for a roll of barbed wire and staples and then to the lumberyard for fence posts and over to the hardware shop for cement mix. I was taking more tomatoes and eggs—Ethan had gone out to the tunnel and picked the tomatoes and collected the eggs for Margaret when he let out the chickens. I had to swing by the vets and get some dog food and pick up the identification tags Margaret had ordered yesterday when she was getting the collars and leads.

I knew their kids loved them. They Skyped all the time and they were all coming for holidays later in the summer.

But I could understand, too, why they didn't want to live on the farm. The whole work and dirt and poo and bugs thing. It wasn't exactly attractive.

The puppies loved the farm…and they loved *me*. Every step I took, they kind of swarmed around me. They were sweet and had silky ears and bristly backs. I loved the shapes they made; endless circles and curves with their spines, big sweeps with their heads and necks. But they were always fighting each other, jumping up on each other's backs, pretending to snap at each other's throats, nipping ears and tails and yelping.

Their teeth were huge and sharp and their claws were, too, because, Auntie Margaret said, they hadn't been worn down enough. Whoever had them first hadn't trained them very well or taken them for proper walks. They were house-trained and knew a few words, but they would need discipline to become good dogs. Well, they'd certainly get that around here, I thought, as I got yet another long scratch down my leg.

'Walk time!' Margaret called. She snapped leads onto their collars. 'Right,' she said. She started walking to the long path that led through the farm. One of the puppies walked with her, but the other two became hopelessly tangled immediately. Margaret looked at me. 'This is going to be a long day,' she said.

She disentangled them, sorted them into position and then started again. They didn't get the whole way across the yard before she had to stop.

But I could tell she was enjoying herself.

The air was fresh and clean-smelling and I found myself humming as I used my leather gloves and pushed through the fence to the coyote pasture.

I had tried to find a way to carry my ballet shoes, and the only way I could do it was to tuck them into the waistband of my shorts...actually into the waistband of my shorts *and* the waistband of my underwear, because if I just used my shorts, they fell right through. I tried about twenty different positions, but there was a spot in the hollow of my left hipbone where they didn't really bother me and stayed put, so I put them there.

The big red cow, who I thought had been getting used to me, now decided again that I was completely horrible. She bellowed and ran at me as I was halfway to the ridge. I could have done without it, really. She was irritating.

In a way, she was terribly slow, with her fat on her neck and chest kind of wobbling as she went. But in a way, she seemed really fast, and I could feel the earth under my feet trembling with the force of her hooves hitting the earth.

I didn't even think about running. I just kind of stood there and was cross with her, and braced myself for the impact, should she actually run into me. I was being charged by a cow, I suddenly thought. People died from that...didn't they?

Dust flew up from her feet as she got closer and I half closed my eyes...and then she stopped short, opened her horrible, slick, gaping nostrils and snorted snot at me. Thankfully, it didn't actually get close enough to hit me, but she certainly tried. And then she lowered her neck, extended her head and bellowed at me for all she was worth. I can tell you right now, a cow's breath is *not* pleasant.

And I'd had just about *enough* of her bullying.

I drew myself up to my full height. I wasn't that tall, but I was taller than *her*. I said, 'What? What is your problem?' and marched right up to her.

Her eyes opened so wide I thought they were going to fall out, and she drew her head back in.

'No, really,' I asked her. 'What seems to be the big deal? Why are you such...such a *cow* to me? Have I ever hurt you? Have I ever chased you? Have I ever threatened your calves?' Now she shrank back on her haunches, rolling her eyes.

'No!' I continued ranting. 'No, I haven't. All I do is walk through your sodding pasture...and you could be a bit more careful about where you poo, by the way...to get to my studio.'

Slowly, watching me with her big, spinning eyeballs, she backed away. 'Just leave me *alone!*' I said, and made a shooing motion with my hands. She spun on her back feet and ran back to her herd.

It was very satisfying.

The weather had knocked over my mirror and my barre, but neither one was damaged. I set them up and ran through my exercises with my ballet shoes on. It was heavenly. My ronds de jambe, the circling movements you make on the floor with your feet at the barre... well, I thought they'd been okay the day before, but with the shoes they were actually fun. I pushed through barre work and then did what few allégros I could remember... maybe I could get a Bluetooth speaker when I got my phone, I thought. I could download some music, and...

The coyote had been in his usual place in the tall grass, watching me. I could see his ears and the top of his head, but not much else. Even so, as I started a nice, long diagonal of pirouettes, trying hard not to fall off at the end (I used to get told off for that quite a bit), I noticed that he'd lost interest in my dance.

And I stopped. I stopped dancing because the coyote wasn't watching.

I was so desperate, I realized, for feedback about my dancing, that I now actually cared what an outcast coyote thought of my technique.

Once I realized that's what I was thinking, I had a little giggle to myself. I was just about to start some pliés when I saw him suddenly move forwards, his head poised, his ears totally intent.

My coyote wasn't bored by my dancing. He was *hunting*. He'd found a mouse or something in the grass.

I stopped moving completely. I think I even stopped breathing.

Suddenly, he sprang into the air. His back was arched. His front legs were stiff, reaching. His head was nearly tucked between them, his ears tilted forwards. It was like a cat's pounce, but also totally *un*like it. He wasn't getting closer to his victim so he could kill it. He *was* going to kill it, with his straight-arm hit.

And he did. He came back up with something big—a rat?—in his jaws. He looked at me as if to say, 'Sorry. I've got to go, now,' and took off for the tree.

I saw my body slump in the mirror. I'd lost my audience's attention to a rat. Realizing what had dragged me down made me laugh—it was just too ridiculous. When I did laugh about it, I saw my shoulders square up and my ribs pull higher. I didn't smile just with my mouth. I smiled with my whole body. No wonder everyone always seemed to know what I was thinking.

And I don't know why, but then I tried to do the jump the coyote had just done. I arched my back and held my arms out stiff and...

Not right.

I tried again and tried to tuck my head into my arms tighter and...

No.

Something was wrong, but I couldn't see what it was. It was something about the way my head was...or maybe my back or my bottom wasn't...I just couldn't *see*. I tried it one way and then worked the other way, but...if I only had another mirror...but they really needed to be big mirrors, because when I moved too much, I lost sight of myself and...

I gave up.

I sank down into splits and raised my arms above my head. It looked lovely. I looked great, really. When I got up, and after I'd dusted down my bottom and everything, I raised up onto demi-pointe in fifth position, with my feet tight, tight against each other and my ribcage up, chin up, bottom in, arms soft and wide and high and... I looked perfect. Just like I used to look—no, *better*. My legs looked stronger and longer. My arms were tighter and something about all the sun and how brown my skin was made me look... really good.

I looked like a proper dancer again. And maybe not 'again'. Maybe for the first time.

But I still couldn't see behind me. I wanted to see how my back looked, now that I'd started properly tightening up my line. I thought about the mirrors at my old studio and the idea nearly made my mouth water... I wanted them that badly. I looked at my ironing board and cracked mirror. I could hear my teacher/audience cracking the bones of the rat to eat it, even though I couldn't see him any more. And in a way, it was all great and I loved it and in a way it wasn't really great at all and I hated it.

I took off my ballet shoes and tied on my trainers. It was getting late.

CHAPTER ELEVEN

'Jules! Jules! Wait up!'

I was loading fence posts into the back of my truck. Uncle Ethan wanted forty, but I was only going to take twenty of them now. I'd have to unload them at the farm and come back for the other twenty tomorrow. The man at the lumberyard told me I'd 'bust my axle' if I tried to take them all, with the two spools of barbed wire and the sacks of cement mix and the dog food and everything I already had in the truck. He meant that the pole-thing that connected the wheels on one side of the back of my truck to the wheels on the other side would actually break and my truck would be really hurt. Once he explained, I'd agreed to make two trips. He put the posts away for me, so nobody else could get them. I guess they were popular in June.

And now someone was shouting my name. I turned, wiping sweat from my forehead onto the back of my leather glove. Carter. Brad's friend.

I didn't smile or anything, but I also didn't made a rude hand gesture and jump in my truck and spray him with gravel, which was what I *considered* doing. I just stood there and took off my gloves.

He said, 'God. I'm really sorry about last night.' He was thinner and less muscly than Brad. He had dark, shining hair and darker blue eyes and, I suppose he was quite nice-looking, actually. Next to Brad, he looked like nothing, but on his own like this, you could see he was actually rather cute.

I noticed this, and I noticed myself noticing, but I didn't actually *feel* anything about Carter. So I stood there some more.

'I mean,' he said. 'Of course it was stupid. We just didn't even think about you not being from here and not seeing...' He shook the hair out of his eyes and looked around, at the sky, the truck the ground, 'I mean, we're all kind of used to...you know...hunting and guns and...stuff.' Finally, he looked at my face. It must not have looked encouraging. 'Anyway, we knew it would gross you out but we didn't know it would actually *bother* you.' He shrugged and kind of tailed off. 'We're sorry. Both of us are sorry.'

He looked *so* uncomfortable that I couldn't keep on saying nothing. I said, 'It's okay.'

Suddenly his smile was blinding. 'Really?' he said. 'That's great.' And then, 'Hey, um...' he kind of twitched his head towards the centre of town. 'Do you get...um...money for lunch? Or a sandwich? Or do you go back to the farm, or what?'

I said, 'Well, it depends. Today they gave me money.' Seven dollars again.

I got the full white Carter smile again. 'That's great because we were all going to meet up at the pizza place? For the buffet? For lunch?'

I nodded, meaning that I knew the place.

But Carter thought I'd actually agreed to come. 'Oh, I'm so glad. That's great. We'll be there in about ten minutes.'

And then he kind of spun around and strode off.

He didn't hear me say, 'But, I didn't mean...' to his back.

Great.

I usually drove through and got a burrito or a burger or something and ate it in the car park and then went on to my next errand on my days in town. I never actually *went in* anywhere. I got into my truck and looked in the mirror. I had a bright orange streak on my forehead, from the dye of my leather gloves where I'd kept wiping my sweat with them. Sweat had also stained a dark V through my sports bra and my vest. I sniffed under my arms, but at least my deodorant was still working. I was still using an English deodorant and I thought it was being heroic...it wasn't designed for that kind of heat and all my physical work. My shorts were dusty. My legs and arms were scratched up by puppies and tall grass and from where I'd tried to help load the barbed wire myself (stupid).

I pulled out of the lumberyard in a kind of panic and then remembered that there was a chemist...a *drugstore*...just around the corner. I went in there and bought some baby wipes and then sat in the truck and pretty much went over every inch of my skin. I had some lip gloss in my handbag and a hairbrush. I ended up sticking my hair back into a bun, but at least I got some bits of grass and a twig out of it and the lip gloss kind of...well...kind of helped.

Well, *stuff it*, I thought, driving to the pizza place and finding a spot and putting the truck into Park and popping on the parking break. I *work*, I thought. I am a *working woman*. My mum never thinks twice about being photographed in overalls and a hard hat when she's off in the oilfields or on an oilrig in the middle of the sea. She gives the same confident smile to the camera she does when she's in a ball gown at a charity function or a chic suit advising MPs on international trade. So I put up my chin and in I went.

'Wow!' Whitney said, after she rushed over and hugged me. 'You look like a real Kansas farm girl.' She told me where to get my plate and how to use the crazily-complicated soda machine.

That's when I discovered that diet root beer with vanilla is the best thing in the entire world. I had a sip of it before I got my pizza and then just stood there and drank nearly the whole cup and filled it up again. It was brilliant.

So, I was kind of happy by the time I sat with them at the table with my big salad and diet root beer. I hadn't had a lot of salad since I'd arrived... Uncle Ethan didn't think it was real food... and I just piled my plate.

Maybe it was because I didn't care about how I looked and actually didn't mind being there, but the whole cool kids gang was really funny that day. Everyone was working, except for Madison B, who had to look after her little brother and sister all summer—they were at their swimming lessons while she had lunch with us. They all told stories about their jobs and then... so did I.

I told them all about Margaret's puppies and they laughed so hard that Chastity snorted soda out of her nose. '*How* big are their paws?' Brad kept asking and I kept showing him and everyone would laugh again.

Then Madison B said, laughing, 'My mom thought Margaret was crazy for taking *you* on, wait until I tell her about...' And all the laughter stopped.

I felt the blood rush up in my body to my face and I suddenly felt very full, like I'd eaten far too much, like I never wanted to eat again.

'Really?' Whitney said angrily. 'Really? You really went there?'

I kind of looked down at my plate, which made me sick to look at, but I couldn't not look at it because if I raised my head, I'd have to look at the other kids' eyes. They knew how horrid I was. I was a horrid person...such a liability...nobody wanted to take me on...my own mother couldn't stand to be with me. I heard Mum's voice in my head, '*Failure. You failed. I failed. Failed, failed, failed.*'

Brad reached across the table and took my hand and the shock of it, of him touching me, made me look up at him. 'It's a little town,' he said. 'Don't take it seriously.'

Everyone chorused that he was right and he kept talking. He said, 'Every single person that I've seen has asked me about showing you that video. I swear.' His eyes were big and sorrowful in his perfect American face. 'How stupid are you?' 'What were you thinking?' he mimicked. 'Didn't you know she was English?' 'Way to go, Brad.' 'You really know how to get the girls interested.' 'Hear you have a unique way of getting a girl's attention.' 'Do all the girls you talk to throw up, or just some of them?'

At first, we all listened in horror. But after the second or third one, everyone started to giggle a little. And by the last one, the sound of my mother's voice faded in my head and even I couldn't keep from grinning. Suddenly, my salad looked really nice again and I picked up my fork.

Sorry, Madison B mouthed across the table.

It's okay, I mouthed back.

And it was, truly, okay. Brad could be . . . kind of lovely. And Madison B? I actually *liked* her.

When I got back to the farm, Uncle Ethan helped me unload and then looked at his watch. 'You mind going back to the lumberyard now?' he asked. I shook my head, no and he said, 'I want to get an early start tomorrow. Robbie's coming over and we're going to try and get most of them in before it gets too hot. Digging in posts isn't any fun in the heat of the day, even with the machine.'

He reached in his back pocket and took out his worn leather wallet. 'Here,' he said, pulling out some money. 'Get yourself dinner at Tasty Queen and ask Robbie to come extra early. I used to practically live on their chilli dogs. It won't do you any harm.'

'Or I could just text him?' I said, holding out my phone, but Ethan shook his head.

'I'd rather operate face to face,' he said.

Which was fine, but it wasn't his face, I thought. I didn't want Robbie to think I was running around after him, some little girl that he just couldn't get rid of.

Still, I went upstairs and changed.

I had glanced for the coyote as I'd driven back to the farm, but I hadn't seen him. On my way back out, I slowed down for a minute and stopped. I don't know why. I was across the road, so I couldn't see into the pasture very far—the ridge and the way the road slanted cut off the view. And I knew that, so stopping wasn't really to look, it was more symbolic, I guess, more me telling myself that the me I'd always been before was still there somewhere, underneath all the American Kids and Farm Girl life I was leading.

And, maybe because I only stopped the truck in that direction when I was coming to dance, the coyote came out to look at me. First I saw his ears, then his head, then he trotted up onto the ridge and looked across the grass, right into my eyes, with his wild golden stare.

It was hot and still. Even the birds were quiet. The sky stretched huge and impossibly far away, lit by the strongest sunlight you can imagine. The air was hazy with heat and moisture being baked out of the grass and the earth. I got that feeling again, that people were watching me, that they could see right into my soul, through the cracked place in the very centre of me, where all the things I didn't like about myself showed.

And I don't know what it was, but something about the coyote being there made me okay with that, with the things getting in and looking at me. He looked at me and I looked at him and the things in the sky looked inside me and...I don't know. It was okay. For a moment.

Then I said, 'Laters,' and put the truck into D for Drive. The coyote watched me pull away.

Back at the lumberyard, after I'd loaded about half the posts, it felt like a splinter had gone right through my glove. But when I pulled my glove off, it was a big bubble of skin on the palm of my left hand. The man came over to see and said, 'Congratulations. You've worked hard enough to get yourself a blister.'

I'd had them on my heels before, from shoes that weren't quite small enough. And a girl I knew got a bad one from playing too much tennis, on the pad of her palm. But seriously, *inside* a glove? I'd been working too hard.

'You need to get a band-aid on that,' he said. I knew what he meant, though I would have called it a plaster. 'There's a drugstore about two doors down and they stay open late.'

So I found myself at the pharmacy for the second time that day. I wavered between two packs of plasters and nearly got the Disney-themed ones, but decided something bigger would probably work better. I walked out, fitting a big one over the blister. It felt a little better straight away. And then, and only because I was looking for a rubbish bin...a *trash can*...for the little paper bits you peel off the back of a plaster, I looked up and finally, finally saw it.

The letters were over a metre high and bright purple. I couldn't believe I hadn't noticed them before. I especially couldn't believe I hadn't seen them when I'd bought the baby wipes before lunch.

FORT SCOTT SCHOOL OF DANCE.

'Summer of Salsa' it said across the big blanked-out window. There was a wall-sized mural of a South American carnival scene, all palm trees and feathered costumes and dark, handsome men.

I had about as much conscious choice in crossing that street as a paper clip has about going towards a magnet. It was like the entire universe pulled me over.

Was it just a ballroom studio? But no, because on the door it said, 'Ballroom. Tap. Jazz. Ballet.' It might have said other things below 'Ballet' but I didn't look. Ballet. There was a ballet teacher *in Fort Scott*.

I pushed open the door and a little bell tinkled. It felt cool and dim inside after the incredible heat of the afternoon. There was nobody around, although someone called from the back, 'I'll be right there,' and then didn't come. I could hear something fall. 'Oh, hell,' the same voice muttered and then, louder, 'I'll be a few minutes. You can come back later, if you want.'

'No, that's okay,' I shouted back. 'I'll wait.'

I peeked in the door to my right. It was a studio. Sprung floor, mirrors on all four sides, a long barre.

Again, I didn't even really think about it. My body was already taking off my trainers and reaching in my bag for my ballet shoes before my mind even *considered* going in. I flicked on the light and suddenly, there I was.

I seemed small and dirty, but I went up on demi-pointe

again, tight into fifth position and yes, I was looking amazing. My back had *never* looked so strong. I had a great line on my shoulders and my bottom was, finally, snug and in the right place. I gave a restrained little whoop and did a couple of cat steps in celebration.

And that made me think…I tried my coyote jump again. I hunched my back and did the straight arms and downed head. It wasn't right. Everything about it looked wrong. The pas de chat had looked fine—they're little sideways jumps—and I tried doing one of those but twisting with the stiff coyote arm and head thing. And that was *almost* right…it made me see that the problem wasn't the arms or the head. It was the jump. I was jumping with just two legs. It made the proportions all wrong.

If I jumped smaller and arched my back right at the beginning of the jump, then…

'May I help you?'

I nearly fell over. It's hard for me to blush, but I managed. I said, 'I'm so sorry. I've been trying…and then the mirrors were…'

It was a man. At first I thought he was around my mum's age, but he was much older. He just carried himself like a younger man. He was looking at me sternly, but then broke into a wry grin.

'What are you trying to choreograph?' he said. 'It looks like a diver.'

I *knew* I was still getting the head wrong. I said, 'Never mind. It was stupid,' and started to leave. 'I'm sorry to come in and start using your studio.'

Without seeming to hurry, he blocked my exit with his arm.

'Not so fast,' he said. 'You used my studio, you have to tell me what you're doing.'

Even though there was nobody else there, I wasn't scared at all. His words were fierce, but he had a warm smile. He said, 'Of course you can go if you want to. And you can tell your Uncle Ethan I tried to entrap you in my evil dance studio.' He put his head on one side. '*Or* you can tell me about your...erm...choreography.'

He came in and sat on a tall stool in the corner and, suddenly, it was every masterclass I'd ever had. I shrugged and then stood properly and said, 'It was a coyote. Hunting mice. You know the way they...' I did the arm thing again and he nodded.

'Back to work,' he said, pointing to the middle of the floor.

'I can't,' I said. 'I don't have any money for lessons.'

He put one elegant hand on his chest, dancing the emotion of being offended. 'Did I ask you for money?' he asked.

It was awkward and kind of cringe-making. But it was so nice being with another dancer, after so long. I shook my head, no.

'Back to work with you, then.' He settled himself down. 'Are you warm?' He was asking if I'd prepared my body for movement—if a dancer tries to dance without warming up, they're likely to hurt themselves.

'Pretty warm,' I said. 'I did barre and floor exercises

this morning and I've been doing physical work just now.'

'Okay, then.' He put his head on one side. 'I think your problem is that your legs bend the wrong way.'

I could see myself look puzzled in the big mirrors. Even my back looked suddenly uncertain.

'For a coyote, I mean,' he explained, and I watched myself understand and relax. 'That's why the pas de chat felt a little more like the right movement. You need to work this move out of a deep plié, to give the impression of coyote legs.'

I sank down into a plié, a deep open knee bend.

'Deeper.'

I sank lower. It hurt a bit.

'Now do your jump out of that.'

I sprang up into the arched back and stiffened my arms before me. My head still wasn't right.

'That's *so* much better,' he said. 'But your head's still not right.'

I thought about what he'd just taught me. My body could make the same moves as a coyote and still not dance a coyote because it wasn't the same body. So the problem with my head was...

'I don't have ears,' I said.

'Good!' he clapped his hands. 'Very good.' We looked at my head for a moment. 'You could use costume or movement, or both. What would you like to do?'

I didn't want to wear big ears on top of my head. I'd feel like an idiot. 'Movement,' I said.

'So,' he said. 'What is the coyote saying with its head at that moment?'

'I see you. I hear you. I'm going to eat you.'

I got another round of applause. 'So how can you make that with your own head? How would you look at someone if you were going to eat them?'

I found myself jutting my head forward, right from the base of my neck, and lowering my eyes so that I was looking from underneath my brows.

'Good. Again.'

'Good. Again.'

'Good. Again.'

'Now with the jump.'

Deep plié. Deeper. Deep until it hurt and jump, shoulders hunched, chin tucked in, looking up from brows, arms rigid. That was it. I did it again and again, without being told.

'Brilliant.'

I stopped to find myself being watched by ten or twelve little girls, one little boy and five or six mothers. The girls were wearing black leotards and pink tights and the boy was wearing a white leotard and navy shorts. They were all staring at me with their mouths open.

'Do it again,' the man said.

I swallowed. I hadn't danced in front of that many people since the school musical. Still, I knew the move, now. I could do it a million times, if I wanted. Or I could not do it for twenty years and still remember how.

I faced my audience and did the move.

'What was that, do you think?' the man asked the children.

'It's a coyote,' the little boy said. 'It's the way they jump.' Everyone murmured their agreement.

I stayed being a coyote. I did his, 'Who me?' look. His crouching in the tall grass. His affronted head turn. The pirouette of his disgust.

'That's amazing!' one of the mums said. Everyone applauded.

I felt... I felt strange and suddenly large and awkward. But I also felt completely amazing. In my dusty shorts and Wallmart shoes, with a big plaster on my blistered hand and scratches all down my bare legs—I was still a dancer. After everything that had happened, I could still dance ballet.

'Don't go anywhere,' the man said. I shuffled to the little reception area as the mums settled the little ones into the studio. I sat on one of the chairs near the desk to change back into my trainers. He got the children doing nice toes and naughty toes and then popped back out.

'Come back tomorrow,' he said. 'Just after lunch.'

'I can't pay...' I started, but he did his offended gesture again. 'You can work,' he said. 'I've got a shi—' he caught himself, 'a great many boxes coming in and my storage is completely f—' he caught himself again, '*messed* up and I really must clear it out. Help me.'

I was supposed to be working for Margaret and Ethan. But... I didn't always work *all* day. Sometimes in the afternoon, I just sat around on the deck or had an early bath. I said I'd ask Margaret and Ethan and the man gave me a quick hug. He smelled lovely. 'I'm Geoffrey,' he said. 'I'll see you soon.'

I was absolutely buzzing with joy when I stopped off at Tasty Queen to sit with Robbie. I ate two corn dogs and some curly fries and we both had a limeade. I gave him the lowdown between bites.

He agreed with the plan for an early morning, but seemed quiet. Finally, I asked him if anything was wrong. 'It's nothing,' he said. 'It's just my little sister has been giving my mom a hard time. She has to take care of the twins when my mom's at work and the boys are getting to that age . . . they don't always do what she says.' He sighed. 'She probably wants to see Mom more than she does, too.'

I suddenly felt very sorry for Robbie's little sister. 'How old is she?'

'She's thirteen. They're eight.'

'Wow.' I thought about myself last year. I imagined having that kind of responsibility and how well I'd have handled it. The twins would have probably actually died. 'How many hours does your sister look after the boys?'

Robbie sighed. 'Well, Mom's got work cleaning the schools over the summer. She helps the janitors get them ready for next year?'

I nodded. 'So that's good money,' he continued. 'But she's also got her normal clients . . . office and houses . . . and she doesn't want to let them go.' He shrugged. 'So she's working six or seven days and doing ten or twelve hour days.'

That's about how my mum works. Not cleaning, but the hours. I said, 'I know what that's like,' and Robbie nodded.

'I can make good money,' he said. 'I'm not working just for me. I give half of everything to my mom and put the rest into savings for college.' He looked at me and took off his hat, waving it around in a circle. 'This is my big luxury,' he said. 'I don't date. I don't go to the movies. I don't go to dances. I just have my limeade and sit here for an hour.'

I smiled. I said, 'And even this is work,' I said. 'We're always getting interrupted.'

Just then, his phone buzzed and he looked at it and smiled. 'She said she's sorry she called me selfish.' He texted back and his phone buzzed again. 'She's making beans and cornbread. The twins are watching tv and she says she's not going to go crazy, after all.'

'What's her name?'

'Rachael.'

He had an older sister, Tanya, but she'd moved away. And a much older brother, Kris, who he barely remembered. 'He died when I was three,' he said. 'He was a football player and a coyote dancer. You know...at powwows.' He looked out and watched the traffic for a little while. 'But that reminds me!'

He hopped down and came back with a thick brick of glass and metal with a charger wrapped around it. 'Ta da!' he grinned. 'You won't be getting the latest apps on here, but it will work with your SIM and it's been upgraded as far as it can go, in terms of memory. I don't know what will work and what won't, but at least you've got a browser and can connect to WiFi.'

Just a month ago, I would have *thrown* that phone at anyone who tried to make me use something so uncool and ancient. Now, I jumped on it like it was the last phone on earth.

'Wow!' I said. 'I wonder if the SIM will really work?'

It wasn't until my SIM was in the phone that I remembered. 'Bother,' I said. 'I don't think I have enough money to pay for this. Not yet. But I can pay you back week after next...'

'That's the best part,' Robbie said, his dark eyes dancing. 'My cousin said that even though he's put hours into it, it's too much of a turkey to sell. Even grandmas refused to carry it. He said he's sick of dusting it. So it's *free!*' He threw his arms up in the air in victory and I threw mine around him in a giant victory hug.

We danced around for a moment like idiots and then settled back down again. It had Skype. It had a couple of games I could remember playing on my mum's phone, when I was too little to have one of my own. It had email and a camera and...it was an actual, actual *phone*.

I was so grateful. I kept smiling, all the way back to the farm.

CHAPTER TWELVE

The next two days were busy. Building a fence is tough work and we did it from from sunup to just after sundown. Robbie didn't have a single cherry limeade. Margaret was busy feeding and watering Uncle Ethan and Robbie and taking care of all the animals by herself and trying to train the puppies. and I had to gather eggs and tomatoes and do other things that Margaret usually did for me.

Even with everything going on, the puppies were much better. Now if one of them jumped up, we turned around and ignored that puppy, very quickly. It was astonishing how that worked—within a day the whole jumping up and scratching us had pretty much stopped.

They had names now. The largest one was Thing One and the jumpiest one was Thing Two and the slightly more calm and rational one was called Genius, because Ethan had said that Thing One and Thing Two made Thing Three look like a genius. They weren't exactly stupid, though, they were just a little wild. But they could nearly walk on the leads already and they certainly knew to lay down in their beds when Ethan told them to do it. When I told them, not so much.

By Friday morning we were all worn out, but we had a new sheep pasture. All the junk was out of the hollow, it was cleared and fenced…and after the morning's chores we walked the sheep down the track from the pasture with the electric fence and lambing shed, turned them loose in the new place, and shut the gate. Genius came along to help and Ethan said that he might even live long enough to make Genius into a sheep dog. He thought Thing One and Thing Two had other talents, so they stayed home. He said it was up to Margaret to see what those talents might be.

We walked through the hay meadow and Margaret and Ethan stopped, looked at seedheads and started talking about mowing early. They said they'd get Robbie in to help. Evidently the seed was setting earlier and earlier in the summer every year. They started talking about the environment and global warming and I kind of tuned out. They were so intent on what they were saying that they didn't notice me lagging behind. I was imagining what it must have been like, flowers like that over all the hills and no fences and buffalo. It made me feel... nice... to think about it. And then I looked up, and they'd gone and I had to hurry back.

When I got back to the house, Margaret handed me an iced tea and we dropped down into chairs on the shaded deck and went floppy. Finally, Margaret looked at Ethan and said. 'I declare a day off.' Counting on my fingers, we'd already worked nearly six hours, so it didn't seem like that much of a day off, but it still felt like a treat. 'Sounds good to me,' Ethan said.

Margaret leaned back and closed her eyes against the sun. 'But I'm hungry,' she moaned. 'I'm hungry and I'm too dang tired to do anything about it.'

I still had twenty-two dollars left of my pay that I hadn't had to give Robbie for my secret smartphone. So I said, 'Come on, you two. Get in my truck.'

Margaret raised one eyebrow and looked at me. 'Seriously?' she asked.

I chased the puppies into the mudroom, said, 'Bed,' and, 'Down,' and I must have meant it, because they did it straight away and didn't get up when I said, 'Good.'

Nobody locked their doors around there. The grownups got into my truck and I very self-consciously drove to town. It wasn't until I passed my coyote's pasture that I realised I hadn't even done my ballet workout that morning.

As of Monday, Geoffrey would be coaching me in the ballet studio every weekday lunchtime, but I would still need to do a morning workout, if I wanted to get anywhere with my extension. Geoffrey had been super nice to me when I'd met up with him and his storeroom really *was* in a mess. He said he hadn't thrown anything away since he took it over in 1984, and I could easily believe it. I don't think he'd ever actually cleaned it properly, either. I was going to ask I could take in a few rags and the tiny vacuum cleaner Margaret called 'the dustbuster'. I was seriously going to need to bust dust in there.

I hadn't told Margaret and Ethan about doing some work at the studio. I thought I'd wait for a good moment to ask. But I *had* to work for Geoffrey. I can't tell you how good it felt just to stand and look at boxes of rosin and packages of tights and racks of character skirts and leotards...

You pass the cinema...the *movie theatre*...to get to the pizza place and Uncle Ethan grunted and said, 'That looks good,' as we drove past. It was some action thriller with a bald man on the poster, but Auntie Margaret got excited.

'Well, let's go tonight,' she said. 'We've got that twenty Jules gave us and we can smuggle in candy.' She turned to me and said, 'Will you be allright minding the farm?'

I could get the WiFi password off the router. I could try out my phone. I tried not to smile too large. 'Oh,' I said, pulling into the pizza place and putting my truck into P for Park, 'I think I can manage.'

Uncle Ethan and Auntie Margaret ate so much pizza and salad that I thought they were actually going to explode as I drove them back to the farm. They kind of staggered up onto the deck, still clutching soda cups, and when I told them I was just going to check on something and left in my truck again, they didn't ask any questions. It had bothered me missing my coyote dance, so I thought I'd sneak away and do a little before sundown.

I still had a big cup of diet root beer with vanilla. Thank goodness Uncle Ethan had thought to install a cupholder for me. I parked up on the correct side of the road, got my ballet slippers out of the glovebox, tucked them into my left hip hollow using my shorts waistband and my knicker elastic, and shimmied through the barbed wire. Before I went through, I was kind of debating with myself, wondering whether or not I should ask Margaret and Ethan about working at the studio when I got back. I was afraid that maybe they'd think I'd taken them for pizza just to soften them up. And I hadn't. At least I didn't think I had.

But, as usual, once I went through the barbed wire, I didn't think about anything but being in the pasture and dancing.

I had never been there so late. The cows huddled near the shade of the tree, too hot to even graze. The grass under my feet felt dry and crunchy and the flies were horrible. I walked towards my platform and even before I saw my coyote, I felt that there was something wrong.

And there certainly *was* something wrong. He hurled himself out of the brush and stood in my path, staring at me.

If his ruff had been up, or if he'd lowered his head and snarled or something, I might have turned and run. But he didn't do anything like that. He just stood there, and looked...I guess a bit *upset*. He wasn't happy with the way he was balanced on his feet and kept shifting his weight around them...I thought he was ready to run away from me if I got aggressive.

He looked uncomfortable, but he was also determined to stand right in my way. His forehead was rumpled up like the puppies' when they were trying to understand something and his elegant eyebrows were drawn together as if he was worried.

Standing like that, out of the grass, I could suddenly see that he was actually *smaller* than the puppies now. He just seemed bigger because he was so...poised...so sure of himself.

He didn't look poised or sure right now, and it was so unlike how he usually was that I stopped for a moment. When I stopped, he kind of relaxed. When I took another step, he bounced a little more from foot to foot and he fake sneezed, as if he was saying, 'No. Really. This is so not cool.'

I said, 'Dude. Get out of my way.' I took another step towards him and he made a little whining sound, but held his place. He clearly was not going to move for love nor money.

So, I tricked him. I walked towards the tree for a moment and then jinked back onto the path behind him. He tracked me without turning and then, when I cut back to the path, he went mental. He shouted at me, a, 'Crckckck,' sound, more gargle than bark.

I stopped and put my hands on my hips. 'I am going to my studio,' I said. 'If you've gone crazy, you're just going to have to bite me or something.'

It seems strange, remembering it now, but I never thought for a moment that he actually *would* bite me. Still, once I'd said it, I couldn't help but think about the puppies' big sharp white teeth and think about how much sharper the coyote's teeth must be, how deep *his* claws would scratch. But I turned my back on him anyway, and kept walking.

He did the same thing I had. He ran in a circle and got in front of me again. Now we were just metres away from the platform where I'd set up my studio. I could see the mirror and the ironing board and the rock I used to get up onto the platform. I wanted to be there, so badly. I said, 'Come on, coyote. Get out of my way.'

And then…he danced for me. He started fighting the air. He jumped back, like the path was trying to bite his feet, and then he jumped forwards, trying to snap his teeth at empty air and jumped back again, as if the empty air had tried again to bite him. He made pounces into the air with his ears forward and leapt back with his head drawn back and his ears flattened in fear. Again and again he did this, far closer to me than he usually came. And then he stopped, and his sides heaved with panting. It was too hot to dance that hard out here. Especially in a fur coat.

When he was done, I applauded. I thought that's what he'd been trying to do, dance for me instead of me dancing for him all the time. That's how totally fixated I'd become on dance.

He'd ended up a little way off the path, so after I applauded, I started walking to my studio again. He moved his head fretfully. When I took another slow step, he started to whine. But as I kept going, he moved further away, until he made that cracking sound again. When I didn't stop, he huffed and turned his affronted head to lay down, about ten metres from me, looking at me from the corner of his eyes with flat, distressed ears.

'Crazy coyote,' I muttered to myself. And I was just about to put my foot on my rock step and grab onto the platform to lift my body onto it, when I thought the word: warning.

It's a warning, I thought, and even though I was still moving my leg to put my foot on the rock, I glanced up at the platform. And there, right at the level of my face, not half a metre away, a rattlesnake sunned its tummy on the floor of my studio.

I immediately seized the movement in my leg and stopped it, but doing that unbalanced me. I stumbled backwards and fell flat onto the path, waking up the rattlesnake.

Rattlesnakes are evidently not morning people. It hissed at me and flipped itself over easily and rapidly. That took my breath away. I was scrambling backwards on my hands and feet, like an extremely awkward crab, when the snake raised its head and its tail and rattled a warning at me. It was so terrifying, I could feel a sudden, sharp urge to do a wee.

I got far enough away that I thought I'd risk it and stood up. I was covered in dust and shaking. I backed up all the way to the ridge, watching the whole way. I had no idea how fast or far a rattlesnake could slither and I didn't want to be caught by surprise.

I stood on the ridge and looked back down the path. There was my coyote . . . just ears in the long grass. I did a deep ballet curtsey to my coyote and hoped he understood how grateful I was. Then, shaking, I shimmied through the wire and into the truck and went home to the farm.

CHAPTER THIRTEEN

I'll never know how I drove the truck back to the farm.

Over and over, in my mind, I kept seeing the snake flip over and coil up, ready to strike. The puppies swarmed over to me when I got out of the car and I sank down onto my knees and buried my face in Thing One's fur while Thing Two licked my ear. It made me feel better, but I couldn't stop shaking.

Uncle Ethan and Aunt Margaret hadn't moved from their loungers on the deck. They were talking about how hot it was getting in the tomato tunnel, debating if they should spend money on a shade or just whitewash the cover they had. Ethan thought the special shade sheet would be better and last longer. Finally, Margaret asked me what I thought, but I could only sit and tremble.

'Jules?' my auntie asked. 'Jules?' But it was like she was a thousand miles away. I couldn't answer her.

Uncle Ethan put a warm, strong hand on my shoulder and somehow, that helped. I said, 'I saw a rattlesnake,' and Auntie Margaret kind of gathered me up until I was sitting on her lap, and Uncle Ethan was still holding onto me. I said, 'It was so scary. I thought I was going to die.'

'It's okay,' Margaret said. 'You're okay.' And it felt nice to be held, but suddenly, I wanted my mum. I wanted my mum and I wanted to be home and I nearly said, *I hate it here*, but I caught the words in my throat and held them until I felt like I was going to choke.

Ethan handed me some iced tea and said, 'I put about six sugars in there. Good for you when you're feeling shaky like that.' The glass was already misted with the cold of the drink and the heat outside and something about that reminded me of the night I had gone out onto the tiles of the roof. It wasn't just me and Archie out there that night. It had been Sophia and Molly Fairclough, too. And the tiles were cold and wet and Archie's white face... terror in it... and his hands scrabbling at the tiles and sliding, sliding...

And now I could imagine how he'd felt, even closer to death than I'd just come, lying broken in the rain...

I want my mum. I want my mum. I want to go home. I want to go back to that night and never do it. I want to just stay in the study room and be bored. I want go back to my ballet class and try harder. I want to not be the girl I was back then. I want to not have to be here, in this dusty, dirty place where there are rattlesnakes and bugs and people who shoot coyotes and strange things that come down from the sky and peck at me. I wish I'd never come here.

All of that was stuck in my throat and I could hardly breathe around it.

'Are you okay? Jules?'

I took a long drink of tea and forced all that regret and sadness down inside the place where I'd been cracked. I stood up and hugged my aunt and my uncle. I said, 'Yeah. Sorry. It kind of freaked me out.' And I went inside for a shower.

When I got out of the shower, I pulled on a pair of jeans without thinking about it. It was cool enough for jeans inside, in the air conditioning, and anyway, Margaret and Ethan wore them all the time, no matter how hot it got. I guess I wanted to protect my legs or something.

Downstairs, at the dining room table, Margaret was looking at something on the computer and making notes. Ethan was cleaning a huge gun...a rifle. He'd laid out felt and was methodically going over every bit of the gun with the same unhurried, steady approach he brought to all his work.

'Where,' he said, as he squinted down a long tube of metal, 'did you see this rattlesnake?'

'It wasn't on your land.' That was the best thing I could come up with at short notice.

Ethan put down the tube of metal and looked at me. He could tell I had a secret.

'Did you know,' Auntie Margaret said, 'That for a long time in York Shyer our family lived on *boats*?'

Ethan was waiting to ask me again. I knew he was. But it was easy to keep Margaret talking.

'Really?' I asked with a whole lot of perkiness.

'Do you know what a canal barge is?' she asked. 'It says here that they were towed by horses. Is that right?'

I nodded energetically, and wracked my brain for anything I knew about the canal systems of England and the Industrial Revolution. I talked solidly for around five minutes. Uncle Ethan's lip did that twitch it did when he was trying not to smile.

'I also found this guy.' She got up and pointed to a bit of pencil on the large sheets on the dining-room wall. 'This is Daniel's father, so I that makes him your great-great-great-grandfather. He was from Michigan, but he became a pioneer. He was a Wells Fargo stagecoach driver, out in South Dakota. He married a Lakota Sioux woman...so Daniel was half Native American.'

Suddenly, I really *was* interested. My great-great grandfather, whose name was evidently Daniel, had been half Native American. 'Do you think that's where I get my looks?' I asked Auntie Margaret. 'Do you think my hair and my skin were like, recessive genes?' We'd done recessive genes in Biology, the term before the term when I got kicked out.

Auntie Margaret blushed bright red and snapped down the lid to her computer. 'I think I'll get the grill going outside,' she said. 'How about some barbecued chicken for dinner? I'd better get moving if we're going to make the movie.'

I was left at the table with my Uncle Ethan, who wouldn't meet my eye. They knew, I suddenly realised. They knew who my father was.

I said, 'What do you think, Uncle Ethan? Do you think I might have recessive genes?' And just from the way his eyes avoided mine and the way he pretended to polish something he'd already polished, I was rock-solid certain.

He knew.

His calm, steady eyes rose and met my own. Now we both had a secret we didn't want to talk about. Without saying a word, we kind of agreed to leave each other alone, and not talk about either of them. I said again, 'The rattlesnake wasn't on our land. Nowhere near it.'

And he nodded. He said, 'Thanks. But it's that time of year. I'd better start having this ready to load.' And I sat there and watched him snap all the bits back into place until a rifle lay on the table between us.

When my aunt and uncle left for the cinema...the *movies*..., Auntie Margaret said, 'We might go out for something afterwards, depending on who we see and how we feel. But we won't be any later than ten thirty.'

Then they left and I suddenly had an entire farm all to myself. I thought about getting the chickens in straight away, so that I wouldn't have to worry about it later, but when I went out to do it, it was still light and they were scratching around. It felt mean putting them away early, just so that I didn't have to think about them. The puppies were running around, too, so I left them all to their fun and went inside to the WiFi router. I'd seen the password taped to the side in Vicky's handwriting.

I'd been charging the big old phone for two days, down the back of my bedside table, so it was on 100%, and I got the WiFi set up in about ten seconds. I Googled mum's name and clicked the 'news' tab. I saw photos of her shaking hands with Russian people. I clicked on the article and it seemed like her deal had come through.

It took forever to set up my Skype details and find her, and I worried that the Skype app would be so old that it wouldn't actually work, but it did. It was one in the morning back home, and I knew she wouldn't answer, but I just had to ring anyway. I just had to. It was nice seeing her photo and hearing the familiar bonging ring. It made me feel normal, like my life wasn't actually divided into before and after, like I had some kind of actual *self* that was the same wherever I was.

And then she answered. She leaned down to the computer and said, 'Just a second,' very quietly. I could hear her say something about a family matter and that it wouldn't take long and then I saw the front of her red suit and cream blouse and a hallway, and then we were in a little office and her face filled the screen.

'Where are you?' I asked.

'Beijing. It's nine a.m. and I was having a breakfast meeting. It's not that important.' She held up a little white bun and a cup. 'I took the breakfast with me.' She said, 'Are we supposed to be talking to each other?'

I said, 'No, but don't hang up.'

'I'm not going to hang up. I miss you too much.' Her blue eyes were light and sparkled with mischief. 'Don't get into trouble, though.'

'Margaret and Ethan are at the movies,' I explained. 'They don't know that I have this phone.'

Mum took a sip of whatever was in the cup and made

a face. 'You've been there a little over a three weeks,' she said. 'And you've already scored a secret smartphone? I know I should be telling you off, but all I can think is...respect!' She fist-bumped her computer camera and I did the same to the phone camera.

I missed her so much it made all those things I couldn't say before come into my throat again. I said, 'I'm so sorry, Mum. I was *such* a jerk. How's Archie?'

'He's okay. Judith says he's starting to milk it. He set up a text group for everyone in the family and keeps demanding food. But he's healing...his legs are healing surprisingly well, even.' She paused. 'He wants to see you. When I told him where you were, he got a bit upset. He didn't know you'd been expelled.'

'You visited him?'

She nodded, had another sip and made another face. 'Ick. God, the coffee here is disgusting.' And then she looked at me. She said, 'Wow, look at you! Cowboy Jules. How are you, darling? How are you, really, really?'

I thought about it. 'I'm kind of okay,' I said. 'I think I've already learned a lot. About work...' I thought. 'And about money...and...' This was going to be hard.

Mum was completely still, completely intent on the picture of me she could see on her screen. I said, 'You were right.' I shrugged. 'It was about ballet school. I was really, really upset not to get in and...' Her face was swimming because my eyes had filled with tears, *again*.

'And you acted out.' Mum looked out of the crappy phone with such love. 'You acted out and...I just didn't know how to stop you. It was like you'd gone away. I just couldn't *get* to you.' Mum's voice dropped a little. 'Are you sure you're okay there, Jules? Nobody's been...horrible to you? Because I'll be on the next flight and...'

God, it was tempting. If I'd just said, 'They're being really mean, Mum. Come and get me,' my mother would have torn the world apart to get me. But it wasn't true. And I was...I was getting better. At *everything*, by being here.

'No,' I said. 'I mean, it's kind of...you know...kind of harsh sometimes.' Mum nodded energetically. 'But it's not *bad*. And I'm learning stuff.' I held up my hand and said, 'I got an actual blister last week, right here.'

Mum grinned. 'Well done,' she said.

'And...'

The door opened and a strong Chinese accent told my mother they'd be starting in ten minutes. She said, 'Okay,' and turned back to me. 'You said 'and',' she said. 'What and?'

I knew it would make her happy. And I loved her and I wanted her to be happy. That's the only reason I told her. I told her I was dancing again. I told her about my platform. I told her about the dance studio and Geoffrey.

She ate her bun, but she was absolutely devouring my words. I told her about my coyote studio. She asked me where it was, exactly, and said that she would look it up later on Google Earth. She told me that Geoffrey Mellon had come to town when she was a teenager and that she couldn't believe he was still there.

Finally, we just sat and looked at each other. And

then the door opened and the Chinese person was back. 'Be careful, darling,' she said. 'And we'd better play by Margaret's rules. I think we get to talk officially in August.'

More than a month away, I thought. I was already down to 60% and the phone felt hot. And then I was just looking at my contacts page.

I hadn't told Mum about the coyote. Not really. If I told her about the coyote, I'd tell her about the rattlesnake...and I didn't want to worry her. She'd looked worried enough when she asked if it was horrible here. It didn't sound like Tuscany was going to happen, but maybe Mum would visit in August and I could take her to see my coyote. I wondered how he'd act if I brought someone else into the pasture.

I Googled coyotes and found out all kinds of things. I should never feed him human food. I should not try and get close to him. I think I kind of knew those things already.

There were a whole lot of things about how to kill them and lots of videos about how to skin them. It was depressing. Then I looked at coyote dancers...there were a lot of Asian girls in tight skirts and then some Native Americans. I watched a couple of videos of the Native Americans. I didn't really understand the dances, but they looked amazing.

I looked through my Skype contacts again to see if I had Archie's number there. I didn't.

And all this time, I was aware of a noise outside, a noise that was getting louder and louder. The dog flap clicked twice and then the noise got even louder and then the dog flap clicked again. All three dogs had come in and gone right to their beds. It made me feel uneasy.

I opened the back door and went out on the deck. The chickens were making a horrible racket.

Stupid birds, I thought. But they were right. It had started getting dark and was time for them to go to bed. I trudged around the corner of the house, ready to try and herd them...and then saw...

It was carnage. That's what people say when something like that happens—it was carnage. But I hadn't really known what carnage meant, until now.

There were ten or twenty dead or dying hens all around the yard. One had its guts trailing out behind it and was still alive—there was blood and feathers and bits of chickens everywhere. Four or five were half-eaten but the others had just been killed, or half-killed...it looked like for no reason at all.

I just stood there for a moment while the live chickens screamed and surged around the coop. I didn't know where to start. I didn't know how to make it right, how to do anything I was going to have to do.

I went over and opened the coop door and all the birds that were okay pushed their way in, flapping and squawking so pitifully that it made my chest feel tight. I shut the door on them and told them I was sorry. Then I went to my truck and got my leather gloves and got a bin liner...a trash bag... from the kitchen.

The puppies cowered to the floor when I walked inside,

like they felt bad about letting it happen. They must not have felt up to fighting whatever it was.

The chicken with the guts hanging out was still alive and making a horrible high wheezing sound. I grabbed a spade... a *shovel*... from the side of the barn and... there wasn't anything else to do. I closed my eyes when I did it and the bad sound stopped.

I scooped up seventeen dead birds and put them in the trash bag and got what feathers I could and put them in, too. I went and flicked on the yard lights even though it was too early for the sensors to make them come on automatically. Whatever had killed the birds, I didn't want it sneaking up on me. And then I thought, and I took the shovel in one hand and a torch... a *flashlight*... in the other and went off to check on the sheep and the cows and pigs. It took a long time to walk around, because I was stopping and getting ready to fight about every time I heard a mouse rustle, but everyone one else was okay. It was just the chickens.

Just the chickens... but seventeen dead chickens was a lot of Margaret's chickens. The egg and tomato money was... it was useful. I knew that much. The farm did well, but it did well *for a farm* and farms these days didn't do that brilliantly. Margaret and Ethan had decent cars and their house was solid and everything, but she got her curtains from Walmart and snuck candy into the cinema.

And I should have put the chickens away, but I'd wanted to play with my new phone. I should have been watching and if I'd heard something strange in the yard,

I should have checked it out. Now there were animals dead, and it was my fault.

I sat on the steps of the deck and waited for my aunt and uncle to come home.

I didn't have to wait long. They must not have run into anybody at the cinema, because they were back before ten. I heard the truck long before I saw it. I heard it coming down the tarmac...the *asphalt* road. I heard it turning onto the gravel. I could smell the dust from the gravel as it got closer and heard the little whooshing noise the tyres made on the rocks as Ethan braked for the turn into the driveway.

They were laughing and talking about the movie. I could hear them when the truck door opened. And then they must have seen some of the blood and feathers because Margaret stopped still. She looked at me in my gloves, with my shovel and flashlight and just waited. Ethan came up and put a hand on her shoulder.

'Something killed the chickens,' I said. 'I heard the squawking and came out and...'

'Why didn't you put them away?' Her voice was calm. Too calm.

I didn't know what to say. 'It was still light and they looked happy, scratching around,' I said. 'And then just as it started to get dark enough...I heard the squawking.' I thought of the not-dead bird and winced. 'It was horrible,' I said.

Auntie Margaret's chin trembled a little, like she was trying not to cry.

145

'I checked on all the other animals,' I said. 'They're all fine. The lambs are fine and the piglets and everything. The cows are good.' I motioned with the shovel to the trash bag. 'I tried to clean up.'

Margaret nodded. 'How many?'

I told her and she nodded again. 'The others were pretty upset,' I added.

'I'm pretty upset, too,' she said. We were standing in the yard just about a metre apart. She'd said that part calmly. But the next part she absolutely screamed, 'What were you doing? What were you thinking? We *told* you there were predators!' She raised her hand and I thought she was going to hit me, but then she stomped off to look into the trash bag. 'What a flipping mess,' she muttered.

Ethan looked after her for a moment and then turned to me. 'What did the dogs do?' he said. 'Did they bark?'

I tried to remember. I'd been talking to Mum and then started Googling coyotes... I'd heard something in the yard, but it hadn't been barking. I said, 'No. I'm pretty sure they didn't bark. But they ran into the mudroom and went straight to their beds and looked scared.' He nodded.

Margaret was looking through the trash bag and crying, but he was intent on me, looking at my face, listening to what I said. I thought deeper. I said, 'I guess I kind of heard the chickens squawking, but I didn't really...'

'Didn't pay any attention to it,' Ethan said.

That's right, I thought miserably. I'd just ignored it as a sound, when it was actually some*body*, an actual other life, being ended. 'I'm so sorry.' It didn't sound enough, even to me.

'I actually started to notice something was wrong when the dogs ran in.'

Ethan looked at me steadily and I apologized again. 'What would you do differently now, if you could?' he asked me.

I'd stay in the study room and not go out on the roof, I thought to myself, so that I wouldn't be here at all. But what I said was, 'I'd go ahead and get the chickens in before I went inside. Or at least I'd run out to see what was happening when I first heard the squawking.'

Ethan looked at me steadily. 'It was an expensive lesson,' he said. 'So learn it.'

I nodded. I wanted to turn into water and sink right into the ground.

Margaret's face was streaked with dirt and tears. She said, 'You are a piece of work, Missy. I don't know what to do with *you*,' and I felt about as small and miserable as I've ever felt in my entire life. She opened her mouth to say something else, but Ethan interrupted.

'Go on in the house,' he said. 'We'll deal with it.'

She opened her mouth, but he gave her a look and she shut it again. 'Get us some rubber gloves, will you, Honey?' he asked her and her face changed again, into a look of smug satisfaction. 'I certainly will,' she said, stomping up the deck stairs.

Ethan said, 'Give me a hand,' and we went to get a table from the barn and set it up by the mudroom door sink. It had a thick white plastic top that had a few long scratches on its surface. He disappeared through the mudroom door into the kitchen. A big light switched on right above us, and then Ethan came back out again with a selection of knives, choppers, pliers and tweezers just as Margaret brought out two sets of blue plastic gloves and told him that she'd have the boiling water soon.

Ethan turned to me. 'Get the bag,' he said.

I don't think I'll ever forget that night. I was sick three times and I nearly cut myself because I was crying and couldn't see what I was doing. It was the most disgusting job you can possibly imagine, cutting up dead chickens and pulling out their feathers and the bits that you can't eat. And when some of them have been half-eaten and some of them have been a little bitten, and you have to cut those bits aside and cut off their... oh, God. It's absolutely horrible.

And I kept saying, 'I can't do this. I can't do this,' and crying. My hands were shaking so badly I could barely hold the tools.

And my Uncle Ethan kept saying, 'You wouldn't have to do this, if you'd done your job.'

Every.

Single.

Time.

CHAPTER FOURTEEN

I woke up to shouting.

'Give me the key!' Margaret was screaming.

I heard Uncle Ethan murmur something that sounded like, 'Calm down.' It didn't sound like my aunt was taking his advice.

'Give me the flipping key, Ethan.'

Yesterday, I'd nearly been killed by a rattlesnake and had been made to cut up mauled chickens. It was pretty much my worst day ever. And today wasn't starting any better.

I stretched really quickly, just splits and a few things where I knew I was tightest in my hips and hamstrings. I could hear Ethan talking in a low rumble for longer than I thought he actually *could* talk.

I threw on a t-shirt and shorts and swirled my hair into a bun pretty much *while* I was carrying socks and trainers downstairs.

'Okay,' Margaret was saying, as I came through the living-room into the kitchen. 'You've said your piece. Now give me the key to the ammo store.'

Uncle Ethan was sitting at his place at the dining table with a cup of coffee in front of him. Auntie Margaret was standing at the back door with the rifle in her hand. She had sunglasses shoved up on top of her head and her jeans were stuffed into big boots.

Uncle Ethan shook his head.

'Damn it, Ethan!'

'You've got to calm down.'

It didn't look like Auntie Margaret intended to calm down. She was shaking with anger and her face was as red as one of the roadside tomatoes.

Then they both noticed I was there. I gave a little wave and said, 'Hi?'

Nobody spoke. They glared at each other some more.

'Can anyone tell me what's going on?' I said. 'Because my aunt has a *gun*.'

'Yeah. I've got a gun,' Margaret said, suddenly sitting down at the head of the table with a slump. 'But I don't have any *flipping* bullets.'

Ethan got up and brought a pot of tea, a jug of milk and two cups to the table and Auntie Margaret leaned the rifle against her leg to pour for both of us. Gingerly, I sat down. I couldn't stop looking at the gun. It was so much scarier in Margaret's hands than it had been in Ethan's.

Ethan said, 'Your aunt has seen a coyote not far from our place. Down near the turning to Highway 69. She thinks it might have killed the chickens, so she wants to shoot it.'

'Well, what else could it be?' Margaret wailed. 'God almighty, give me strength! Should we hold a jury trial? Just let me shoot the flipping thing.'

I could still hear her words and I could still feel the hot cup under my fingers and the wood of the table under my arms and the chair cushion on the backs of my legs. I could still see Ethan's face and hear him as he said, 'I'm not going to give you any bullets until you *calm down*.' But it felt like I was a long, long, way away. Farther away than the pasture. Farther away than England. Maybe somewhere out in space.

And from there, I made my mouth say, 'You can't shoot that coyote.'

Margaret was already talking, but she stopped and looked at me. 'What did you say?'

Still out in space, I said. 'You can't shoot my coyote.'

Uncle Ethan turned to me with the same serious face he'd shown last night, when he was asking about the chickens. '*Your* coyote?' he asked. His voice was quiet, but rock steady, and very, very firm.

It was so firm that it kind of pulled me back from space, through the atmosphere, around the Northern Hemisphere and down, down to the middle of nowhere to the state and the farm and the table.

During my journey back into my body, Margaret started to splutter, but Ethan just raised one hand and ducked a little and she immediately shut up and...and I realised that Mum had taken that gesture from Ethan. She'd copied it. They knew each other so well that she had seen it enough to...to make it her own.

And I was distracted in my journey, by thinking, just for a moment, that they all three knew each other in ways I couldn't even imagine. That they'd had all this *life* together that I didn't know about, that I might never really know about or understand.

And then I clicked back into my body and everyone

was waiting for me to say something. I said, 'He saved my life yesterday.'

It took two pots of tea and a big stack of pancakes before I'd told the whole story about how the coyote had warned me about the rattlesnake. Margaret kept saying, 'I'll be damned. I'll be damned.'

Ethan just made the food. The rifle was back in its corner near the door.

But when I got to the bit where I did the coyote dance for Geoffrey, Ethan said, 'Show me.'

'Oh,' I said, suddenly embarrassed. 'It's not a real dance or anything.'

'Show me.'

I said, 'Okay.' I stretched a little bit more and ran in place behind my chair for a minute, and then went to the bit of the kitchen where the big arch went through to the living room. There was a good space there on the wooden floor. I went into first position legs and arms—it's always a good way of letting your body tell people, 'I'm going to dance, now.'

They'd been talking quietly, but now they fell silent. My mouth dried... it felt like another audition and for a moment I didn't want to do it. But then I thought about my coyote and Margaret wanting to shoot him and... it was too important not to do it.

I started with the scornful head and the twirl of disgust. I did that both ways and added some trotting through long grass and hiding and watching. Then I saw a mouse and did the coyote jump to kill it. I danced carrying my mouse and Margaret cried, 'Oh, my Lord! It's just like when we saw it with a rabbit!'

That made me feel warm and strong in my middle, where the crack was. I said, 'Now this is how he told me about the rattlesnake,' and I tried to dance that, darting at the ground and leaping back in fear and darting in again and circling out of harm's way.

And then I stopped and bowed and sat back down, tying on my trainers so that I wouldn't have to look at either of them. Margaret clapped and said, 'That was really good, Julia. You are so talented.' I was about to dare a look at Ethan's face when I realized I'd been hearing something for the last few minutes.

Chickens squawking.

I think we all realized at the same time. I don't know who went out the door first, it was pretty much a mad scramble. I know I was still on the deck when Ethan had made it down into the yard, with Margaret right behind him.

Thing Two looked up at Ethan and let the chicken drop from his mouth. Thing One and Genius were hiding under a chair on the deck, quaking, with flat ears and shivering coats. They knew their brother had done something terrible. They must have known last night, too, I thought. The first and second flap of the dog door were probably Thing One and Genius, trying to get away from the scene of the crime.

Ethan sighed. With one hand, he picked up Thing Two by the scruff of the neck. With the other, he got the dead chicken. He walked off towards the old sheep pasture, the one with the lambing shed.

'Where's he going?'

Auntie Margaret turned to answer me. 'He's going down to the electric fence,' she said. She shrugged. The chickens all wanted to get back into their coop and she went and cooed to them and got out the hose to top up their water.

'What will he do to Thing Two?'

'He shows him the dead chicken and holds him against the fence for a few seconds,' she said. 'He'll do it two or three times. Usually, that's all it takes.'

'He's electrocuting the dog?'

She shrugged again. 'Mom would have just shot him,' she said. 'At least we're giving him a chance.'

I heard a sharp yelp off in the distance.

We went inside and I started cleaning up the kitchen.

In the mudroom, Margaret packaged up what few eggs we'd collected and began to wash and pack up the tomatoes. 'I reckon it would be okay if you did some work down at Geoffrey Mellon's place,' she called to me.

I said, 'Thank you,' and really meant it.

She finished up and leaned against the kitchen doorjamb. 'Be careful dancing around in that pasture. I'd tell Mark Palliser you're using it, but there's no use—he's never here. He leased that land to Terry Short and all Terry will do is make sure the water trough is working and haul the stock to market.' She looked at me. 'So there's nobody to shoot the snakes or scare off the coyotes.'

'There's only one coyote,' I said. 'And I don't think he'd bother the cows. There's a really scary big red mother cow that would probably stomp him to death.'

She smiled at me. She said, 'Well, take a stick for snakes and keep your phone handy. And be careful of the mama cow, too.'

Then the dog door flapped and Thing Two shot in and went straight to his bed.

He didn't smell singed or anything. He didn't look marked. But he certainly was shaken.

So was I.

My hands on the wheel looked like the chicken feet I'd had to... God... the night before. I was hyper aware, as I drove out with the eggs and tomatoes and a list for the grocery store, that I was made of the same fleshy stuff as the chickens, that the same unspeakable gooey mess was inside me. I seemed to see it everywhere. A bird flew over and my stomach kind of turned thinking about its head and its...

I was shaken.

My leather gloves were stiff with dried blood from picking up the chickens the night before, but I put them on anyway, and got my broom from the back before I went into the pasture. I couldn't see the cows, but there was lots of cow poo. It seemed like every day I had to tiptoe around more of the stuff. There were giant flies that settled all over, eating it. One of them had bitten me, just on the back of my knee and left a giant lump.

The cows had gone over the ridge. I guess the grass on the front side had run out and they'd pooed everywhere they wanted to poo there, so they'd come over to give us some flies on our side. The big red cow didn't like it when I topped the ridge and looked at them. She mooed at me and I told her not to be so silly. They weren't over by the tall grass or my platform, though. They were kind of spread out around the path and down to the left by the big cottonwood tree.

I couldn't see my coyote anywhere. Carefully, carefully, I crept towards the platform, with my broom out in front of me.

But it was all snake-free.

I couldn't believe how hot it was. I'd been in some hot weather before, but that day was far hotter than anywhere I'd ever been. I found out later it had been a hundred and seven degrees Fahrenheit that morning...that's forty-two degrees in Celsius. I brushed off the floor...It was surprising how dusty it got, how quick. I did my floor work and stretched on the ironing board barre and did some ronds de jambe. It felt like the heat was actually pushing me down and my barre was starting to get hot, too.

Then, deep into the shade under the tree, I saw two sandy-coloured ears and my heart leapt up in my chest. I tried to dance 'thank you', doing arabesques...big back leg raises...in steps and then a chain of quick pirouettes and then sank into a curtsey, down, down, so low that I sank to my knees and then slid my arms forward and put my head down on the gritty wood of the floor and held, held, held and then slowly raised up my arms and my head into a kind of triumphant 'yes' gesture.

He'd sat up in the grass, to see me better.

I stood up again, too. It was so hot. The air between us seemed to shimmer, like it had yesterday in the hazy heat. I couldn't imagine wearing all that fur in weather like this. He was panting, just sitting still in the shade. At least he had access to water in the cattle trough by the road.

I did my reverence and felt like my head was full of bees. It was so...bright...and the air felt heavy, like it couldn't actually move in and out of lungs any more. I was halfway to the ridge when I realised I'd forgotten my broom and went back for it.

I was hot and squinting in the sun and my head felt faint and buzzy. And then, in an instant, I was sharp and clear and perfectly strong and able. Because the rattlesnake was on the path.

He was moving towards the platform, in the dust of the beaten-down track, about three metres away from me. His peculiar swooping wiggle is what had attracted my eye, but now I saw the brown lozenge pattern on his back.

He must have sensed I was there, because he stopped and raised up a little, moving his head in a circle and tasting the air with his flickering tongue. I stayed perfectly still, and he didn't see me. You could almost see him do the equivalent of a rattlesnake shrug and decide that it had been nothing and that he should carry on. He started again with his energetic slither away.

I left the broom.

Back in my truck, my hands shook on the wheel. Again, I was hyper aware that I was just a thin skin covering bones and goo and...

I was mortal, I told myself sternly. It was possible for me to die. Just like the snake, and the coyote and the cows and the...I swallowed dryly...the chickens. I was a body. It was made of...stuff and some of that stuff was unpleasant. And none of this is *news*, I told myself. You *knew* all this *before*.

But it was different. Before, I knew it in my mind, but I didn't really believe it. I didn't know it in my body. Sitting in the hot truck, I realized that I don't really believe anything until I know it with my body.

I thought about the night before, about how many times I'd been sick. My body certainly understood the concept of mortality now.

It was too hot to sit in the truck and think. Even with the windows down, the truck was a metal box and the air inside was boiling.

The moment I started to move, everything was better. By the time I pulled out on Highway 69, and got up some speed, the air had lightened, the heat had shifted a bit, my thoughts were sorted out and it was all nearly bearable. I dropped off the eggs and tomatoes and completely understood why the roadside stand people had big fans going. Without them, I thought the eggs might boil right in their shells.

When I passed the Tasty Queen, I drove into my spot under the tree without thinking twice. I needed something to drink.

Inside, the air conditioning was amazingly nice. I felt better just standing at the door. There were only three or four people there, all at separate tables, drinking coffee. I got my phone out of my bag—it wasn't even ten o'clock.

So much had already happened that day.

The lady at the counter took one look at me and left, coming back with a little paper cup of water. 'Drink this,' she said and I did, and felt better.

I wanted a big drink, though, and I didn't know what I wanted. Coke gave me that gloopy feeling and Robbie's favourite cherry limeades were just too cold for right now.

'Do you do root beer?'

'In a frosty mug,' the lady answered. 'Do you want just plain root beer or a root beer float?'

A root beer float goes in a huge glass mug that has been in the freezer until it is covered with a film of ice. When they fill it with root beer, they don't add ice. Instead, they add a big round scoop of vanilla ice cream. It makes the root beer foam with vanilla cream. It's...it's amazing.

'That looks awesome.' It was Brad, looking less-than-perfect in a sweaty t-shirt with the arms ripped off and a bandana around his head. He shone with perspiration. He put his sunglasses down on the table opposite me and went up to the counter.

Soon, he was back with his own root beer float. He took a deep drink through the huge straw and then pulled out the straw and licked it. 'Oh, man,' he said. 'That hits the spot.'

I had forgotten what he was doing for work that summer, so I asked. 'I've started my own lawn mowing business,' he said. He reached into the back pocket of his cut-off jean shorts and gave me a card. 'But it's just too dang hot out there right now. I had to take a break. I'll get back to it late this afternoon.'

I said, 'It's stupid hot out there. Does it get this way often?'

He rolled his eyes. 'For *weeks*,' he said. 'When we were little, we'd either be inside, in the air conditioning or in the pool.' He took a big glug of his float and got ice cream on his upper lip, wiping it off with the back of his hand. He was completely unselfconscious about all of it. 'But now we're all old enough to work.'

I wondered, not for the first time, what it would be like to have brothers and sisters. 'How many of you are there?'

He grinned, 'One sister and three brothers,' he said. 'I'm the baby of the family. They pick on me all the time. They say I'm spoiled.'

He *was* spoiled, I suddenly thought. That's why he was so... irritatingly confident. 'Really?' I said, 'What do they say about you?'

He looked at me shrewdly, like he knew what I was thinking. 'Oh, you know,' he said. ' "You always get your own way," "You need to learn to compromise," "If you don't learn to back down, you're going to end up in jail."' He'd put on a funny, sing-song voice to do his family. He stopped and scratched behind his ear and then hunched over the table, looking into my eyes. 'I really do need to learn to back down,' he said. 'Even Coach says I'm too competitive. It must be bad when a football coach tells you to be less competitive.'

His big blue eyes had little green flecks in them. Every time I met Brad, I found out something more I didn't like about him and noticed something else about him that was utterly beautiful. I made myself look away.

The conversation dropped into an awkward silence. I got my long silver spoon and poked at the ball of ice cream that was rolling around in the half of my root beer I hadn't yet drunk.

'Anyway,' Brad said. 'It's too bad about your chickens.'

I was astonished. 'How did you know about that?' I asked.

He grinned. 'It's a small town. You'll get used to everyone knowing your business.'

He pointed his spoon at me. 'Coyote got them, I hear,' he said.

I started to protest, but then didn't, I suppose out of loyalty to Thing Two, or maybe because if I'd said it was one of the dogs, I'd have to admit what Ethan had done to punish it.

I put down the spoon and used my straw to drink the last of the root beer.

'I told you,' Brad said. 'I know it seems kind of...
cruel...but you can't let coyotes just wander around
farms. You've *got* to kill them.'

The frosty glass mug was huge and heavy. I imagined
how satisfying it would be to swing it right into the side of
Brad's head. But then I thought about bones and goo and
what it would actually do to his beautiful head.

Suddenly, I just didn't want to be there any more. He
made me feel cross with myself. I was always a bit horrible
about Brad. It was the way he *assumed* I was really into
him. It brought out the worst in me.

I stood up. 'I've got to go,' I said.

He stood up, too. He said, 'I'm looking forward to
seeing you tonight. I'm glad you aren't grounded for it.'

Saturday night? It wasn't a softball game, or a practice.
I blinked at him.

'Church disco?' he said. 'Earth to Jules?'

Oh, God. I'd pushed *that* out of my mind. 'Oh. Yeah,' I
said, wondering if I could get out of it.

Then he looked at me again, in that way he sometimes
had, with big, wide-open eyes and said. 'I've been wanting
to get to know you better.'

He was so...different from me. And sometimes I just
wanted to...smack him. But then he'd say something
nice and...he looked so beautiful, always.

I didn't know what I thought about Brad. I supposed I
wanted to get to know him better, as well. But I surprised
myself when I said, 'Me, too.'

He looked at me and I looked at him and there's no

use saying that there was nothing going on between us, because there was. There was a moment, like at the pizza place, where I saw another boy in Brad—somebody vulnerable and kind. Somebody I might actually want to know quite well.

Then he made one of those stupid gun shapes with his hand and fake shot me with it. He even said, 'Pow!' in this totally thinking-he-was-so-cool way that made me feel a little sick. I walked back out into the heat and immediately forgot he even existed.

CHAPTER FIFTEEN

I tried very hard to be grounded for the disco.

I reminded Margaret how irresponsible I'd been the night before, but Ethan said that I'd already been punished for that. I even thought about showing them my smartphone.

But that would get Robbie and Mum into trouble, too. So I had to go.

I got ready as slowly as possible. I didn't have a ton of clothes to choose from, but I found a t-shirt near the bottom of my stack with sequins all over the front. It must have been in the stack of t-shirts when Mum or Marta was packing my things.

We'd bought it last summer, in the Oxford Street sales. Mum had taken an afternoon off and we'd had enormous ice creams at the John Lewis counter and walked the entire length of the street *and* had done New Bond Street for Mum, as well. We'd had to get a taxi home because we just couldn't physically carry all our bargains through the tourists on the pavements.

I hadn't actually wanted the shirt, but Mum had said that orange suited me and that it would be good for things like school discos. It smelled of the laundry stuff Marta used and her ironing water.

I wore it with jean shorts and my brown sandals and actually dried my hair with a blow-dryer and put on lipstick and eye make-up. I looked...like me again...like who I was just a month or so ago. I just didn't *feel* like her any more and I wasn't sure I liked her...or that I ever had. I sprayed my hair stuff on, so that my high side parting wouldn't flop into my eyes and then it didn't matter if I looked like the me I was now or not. I was late. I grabbed my handbag and went downstairs.

'Lord, have mercy!' Margaret said. 'You look like a model.'

I told her I was too short to be a model.

Ethan asked me to turn around and to touch my toes. He grunted. 'Well,' he said, when I did. 'Your butt stays covered. Just.'

'Oh, Ethan!' Margaret socked his arm. 'You look lovely. Don't listen to him, he's an old grump.'

It wasn't on farm business or part of school or anything, so Ethan had to drive me into town. He didn't turn on the radio. I didn't want to roll the windows down, because of my hair, so there wasn't even the noise from the birds and animals. We had the air conditioning instead...it was quiet in the big truck...awkward.

He must have felt it, too, because he cleared his throat like he was going to say something, but then didn't.

Finally, he said, 'Farm life must seem a little weird to you.'

You think? I bit back. I thought about him making me cut up chickens the night before and how many times I'd been sick, about him electrocuting a dog, about the gun and the bugs and the smell of poo. About driving myself around in a huge chunk of metal and lifting things all day. I said, 'It's a bit different.'

'Yeah, I'll bet.' We passed the coyote pasture and he slowed down. 'That the place?' he asked.

I nodded.

'Huh.' He sped up again. Another long silence and then, after he'd turned onto Highway 69, 'You remind me of your mom.'

He glanced at me sideways. I don't know what was in my face. I didn't know if I wanted to have this conversation.

'I knew her before I knew Margaret,' he said. He shook his head and smiled. 'She would have done something like that—made her own ballet studio.' I can't tell you how strange it was to hear Ethan say the words 'ballet studio'. He was clearly uncomfortable saying them and put a kind of ironic spin on the phrase. 'But I don't think even Annalise would make friends with a coyote.' He said 'coyote' like 'kai oat' instead of 'kai oat ee' like everyone else. He glanced at me again.

I never minded being compared to Mum. Lots of my friends hated being told that the looked like their mothers, or acted like their mothers. But I've never been ashamed of my mum. I said, 'I miss her.'

We pulled off the main drag and Ethan pulled up in front of the church. 'Yeah,' he said. 'I miss her, too.' And then he looked at me and said, 'You look real pretty. Watch the boys. I'll pick you up at ten.'

Ethan needn't have worried about boys, I thought, as I crossed the room at the church under-age disco. It was starting like every school disco ever, all the boys on one side of the room and all the girls on the other. I looked in, groaned, thought briefly about running away and hiding in the park for three hours, and then pushed open the doors to join Whitney and her group.

Halfway across the floor, I realized most of the other girls were wearing dresses and heels and had their hair in buns and things. Like it was a big deal. The boys were in shirts and jeans... maybe buttoned shirts instead of t-shirts, but still wearing trainers or boots... or even flip-flops. The girls, though, seemed to have made a really big effort.

Like I actually cared what school dance fashion was in Fort Scott, Kansas. I put on my bored face, which wasn't hard, I can tell you, and walked all the way across the hall to get to Whitney's group.

'Oh my God, you look *so* cool,' Madison B said. 'I *love* that top.' She herself was wearing a cream chiffon thing with a sparkly belt. 'Don't look at me,' she begged. 'My mom got me three of these for the summer discos. The next one is *pink*.'

I put my bag down on the floor with theirs and joined in on some more dress chatting. Well, I kind of joined it.

I listened, anyway and made the right faces.

'Oh, you don't have any punch,' Whitney said, indicating yet another cup of some squash-like substance in her hand. 'Go get some punch.'

There was a long table covered in a silver tablecloth at one end of the hall. At the other end was another table with the DJ and above us was a silver disco ball. Other than that, it was just the church hall, where I had tea and cookies every Sunday morning, wearing my yellow cotton dress and trying not to become suicidal. I wondered if every time I came here, I would be bored out of my mind.

If there was suddenly a Zombie invasion, would I still be bored, because it was in the church hall? If my hair suddenly caught on fire, would I kind of yawn as I patted it out?

On the silver table was a large plastic bowl. Behind it was a large woman in a flowered dress. 'You want some punch, honey?' she asked and I nodded and tried to smile.

'God.' It was Freddie and the pink-haired girl, and they were talking to each other. The girl was the one who'd said, 'God.' She continued, 'Every time we come here it's because I can't think of anything better to do. But once I'm here, I can think of about a million things.'

'Punch, Honey?' the lady said to her.

'Got any hemlock?' she answered. 'No? Then I'll have the punch, thanks.'

Then Freddie recognized me. 'Oh!' he said. 'Jules! Hey!'

'Hey yourself,' I said. 'Who's your funny friend?'

The pink haired girl stuck out her hand. 'I'm Clarissa,' she said. 'Also known as Pinky. For obvious reasons.' She was wearing black leather jeans, Doctor Marten boots and a baby blue chiffon top. I liked her straight away.

The music, all this time, had just been a faint hum in the background. Now the lights went down and a bank of coloured lights started flashing, while another beam of coloured lights hit the disco ball.

'Ladies and Gentlemen,' Pinky said, right before the DJ said, 'Ladies and Gentlemen.'

'Fullbright Productions is pleased to announce,' Freddie said and again the DJ echoed him. They did it all the way through the DJ's speech and I was giggling by the time it was done.

'And now he'll drop some big stupid 70s disco tune,' Pinky warned me and I braced myself. But it was Blondie's 'Heart of Glass,' and Pinky's face opened up into an 'O' of wonder and delight. 'This is my jam!' she cried and put down her punch. She tried to drag Freddie onto the floor.

'No way,' he said. 'I'm not going first.'

Well.

She didn't even have to ask.

Pinky was a pretty good dancer and what she lacked in technique, she made up for with enthusiasm. After the first chorus, I went over and dragged Whitney and her bunch onto the floor and they came, giggling. The boys were glued to the wall. I didn't even try.

And then came the big stupid 70s disco hits, and by that time, we didn't care. The girls dropped out, one by one, but Pinky and I kept going. We weren't wearing heels.

Even I stopped to drink some squash at one point and it was just when the DJ put on some hip-hop. Most people left the floor but some people came onto it that I hadn't seen before...and yet, I *had* seen them, at Walmart and at Drivers' Education and there were even two girls on our softball team—Amelia and Tara. But I never ran into any of the black kids at the pizza place or Tasty Queen and they never sat with us or talked to us or anything. So when they came onto the dance floor, it was like they'd just suddenly appeared.

Pinky was looking a bit lame out there. Rhythm wasn't really her strong point. I downed my squash and went out to lend moral support. Freddie arrived at the same time. All the songs were from eight or nine years ago, like the DJ once asked someone what to play and never spoke to that person again. And despite that, the sound felt like home...it was the sound of the city, of people pushed in together and trying to get on and it was gritty and real and...I didn't really think any of that at the time, but I *felt* it, in the beat and the grinding sounds and the raps and melodies.

Freddie knew all the words to all the songs and was giving it large on the moves, freestyling. Everyone else on the floor looked tolerant of his enthusiasm. Then this one kid with an afro even bigger than Freddie's stepped up and did some locking and popping and everyone else formed a circle and then applauded. Even the people talking against the walls clapped when the guy did his stuff. And that was meant to be that, I guess. He was the best and he did his thing.

But of course, I couldn't let it go.

When I was little, like about eight or nine, I went to a school disco and came home in tears because I couldn't dance *that way*, so Mum, being Mum, had sent me to the best street dance club in London. It was down in Camberwell and the kids there had been a properly fierce crew.

I stepped up hard and got into the popper's personal bubble to stare him down.

All the other black kids started to laugh and I guess it did look kind of silly, me in my sparkly orange top and little brown sandals going in big. He stepped back and waved at the floor, like, 'Okay, show me.'

I can lock and pop a bit, but what I really liked was krumping—a kind of compact but really rapid lock and pop. It had taken me about five hundred years to learn to work my hips and swivel and drag my feet using my ankles, but I'd done it. I never danced in the crew down there in South London—I wasn't really good enough and I never had time to rehearse, but I only left their classes when I…when I quit dance and went off to boarding school.

So, let's just say I knew what I was doing. I did a bunch of body pops and then some swivels and a bunch of fancy stuff and then broke out into bigger wave moves and shut down again into tiny pops and locks. The kid with the afro was smiling all over his face and we high fived and Tara and Amelia came over and hugged me.

Then we got some more 70s disco hits and they all stayed on the floor.

And it was…fun. The squash…the *punch*…was actually nice-tasting for once. And then the lights came up a little and there were sandwiches and crisps and dips and everyone stood around talking and I mean *everyone* was actually talking to *everyone*, which I had *never* seen before in that town. Carter talked to Freddie. Whitney was joking with Amelia and Tara, and Madison B was complaining to Pinky about her three disco dresses. I ate about three hundred sandwiches and just stood there watching everyone and being happy.

I went to the loo and brushed my hair, to get ready for the next set.

Brad and his boys had been glued to the wall and then the food table the whole time but he followed me to the corridor where the loos were and waited. He must have done—there was no other way he could be waiting for me when I came out of the loo, after sharing my brush with about fifty other girls, all crowding around the mirror, repairing lipstick and eye make-up. Mine was fine. I only used waterproof for discos.

'Hey,' he said.

I said, 'Hey,' back to him and he said, 'We haven't had much time to talk. You're always dancing.'

He was standing close to me, leaning over me. It was…disturbing, but I wasn't sure if it was disturbing in a good way or a bad way. He was waiting for me to say something, so I kind of shrugged and said, 'I like to dance.'

'Yeah, I kind of figured that out.'

He took his index finger and ran it down my bare arm,

from my shoulder to my wrist. Then he circled my wrist with his hand for a moment, before letting it go. I could feel my heart start to pound, and again, I wasn't sure if it was because I liked it so much or because I really, really didn't.

I looked up into his face, wondering if kissing him would be a way of sorting out my feelings. He moved a little closer, and said, 'Will you save me the slow dance?'

I swallowed and moved back a little bit. Get a grip, Jules, I told myself sternly. Then I heard myself saying, 'Yes. I'd like that.'

Would I like slow dancing with Brad? Really? I guess I was going to find out.

The music started again, just as I'd put my brush back in my handbag, and I didn't think about it any more. I didn't think about anything, except how well Madison B and Pinky were getting along and how I really needed to learn the Madisons' surnames.

Then, about four or five songs later, the lights suddenly dimmed and turned a deep shade of blue. All the boys who had been stuck to the wall unpeeled and I found myself face to face with Brad, just as the DJ dropped a slow country number.

I went to put one hand on his shoulder and one in his hand, but they didn't dance like that there. The boys held the girls by their waists and the girls put their hands around the boys' necks. It was more like cuddling than dancing. Suddenly, I was very close to Brad.

He bent his head down to me. 'So,' he said. 'What else do you like to do? Besides dance?'

I thought about it, as much as I could think with Brad that close to me. What *did* I do besides dance? Nothing. Not really. I shrugged. I said, 'A lot of the things I used to do I just can't do here...' He nodded, waiting for me to say more. 'I take long baths,' I told him, and then felt incredibly stupid for saying it.

But he grinned. 'What?' he said. 'With, like, bubbles?'

I nodded and he held me a little closer. 'That's so cute,' he said.

But something about the way he'd pulled me so close bothered me. I pushed away, just a little, and cleared my throat. A lot of the other couples were kissing. I asked, 'What do you like to do...besides play baseball?'

He looked at me. 'Really?' he asked. 'You don't know?'

I just looked back at him. I had no idea what he was talking about.

'I'm a quarterback, baby,' he said. 'Youngest varsity quarterback in the history of the school. I took us all the way to the state championships last year. I have seven colleges already calling my dad on the phone.' He briefly let go of my hip to cross his finger on his heart. 'Honest,' he said.

And now that he'd said, I could kind of see it. His body really was perfect. He was balanced and sure of himself. He was smooth and whole. In fact, I could see myself in him. And maybe he could see himself in me, too. Maybe that's why he said, 'I want you to be my girl.'

But what I saw of myself in him, I didn't like. I said, 'I don't think that's a good idea.'

He stood up straight and looked down at me. 'What?' he said. 'It's a great idea. We're made for each other.'

I took my hands from around his neck. 'I don't think so, Brad,' I said, but he wasn't listening.

'You know you want to kiss me,' he said. 'I could see it in your eyes earlier.' He pulled me tight again and tried to push his face onto mine.

'Get **OFF**!!' I was much louder than I'd meant to be. Everyone stopped dancing and stared at us.

Brad's face had looked shocked and hurt, but when he realized everyone was watching, it started looking angry.

I said, 'Sorry,' and marched over to where the bags were, looking for mine. Pinky left Freddie on the floor to run over.

'Are you okay?' she asked.

I had picked up my bag wrong and hadn't shut it properly before. Everything went everywhere and Pinky and Freddie helped me pick it all up, using my phone's light. Then the three of us went outside. The lady in the flowered dress told us that once we went outside, we couldn't go back in and Pinky said that was absolutely fine.

Pinky took my number, so she could check I was okay tomorrow and so that we could maybe get together and then Whitney was there, too, telling me that Brad was really angry and that the man in the suit who had been standing in the corner all night had made Brad go into the kitchen and explain himself. 'As if he's some kind of criminal,' she said. 'You were a bit of a drama queen.'

Freddie snorted and Whitney rounded on him. 'Do you have something to say?' she asked.

'Yeah, actually,' Freddie said. 'Brad just thinks he can have whatever he wants. It's about time somebody stood up to him.'

Whitney's eyes narrowed and she put her hands on her hips in fists. 'Is that right?' she said. 'Well let me tell you—'

Just then, Ethan pipped...*honked*... the horn on the truck and I was absolutely delighted to climb inside to the awkward silence and go back to the farm.

He didn't say a word until we turned into the drive, and then all he said was, 'Yep. You're *just* like your mom. Never went to a dance without a drama.'

I didn't say a word. Margaret called out, 'How did it go? Did you have a good time?' but I just marched straight up the stairs. I took off my make-up, brushed my teeth and went to bed fuming. I lay there rigid, straight as a broom pole, and stared up at the ceiling as if I could shoot lasers out of my eyes and burn a hole to the sky.

Of course, Margaret knew all about the disco by the time I came in from picking tomatoes and getting eggs the next morning. In fact, she'd sent me out to do those things so she could talk to Mrs Hall on the house phone.

By the time I came inside, Margaret had already heard the whole story and made up her mind about everything.

'We are nipping this *right* in the bud,' she said to Uncle

Ethan over breakfast. 'Can you please get Wayne on the phone?'

My uncle rolled his eyes and reached for the house phone, dialling the number. He didn't believe in speed dial. He kept all the numbers he needed, he said, right in his noggin.

We listened to the conversation, so I knew they'd be over at eleven. It just gave me time to deliver to the roadside stand and go to my ballet studio on the way back.

There wasn't a sign of the rattlesnake. It had rained a little overnight, Ethan said, and the marks the snake had made on the path were gone. It was still early-ish, so even after delivering to the stand, it smelled fresh and clean.

This would have been flowers, too, I thought. A sea of grass and flowers. And the cows would have been buffaloes. And there wouldn't have been any fences.

My coyote trotted out of the shade of the tree and sat in his normal spot. I guess he'd got used to the cows being on our side. His ears were interested in me again. There still would have been coyotes, I thought. There had always been coyotes and I guessed there always would be.

I kept kind of thinking about it as I did my exercises. It was easy to get down into splits now, and I was nearly, nearly at Russian splits. My thighs were always sore from stretching, but it was a nice soreness, a kind of soreness I didn't mind. Still, I knew that I'd better not push too hard or I'd hurt myself.

And then I had some time, so I decided to dance the grass. I did the pre-school thing, where you are a seed and grow, but that felt stupid. It wasn't what I was trying to do. From my platform, I could see the next bit of pasture on one side. On the back side was a wheat field. I didn't think it was one of ours, it must have been the Gundasons'.

There was a faint breeze that morning and the wheat was nearly ripe. The breeze cut a ripple in the wheat, just exactly like a ripple through water. And then the wheat swayed back upright. And I suddenly thought that just one stalk of wheat would probably be bent over, but the other stalks help to hold it up. And that made me think of me and my coyote, and how much we needed other people . . . or other coyotes, I guess, for him.

And then I was dancing the wind and the wheat and the grass, and dancing Margaret hanging laundry, and Ethan wiping his forehead with his bandana, and the tractors and the fence posts and the long, long, straight road that was Highway 69. Suddenly, I was dancing the whole of Kansas. My coyote watched, with his head on one side. He didn't really understand. But he liked it.

Of course, all that dancing meant that I was late coming back out of the pasture. I had my broom and my gloves on, and I was trying to whistle as I walked along with my ballet shoes shoved down that perfect place in the hollow of my left hip.

Ethan whistled around the farm and I remembered my cousin Vicky whistling around the house when she stayed with us in London. I could whistle, a little, but not very well. A meadowlark bird hung out on the back fence in the coyote pasture and he sang so sweetly . . . I was actually trying to whistle like the meadowlark that day. I was terrible at it.

Just as I was coming through the barbed wire fence, a red truck sped by. I don't think Brad's father saw me...he was on the other side of the truck.

But Brad did.

When I got back to the farm, everyone was sitting around the dining room table with iced tea and sugar cookies. I sat down about as eagerly as you do at the dentist's.

The last time I'd seen Brad, he'd been grabbing me on the dancefloor. The last time I saw Wayne, Brad's father, was on a video, killing a beautiful coyote by luring it with the sound of puppies in trouble.

I'd been dancing, so I gulped about half my iced tea before I noticed everyone was watching me.

I had to tell my side of the story. Brad had to tell his side. Then we had to agree what to do next.

It wasn't really us agreeing it, though. It was Wayne and Margaret and Ethan agreeing it. Finally, it was done. Brad had apologized. I had officially forgiven him (though I hadn't, really). Everyone had shaken hands, all around.

It was on the front porch that Wayne turned back around. 'Oh,' he said. 'I hear you've got a coyote problem. I'd be glad to come and take care of it for you in the winter...when I can get a good coat off of it.'

Margaret's face was tight. 'Thanks,' she said. 'But I think we're good.'

Then Brad turned around and looked at me, even though he was talking to his father. My face must have shown how stricken I was by the thought of Wayne luring and killing my coyote, because Brad kind of smirked.

'I think I know where there's a coyote,' he said. His eyes met mine and he was laughing at me, laughing at the fear he must have seen in my face.

Wayne had waved to Margaret and Ethan and was opening his truck door. 'Well, you'll have to shoot it without me,' he said. 'I'm all about the pelts.'

Brad *knew*. He had put two and two together and he *knew*. He knew I'd got in trouble for parking on the wrong side of the road just there. He'd seen me coming out of the pasture. He'd seen how terrified I'd been, at the thought of Wayne shooting my coyote. He'd put it all together in his mind.

Just then, his face started to twitch. He could see that I'd figured it out and it had made him giggle. He got into the truck, trying to stop laughing, trying to answer his father when Wayne asked him what was so funny. I could see his shoulders shaking.

I stood on the porch step with Margaret and Ethan above me and glared at him as, still laughing, he waved goodbye.

CHAPTER SIXTEEN

On Sunday, the church service was all about forgiveness. Margaret kept nudging me, and telling me that she was proud of me for forgiving Brad the way I had.

I thought about trying to tell her about the way Brad had kind of threatened my coyote, but the more I thought about it, the less I felt like I could say anything. He'd acted it was all a big joke. Maybe I was taking it too seriously. But I was back to wanting to smack him in the head with a glass mug, and didn't want to be praised for forgiving him.

Instead, I took advantage of her good mood by asking if I could quit softball. I told her I was stretching so hard that I didn't want to hurt myself. I also said that I was going to be busy with my new job and didn't want to do softball if I couldn't give it one hundred percent.

She nodded thoughtfully, asked me if I thought it would hurt me socially, and accepted when I said that I was already friends with Whitney and the Madisons and Chastity. I also told her about Freddie and Pinky and that I liked them, too, and had met them on my own. She asked me about five hundred questions about Pinky and Freddie and didn't look terribly impressed with my answers.

We were sitting at a little table in the church hall, having tea and cookies. Ethan was over in the corner, planning part of the upcoming church barbecue with some of the other men. Margaret had already talked to all the ladies she needed to talk to and was finally eating a cookie and chatting to me. As we chatted, a man I hadn't seen before crossed the room to our table.

Margaret stood up when he got there—he was that kind of person. He looked terribly important and unnaturally clean, like all really rich Americans, but he hadn't bought his suit in America. It was totally British tailoring, and it made me homesick with a sudden pang that took my breath away.

His hair was silver and his back was straight. He put out his hand to Margaret and asked after my mother. He called my mum Annalise, not Lisa Ann. He said she was doing a superb job for her company. And then he turned to me.

I'd stood up, too. I hadn't meant to, but I got swept up in the moment. He said, 'I know you're Jules. I must have seen two hundred photographs of you.' I found myself shaking his hand, which wasn't as smooth as I thought it would be. 'I hear you've started dancing again.'

I don't know what I said. I said...something, and he said. 'You ought to be proud of your mother. She saved over three thousand jobs with that Russian deal. That's a lot of families living happy and secure lives because of her hard work.'

I looked him right in his deep-set brown eyes. They looked calm and clear and very, very clever. I said, 'I *am* proud of my mother, Sir.' I don't know where the 'sir' had come from. Kansas was rubbing off on me.

He nodded at me, told me I was a good girl, said something to Margaret and left.

Margaret flopped back into her chair and drained her cup of tea. 'Lord,' she said. 'He scares the bejeezus out of me. Always has. I don't know how Lisa Ann had the nerve to go right up to him and ask him for a job, but she did. *And* she got it.' She fanned herself with her hand and then explained.

'Euan Stuart,' she said. 'He's... well, he pretty much *is* Bell Oil. His family were ranchers here.' She gulped the very last dregs of her tea and said, 'I don't even know why he *comes* here any more. They're all *dead.*'

'And he and Mum are still friends,' I said.

'Obviously,' Margaret said. She lowered her voice. 'Everybody thinks that they were more than friends, but I've never believed it. I think he just likes her.'

His eyes had been brown and his skin had been deeply tanned. But I didn't think I had just met my father.

I thought about it on the way home. It would be... better... I thought, when I knew who my father was. I kept changing... like suddenly saying 'Sir'. It would be kind of nice to know who I actually *was*, in some kind of way.

I *was* proud of my mum. And I wasn't angry at her... she probably had some really good reason for not telling me. But...

... it would still be nice to know.

There is no way I could have also managed softball. My new routine was even more gruelling than the old one. Wake up, stretch, clean the kitchen after breakfast. Get my list of errands and chores, pack up the truck and take off for the pasture. Dance for my coyote, run my errands and do my chores and either drop back to the farm for lunch, or grab lunch in town. Then over to the studio.

Life at the studio felt completely normal. In no time, I was answering the telephone, signing up dancers for autumn classes, posting out kit lists and timetables, and sorting out the total mess of Geoffrey's storage area. I came home late for dinner most nights, with cobwebs in my hair and so dusty I looked as pale as Chastity. But I also came home with treasure.

As we went through stock, Geoffrey would say, 'Oh, I've had that for years and nobody's bought it. You have it.' I'd then become the proud owner of 80s neon legwarmers, or a deep purple satin leotard with a strangely complicated strap arrangement or a pair of leopard-print velvet ballet shorts. I got two grey sweatshirts with FAME printed on them in swirly foot-high pink letters (I gave one to Pinky) and some cropped t-shirts in mad bright patterns that were popular, Geoffrey said, in the 1990s. One of my new leotards had a lace keyhole cutout at the back and was fire-truck red. Another one had a matching ballet skirt and was the most revolting shade of mustard yellow. It was all so ugly it was great.

But if he was a good boss, he was an even better coach... once you got over his total lack of tact.

'Superb technique,' he said on my first day. 'And you look perfect. But your extension is still pretty sucky.' He disappeared in the back and came back with a resistance band and taught me how to use it to pull my legs higher. He made me hold my developpés for a count of thirty-two instead of eight. He taught me this horrible exercise where I have to raise my foot off the barre and hold and hold and hold.

But mainly, through those weeks, he just kept running me through my RAD Grade 5 syllabus again and again. He said I could do something else when I was perfect.

On the way home from Geoffrey's, if I wasn't too dusty or late, I'd stop off for a root beer float and a chat with Robbie. He wasn't at the Tasty Queen *every* night, but he was there most nights and my heart gave a little flutter whenever I saw his rusty truck under the tree.

When I was, like, eleven or something, I'd 'gone out' with a few boys, but it wasn't actually dating. It was just because everyone was 'going out' with somebody and I didn't want to look like a loser. And then, I'd had a huge crush on one of the fifth formers at school . . . had crushed so badly that my knees would shake if I was behind him in the queue for lunch. Once, when we'd had exchange students in from Germany, all the seating in chapel was messed up and I actually got to sit next to my crush for an entire hour. I literally thought my heart was going to explode. He *touched my hand* when he passed me a hymnal and I could feel the place for days.

It wasn't like that with Robbie.

I didn't feel the nothing that I had with the boys at

school I'd 'gone out' with. But I didn't feel the paralysing, overwhelming physical thing I had with my crush, either.

Mainly, we talked. I showed him the things that Geoffrey gave me and he laughed at them. He talked about the trouble the twins got into or what he'd been doing that day. He said he wouldn't gossip about his clients, but sometimes he told me funny things they'd done or said.

And sometimes, we got talking about things that were a bit more personal. We both knew what it was like, growing up without a father. We knew what it was like to be away from home and to have complicated families.

One night, I found out that his sister and the twins weren't even his sisters and brothers, not really. They were his cousins that his mother had adopted. None of them knew that... they called her Mom and couldn't really remember their real one.

His mother was cleaning for a living and had taken over raising even *more* children. I asked him if that had been a good idea and he shrugged and flipped his hair over his shoulders. He said, 'It was bad in their family. My uncle was drinking too much... and really for most of us Indians, any is too much. And my aunt was... she was desperate for money and making some bad decisions.'

I thought about what it must have been like for little kids in a situation like that. I remembered when Margaret got puppies, about her not being able to take just one.

'I'd like to meet your mother,' I said and Robbie smiled. He said, 'I'll ask her tonight.'

But the next night, Robbie wasn't at the Tasty Queen. Or the night after that. I texted him, asking if he was okay, but he didn't reply. At dinner, Ethan asked if I'd seen him and I told him no. I even told him about the texts, and Ethan's eyes narrowed slightly in a way that let me know he was worried.

'Huh,' he said, in between mouthfuls of mashed potato. 'I'm going to head over to their place after dinner,' he said, and then to me, 'Do you want to come?'

'Ethan,' Margaret said, in a kind of warning voice, and he looked right into her eyes.

'Is there a problem?' he asked. 'Do you want to talk about it?'

Although she still had food on her plate, Margaret pushed her plate away and stood. She said, 'No. You know what I think,' and began to clean the kitchen.

I had no idea what all that was about.

I didn't think about it much, though. I ran upstairs, washed my face, brushed my teeth and hair and was back downstairs in a clean shirt and a pair of jeans in about five minutes. I tied on my trainers watching Ethan nosing around in the cupboards and putting things in one of the paper bags they gave out at the supermarket.

At first, Margaret just shot glares at him from where she was loading the dishwasher. But then she came over, looked in the bag and took something out. 'Don't give them that,' she said. 'Give them the good stuff.' She pulled out a jar of the slightly-too tart apricot jam she'd made last year and put some of this year's strawberry jam into it, instead. Then she looked, and added another jar of it and went outside. She came back in with tomatoes and a head of lettuce and then pulled some of the chicken out of the freezer and wrapped the package in bubble wrap and aluminium foil, to keep it cold for the drive. On top of that, she put a loaf of bread and some of the farm's good milk in another big glass jar. Ethan was grinding down his special coffee beans and spooning the ground coffee into a plastic sandwich bag. Then he picked up the lot. 'Ready,' he said and Margaret raised up on her tiptoes and kissed him under his right ear.

'Mule,' she said quietly.

I had more time to think as we drove silently into town. Ethan didn't bring Margaret flowers or sweep her off her feet or cover her with kisses all the time. And Margaret didn't hang on his every word or sit on his lap or anything. And they fought nearly every day...over the dogs or me or the farm. But their fights never seemed serious. They fought about serious things sometimes, like when they were talking about how to pay for something new the tractor needed, or Ethan thought it needed, anyway. But they got over it quickly.

They just let each other be themselves. And stayed together—knowing they'd probably fight again the next day. I didn't know why Margaret hadn't wanted Ethan to take me over to Robbie's house, but she hadn't. And yet, she helped him pack up food for Robbie's family...had even given him extra things, things she'd probably been saving for herself, or to sell. And then she'd kissed him.

And I thought that was maybe what real love was... letting each other be how you are and not minding that it gets irritating sometimes. Getting over the irritation, even though you still thought the other person was wrong.

Ethan pulled up at the convenience store and came out with another bag...this one had a huge box of orange soda tins...*cans*, bags of sweets...*candy* and crisps...*chips*. It also had a teen magazine with a boy band on the cover.

I noticed all that, but I was still thinking—mainly about me and Mum and how we treated each other. I'd wanted her to be different from how she was my whole life. Part of me still did. I'd thought it was because I loved her so much, but now I wondered if it was because I hadn't really known what love was at all.

CHAPTER SEVENTEEN

Fort Scott isn't a big city, but it is a city and it has its nice parts and its not so nice parts. I'd only been to one or two houses—usually when I'd been carpooling to or from an away softball game—and they'd both been in the nice parts. There were some big old Victorian houses near the fort that were lovely and there was a very Americans-on-television suburban area with huge, perfect lawns and gleaming painted houses in another part.

Robbie's house wasn't in those neighbourhoods. The lawns here were yellowing from the heat and the gardens were untidy, with a lot of old cars or play equipment that had faded in the sun. There were hardly any flowerbeds, although there were quite a few vegetable gardens.

Ethan knew right where he was going. There's a way people drive when they've driven the same way hundreds of times and he drove that way. Something about that made my stomach tighten up hard with tension.

When we got there, the air felt hot after the air conditioning of the truck and I wondered why I'd put on jeans. There was a doorbell button, but Ethan ignored it, opened the screen door and pounded on the wooden door. 'Bell hasn't worked in thirty years,' he said. 'Keep meaning to fix it.'

The door was flung open and a short brown girl stood there. You could tell she was terribly cross and she put one finger to her lips and shushed us. Ethan grinned as we crept inside and she carefully, carefully shut the door.

'You got them in bed already?' he whispered.

She nodded and Ethan reached into the plastic bag and gave her the boy band magazine. Her eyes widened and she hugged Ethan around his tummy, hard, before he even managed to get the rest of the stuff onto the counter. Then it was like she'd seen me for the first time.

She was short, around five foot, and I'd been taller at that age. She was rounder than I'd ever been, too. Her hair was black but curled in that frizzy way that only natural hair curls and her face was rounder with different features than Robbie's—a flatter nose, more deep-set eyes, fuller lips. But I could tell she was Native American straight away and I suddenly felt self-conscious that she was looking at me, assessing my own genetic background while I was assessing hers.

'I'm Rachael,' she said in a low voice, putting out her hand to be shaken.

I still found that whole hand thing awkward, but I did it and said, 'Robbie's told me a lot about you.'

She looked delighted. 'Really?' she said.

I said, 'I can't believe how responsible you are. I couldn't have done it at your age,' and she was suddenly terribly shy, dropping her eyes and my hand at the same time. 'I'll go get him,' she said and went down the hall.

It was a bungalow, like most American houses, and looked to have been built in the sixties or seventies. It still had those horrible plywood hollow doors and green linoleum in the hall. The walls were scuffed, here and there, and the furniture kind of sagged. The air conditioning worked, but it was noisy. Still, everything was sparklingly clean, and the kitchen definitely smelled of lemons.

Robbie came out and Ethan started talking to him about helping with the hay. The big fields could maybe be cut twice and they'd use the baler and he and Margaret could do that on their own, if they had to, but the special field had to be cut and then put in the sunshine until it was bone dry. A special lorry had to come to collect it, sucking it up right off the ground with something like a huge vacuum cleaner, so they had to time the whole operation with the weather and the available collection times. Evidently, tomorrow would be the best time to cut it.

Robbie made a few phone calls...in fact, it sounded like half the county rearranged their week so that Margaret and Ethan could cut their fancy hay tomorrow. I was half listening to Rachael talking about the boys in the magazine band and half listening to Ethan and Robbie thanking six or seven people for moving their schedules.

Finally, they finished and Rachael must have been half listening, too, because she suddenly begged Ethan to play her at chess.

'Oh, no,' Ethan said. 'It's getting late and I haven't played all summer. You'll kill me.'

'Please?' she begged. 'There's *nobody* here. Mom and Robbie are just *terrible*.' The way she flung her head in disgust reminded me of my coyote and made Ethan chuckle.

'Well,' he said. 'I guess I'm better than *nobody*. Get the board.'

Robbie looked at me for the first time and his eyes seemed dark and sorrowful. He walked to the front door and looked at me with those big sad eyes again and I knew what he wanted. I followed.

It was finally dark, the dark I hardly ever saw, because I fell dead into my bed after my bath every night, while Margaret did her genealogy and Ethan watched baseball. I couldn't see many stars, here in town, but the moon was amazing—huge and full and pinky-red.

'It's the Strawberry Moon,' Robbie said. 'It'll be the Fourth of July soon. I'd better get the twins some firecrackers so they can drive Rachael crazy.'

We were sitting on a bench on the narrow porch. Even in the moonlight, I could see his eyes were hooded with something. He sighed. He said, 'I was going to ask if you wanted to go see the fireworks at the fort, but now...'

I'd had it with his man of mystery act. I said, 'Just tell me what's going on, Robbie.' I could hear the same impatience in my voice that Margaret often had when she was talking to Ethan. I said, 'Sorry,' but he shook his head.

'No,' he said. 'You're right. I need to tell you.'

He turned to face me. Behind us in the house, I could hear Rachael giggling and Ethan's slow laughter. He said, 'Remember the night we met, when I said we were probably related?'

I nodded. I'd probably never forget anything about that night.

He continued. 'Well my cousin came by, the one that does the phones. And Mom said something about us seeing each other and about me having feelings for you.' He stopped for a moment.

I said, 'Go on.' It wasn't really news that Robbie had feelings for me. I didn't get wildly excited on the one hand or grossed out on the other. It just felt...normal. I had feelings for him, too. It was just a fact.

He kind of smiled a little, but then the smile fell off his face. 'They didn't know I could hear,' he said and then kicked a little rock off into the grass. 'But you can hear anything in our house, if you listen hard enough. And I was listening, I can tell you.'

He took a deep breath and looked back out at the moon, as if he was having a conversation with it, not me. 'They talked about how your mom used to date Kris—my brother Kris. They said that they kind of kept on... well...being serious with each other on and off for a long time.'

He looked at me again. He said, 'I already told you that Indians and drinking don't really go together. Drugs and Indians don't go together, either. Evidently, we just don't have as much resistance. We get addicted quick. My brother Kris went to college on a football scholarship and came home addicted. Bad.'

I couldn't really think clearly. Mum and Kris. Dated. That's what kept going through my head, like I couldn't really understand the words. Mum. Kris. Dated. Mum. Dated Kris. Kris. Mum.

But Robbie kept talking. 'So, Kris would get clean and

get a job and your mom would talk to him. And once they started talking, they evidently would start seeing each other again...in a kind of serious way.'

I wasn't stupid. I knew what he was trying to say.

'But then Kris would start up with the drugs again and your mom would dump him. My mom said it used to break your mom's heart.' And now Robbie reached out and took one of my hands and held it tightly, so tightly that it hurt a little bit. 'They think Kris was your father. Your mom was here visiting at the right time, they said. But then Tanya got hurt and Kris got in a big fight and...he died. He...he drove off the road and he died.' And now I was holding onto his hand as tightly as he was holding onto mine.

'I think,' he said. 'I might be your uncle.'

Although I could barely see him in the moonlight, I already knew every inch of Robbie's face. And I suddenly recognized that his eye sockets were the same as mine and his jawline was the same as mine and his cheekbones were the same as mine and his long, black, poker-length hair was...the exact same as my own.

I dropped his hand and jumped up to my feet. I didn't know what I was planning to do or what I felt. It was all jumbled up in my head—my mother dating Robbie's brother was enough to deal with. That Kris might be my father seemed to be too huge to actually fit into my brain. And that Robbie and I were...that I was Robbie's *niece*?

'Ready to go?' Ethan and Rachael came out onto the porch, smiling. 'She wiped the floor with me,' he said to Robbie.

Robbie stood and rubbed his eyes. 'She's a holy terror with that chess board,' he said. 'I keep telling them at school. They can't wait to have her.'

I congratulated Rachael and got into the truck in a kind of a dream, and we drove home with the big strawberry moon hanging above us.

After a while, Ethan cleared his throat, but in the end, he didn't say anything. And that was fine. I didn't want to talk. Because it had finally occurred to me...if this Kris was my father and my mother was my mother...I wasn't British at all. Except for that little bit from my grandfather that Margaret had told me about, I was completely American. And more than American. I was *Native* American—more than half of me was Native American.

And that was pretty amazing. It was nothing I'd ever imagined, but it was...cool...and it came with this big, important history. It was a proper *heritage*, and I found that I wanted a proper heritage really badly. But it was also a bit terrible, because England was my home and I loved it and it suddenly seemed like I didn't belong there...that I'd never actually belonged there.

All those, 'Who am I really,' feelings that I'd had since the airport came back hard. The moon filled the truck and Ethan said, 'Wow. That's really something.' I don't know what I said back. But he'd said exactly what I felt. All of this was something—something big, like the huge red moon. It was impossible to swallow it all whole and try to hold it inside my cracked apart heart.

I thought I'd never get to sleep that night. After my bath, I lay on the floor in my splits stretch and felt electricity whirring around in my brain, like it was busy making about a million new connections and concepts. But it wasn't telling me what they were...my mind felt stupid and thick with it all.

I lay down. I couldn't see the moon from my window... it was right above us, but the bright of it made huge shafts of light across my floor, my bed and my walls. It wasn't like it was trying to push inside me any more, because I didn't have an inside any more. Without noticing, my cracked middle had become so wide and open that I was outside now, all outside, spilling out my light like the strawberry moon.

CHAPTER SEVENTEEN

When I came down, Ethan and Robbie were already out in the hayfield, mowing.

'Honestly,' Margaret said. 'He's got Robbie out there guiding the tractor like he's never mown before. I swear if I'd let him he'd cut it with nail scissors.'

I said something about the money being good and Margaret shook her head. 'It's not that,' she said. 'He just *likes* it.'

That morning, Margaret did Ethan's chores and I did Margaret's. I still spent a lot of time apologizing to the chickens when I collected eggs and I was slow judging the ripeness of tomatoes. There were also about five million ripe strawberries and I hadn't allowed time to pick that many. So, I was late when I got back into the mudroom to wash my hands. Everyone else was already finishing breakfast.

I had heard, in a kind of not really listening way, Margaret saying something about Sunflower the cow's top left quarter. It turned out that was part of her udder and it was looking a bit not right, so straight after I sat down and filled my plate, they went to look at her. They only had two cows and Margaret was kind of attached to both of them. I watched Ethan and Margaret walking off to the barn to look at Sunflower and Ethan put his arm on Margaret's shoulders for comfort.

All that thought about what love truly is came back to me as I looked across the table at Robbie.

Robbie's hair was in two tight plaits under a green John Deere baseball hat and his old brown t-shirt was dusty. He also had a bit of ketchup on his chin from his breakfast. He was, I noticed, amazingly beautiful. He was looking intently at a big book, so as I mechanically ate my hashbrowns, eggs and bacon, I had all the time I wanted to look at his broad, flat shoulders, the long, lean muscles in his arms and his strong hands.

I noticed that Robbie was beautiful, but I also noticed that I didn't actually feel much about it. It was just nice to look at him. So I did.

I was nearly done eating by the time he got up and took the chair next to me. 'Look,' he said, pointing.

If it hadn't said, 'Kris Slater,' under the photograph, I would have thought it was a photo of Robbie himself in fancy dress. If you could get rid of the tie-dyed t-shirt and the wide jeans...and the horrible 90s hairstyle that looked like he was wearing curtains on his head...he looked just like Robbie.

He was goofing around in a school corridor with his arms around the necks of two other boys. I looked closer...and he was a bit more muscled than Robbie— gym muscles, like Brad had. He was taller. His hair had a slight wave that reminded me of Rachael. But it was close. God, it was close.

Robbie pointed to the other names. Ethan Buchwald wasn't wearing tie-dye...he wore the same kind of front pocket t-shirt that he wore now and the same Levi 501s...but they were a lot tighter and he was a lot slimmer with a flat tummy over his big belt buckle. His hair was blonder, but in the same long on top and short back and sides he wore now, in the rare moments I saw him without his feed cap. The other boy was Brad's father, Wayne, in a shirt with a collar and a logo, chinos and loafers without socks.

The caption read, 'Football stars stick together on and off the field,' and suddenly, it all kind of clicked in my head. The way Ethan knew Wayne's number by heart. The way Ethan had driven over to Robbie's house hundreds of times. They'd been friends, maybe best friends, in school.

It was a yearbook, Robbie explained. The school put it together for the kids to buy. Kris hadn't bought one, but Ethan had. He flicked past individual school photos, like the ones we had in England, only in rows and bound into the book, to get to another photo. Homecoming King and Queen. There was Ethan again, looking very handsome in a dinner jacket. And next to him, wearing a glittery crown and a long red satin dress, was my mother.

She looked nearly exactly the same as she did now. Same hair. Same hair*style*. I'd seen it in an updo just like that one, hundreds of times. She was a little thinner, maybe, and maybe an inch or two shorter, it was hard to tell with heels, but the shade of red was the same as her red suit and a red cocktail dress and a red jumper she had in her wardrobe now. The caption had her name as 'Annalise,' so she'd already changed it.

She'd been clumsy. She'd been lazy. She'd been the loser of the family. But like Margaret had said, at seventeen she'd become someone else, the person she was going to be all the rest of her life. Ethan held a sceptre in one hand and her hand in the other and they smiled confidently out of the photograph.

'But that's messed up,' Robbie said. 'They said she was going out with Kris, not Mr Buchwald.'

I looked out the big glass back door past the deck and saw Ethan and Margaret walking back from the cow shed with all three puppies scampering around their feet. I should have cleaned up the breakfast things by now.

'Run upstairs,' I said to Robbie, 'And shove this under my bed. I'll have a look at it later.'

He was fast, I'll tell you that.

By the time Margaret and Ethan came through the door, he was sitting drinking juice like nothing had happened and I was putting plates into the dishwasher. Margaret opened the drawer she always had ready with all that day's stuff and got out my envelope and a big bandana that she tied on her hair before she put on her hat. When she gave me my envelope, she nodded at the strawberries and said, 'I'll make jam later. I'm going to help spread the hay.'

She tapped the envelope at a circled list. 'I called an order to the deli counter last night but tell them I forgot to add two of the big coffee cakes. Make some iced tea and put out the sugar cookies before you go, just in case somebody comes by early, but most people come in the afternoon.'

People. Coming. Because, I slowly realized, of the hay. The hay was a big, cool deal. People rearranged their work for it. They came by and *looked* at it. It was an *occasion*. I suddenly wanted to go and look at it, too, and decided I would, in the afternoon. And then I remembered I was meant to be at the ballet studio in the afternoon.

As if she'd read my mind, Margaret said, 'I also got Geoffrey Mellon on the phone last night,' Margaret continued. 'He's got time for you to do your studio stuff at ten, instead of noon and you can go to the deli and home after that. He says he understands about you not working there this afternoon.'

I got that familiar feeling that everyone knew my life better than I did...but now I knew that was just what it was like when Margaret was raising you. There was nothing else I could do, so I just nodded and said, 'Okay.'

'When you get home, put out the deli stuff, make some coffee, top up the iced tea, put out some plates and napkins...no, better pick up some paper plates.' I scribbled it all down on my envelope. 'Just make it look nice.'

'How many people will there be?' I asked, trying not to sound scared. It didn't work. Robbie and Ethan grinned behind Margaret's back.

'Oh, not many. Probably twenty or so. Though we had fifty the year before last.' I could feel my mouth open in shock and shut it with a snap when Ethan and Robbie grinned wider.

I could cater for fifty people. After running errands and dancing. On my own. For the first time ever. Yeah. Sure. Of course I could.

My head was full of things to remember as I drove off that morning. I actually stopped and waited before I turned onto the asphalt road because I knew I wasn't concentrating on my driving. I could hear Mr Hanson's voice in my head, telling me that I always had to pay attention, and suddenly remembered again what it had been like, holding onto the wheel and waiting for a crash.

I closed my eyes and did some of Mum's deep breathing exercises, and for once, they actually helped. I made the left hand turn (which wasn't tricky, because there was hardly ever anybody else driving along there) and drove on.

And I don't know how I'd missed it before, if I had—and I also don't know how it had happened overnight, if it had—but there were sunflowers along the sides of the road, in the place where the tall grasses grew outside of the fences. They weren't as big as the ones you grow in primary school, but they were big enough—six or seven centimetres across. And they'd just popped into view.

There were literally hundreds of them, with fluffy brown centres and shocking golden petals, and of course they were all facing me, since I was driving West and the sun was still in the East. It was lovely.

I got out of the truck, stuck my ballet shoes into the hollow of my left hip and secured them with my panty elastic, put on my work gloves and grabbed my broom. I didn't even have to think about any of it any more.

I noticed, as I walked through the pasture, that all the old cow poo had dried up in the hot sun. Although there was a bit of new stuff here and there... they hadn't been able to resist letting go of some on their way to and from the water trough... most of it was crumbling in the heat. I thought that, and then almost stepped in a huge new pat right on my path. I would have bet money that the red cow had dropped it.

The cattle were all cropping grass on the other side of the tree when I came over the ridge. I walked carefully, tapping the path with my broom, because Robbie had told me that was a good way to scare away rattlers. A couple of the huge carrion eaters Ethan called 'buzzards' rose up out of the grass and flew away with big lazy flaps. They looked at me appraisingly as they passed, as if it was only a matter of time for me to be dead enough to eat. It was insulting.

There was not a breath of a breeze that morning and the sun was baking hot already. I didn't think it would take long for the hay to dry. I started to sweat just brushing the dust off the platform.

When you take ballet class every morning, my old teacher had always said, you don't have to even think about the exercises. Your body just starts to do them.

For the first time in my life, that was true for me. I realised it halfway through my ronds de jambe, and for a moment lost my place in the movement. Then I just let my body take over again and stopped trying to control it.

It wasn't until I was doing some central exercises that

I saw my coyote. He'd been laying in the tall grass, but had decided to creep forward a bit on his belly. The way he did it made me afraid, at first, that he'd been injured. But then I was pretty sure he hadn't. He didn't look as healthy as he had when I'd met him, though.

As I worked through the whole round, I remembered all the things I'd read on the coyote website. Lone coyotes don't last very long. Coyotes suffer when they're not in a pack. Coyotes need large territories or they will 'hunt out' all available food.

He always resented the loud noises jetés—ballet jumps—make. Whenever my feet landed hard, he'd always give me one of his 'must you? really?' looks. Today, he just gave a tiny little flick of his ears, like he couldn't be bothered to complain. And then he put his head down on his paws and I realised he'd crawled forward so that he could watch me while laying down, so that he didn't have to keep sitting up.

I couldn't see that much of him. Even the short grass was tallish. But what I could see of his back and his flanks looked thinner than they'd been when I'd seen him that first day with a rabbit in his jaws. Of course, it had been hot lately. But...

I went to the top of my platform to do a diagonal of pirouettes. I didn't think any more about it while I was doing them...you just can't think about anything when you are doing a long diagonal of pirouettes. But once I'd stopped and pulled an attitude, I thought again. He should, I realised, have moved on. Ages ago. He shouldn't be here any more. He had to find a pack.

It seemed very hot right then, and I went to the edge of my platform and sat down, dangling my legs over the edge. The coyote and I looked at each other carefully.

Neither of us could keep going the way we were, I realised. Not the coyote. Not me. And I could add Robbie to that list, too. Margaret liked to talk about 'sustainable' agriculture and that word came to me as I sat there. There was nothing sustainable in what was happening. I could suddenly see it quite clearly. None of what was going on in my life could last, not the way it was.

It made me feel sad. I lay back and looked up at the enormous blue sky, wondering if we were all about to lose the things we'd found.

CHAPTER EIGHTEEN

It's easy to do catering in America. By the time I'd locked out the puppies and gone down to the hayfield, the table looked amazing and it hadn't been any problem at all. The food actually came in really nice-looking serving dishes. I just had to arrange them on the tablecloth (red and white checked, paper, bought it without being told), put the plastic knives and forks (bought without being told) in Mason jars, stack up the paper napkins (blue) and plates (yellow) artistically on the table and put the big Mason jar full of sunflowers in the middle of it (cut on the way home with one of the plastic knives and well examined for bugs). There was enough iced tea in the iced tea dispenser to float a ship. There was coffee in the coffee maker. There were cups and glasses in neat rows on the kitchen countertops. And I was, officially, a total goddess.

Down at the hayfield, Margaret told me things were going well. All the flowers would make little specks of colour in the hay when they dried, because it would dry fast enough, which was what the client liked. Robbie and Ethan and Margaret kept poking it, tossing it up in the air and turning it over. There were spare pitchforks and rakes if you wanted to have a go. I didn't.

People came and went 'oooo' over it. They went 'oooo' for a really long time and it was terribly boring. So, I went back to the house. I fed the puppies and locked them back into the mudroom. Margaret was going to have everyone wash at the sink outside and so I put out nice little soaps and about a hundred hand towels and a laundry basket to catch the dirty ones. Nobody had told me to do that, either.

And then I went upstairs, washed myself a bit, got the yearbook and went downstairs with it so that I could snoop while I waited for the people to come in. I just glanced at the long note the principal had written on the first page and skimmed over the photos of the kids on the 'yearbook staff'. It seemed like every teacher had written a bit, as well, but apart from marvelling at the truly dreadful fashions, I flipped through all of that. Until I got to the librarian's bit, because under her list of the top books of the year was a photograph of Mum and Kris.

They were talking at a library table and obviously completely unaware anyone was taking a photo. There was a stack of books between them and some paper and pencils, too, but they had leaned over all of it. Their faces were close. They looked deeply into each other's eyes. Their expressions were tender and completely serious.

The caption read, 'The library is a great place to—ahem—study.'

Mum has dated, of course, in the fourteen years I've been on earth. But I have never seen her look at a man that way. I was now rock-bottom certain that I was looking at a picture of my father.

Julia Slater Percy . . . or Julia Percy Slater. Either would look good, I thought, on ballet programmes. Slater was a nice name. A solid name.

And that was the feeling I got. I got a solid feeling. As

if I'd been floating around in the air my whole life and had just now been able to stand on the earth. I got up and walked around in circles for a little while.

I'd been so concerned with Robbie and me-and-Robbie that I hadn't noticed. I *had a father*. I had a father who had totally loved my mother. And who would have loved me, too. It was all in his face. It was in the story of how hard he'd tried to fight his addiction and keep Mum.

But I wanted to see more.

Feverishly, I sat back down and flicked through pages. Then I remembered, and went back to the formal, posed photographs. I found Ethan and then Mum and...and Margaret. Right next to each other as 'Seniors'. But that wasn't right. Margaret was three years older than Mum...she shouldn't have been in the yearbook *at all*.

I looked through the big glass doors. Even with the air conditioning on, you could kind of tell when people were talking behind the barn. Under the photographs were little numbers. There were dozens under Mum's photo. There were three under Margaret's. I thought quickly and flicked to the page number that went with the first of Mum's numbers—it was the photograph with Kris in the library.

So then I flicked to the first one under Margaret's picture. 'Champion Jam from Home Ec Leader' was the caption. Margaret was smiling, holding a ribbon and a jar of jam in front of a sign that read 'County Fair'. Her hair was in a ponytail, but shiny and well-brushed and long. It curled at the end in her natural wave. She was thinner, but she already had her big, open smile and she was wearing a dress that didn't look too hideous, even for today.

I flicked back to their small photos to find the others. Mum was Homecoming Queen. Mum was a Letter Girl. Mum was the President of Science Club. Mum was Class President. Mum was Valedictorian. Mum won an essay contest.

Margaret won the jam thing. Margaret was in a practical accounting class. She looked pretty in both of them, but... it wasn't great, was it? It wasn't like Mum.

Margaret only had one more photograph page and I kind of hoped she was doing something more interesting than she had in the others. I could hear laughter and talking by the mudroom door so I turned to the page quickly. Prom King and Queen... Ethan Buchwald was king and the queen was Margaret Percy. This time, Ethan wasn't looking out at the photographer. He was looking at Margaret, who was shining and radiant and... just lovely.

And beneath it were two more pictures—this time of all four of them. They'd travelled to prom together, arriving in a farm trailer pulled by a tractor. The trailer had been decorated with crêpe paper streamers and paper flowers. Inside they'd put quilts and rugs over haybales to seat the girls. Ethan had driven the tractor in his tuxedo and Kris had somehow crammed into the glass cab with him in his. In the second one, Ethan was lifting Margaret down, while Mum looked on, laughing. Kris was standing behind her, and she was wrapped up in his arms.

'Doesn't this look nice?' They'd come in. I could

tell Whitney's mother Elizabeth had spoken. I'd know her voice anywhere after all the times she'd told me to keep my glove up or to swing with my hips at softball. 'Margaret, you are a wonder. How ever did you manage to get all *this* ready?'

I kind of shoved the yearbook on the coffee table and hustled to start handing out drinks. My mind was reeling…with questions, with answers, with all my feelings.

'Nothing to do with me,' Margaret said. 'It's Jules. I forgot to put the knives and forks on the list and would *never* have thought of the sunflowers.' She came over and put her arm around my shoulders and squeezed.

It felt nice to be hugged, to be displayed as good and worthy to the same people who thought Margaret had been insane to take me on. But I also felt horribly guilty. I had seen something in those photographs, something I couldn't put into words, not even in my own mind. There was a pain and a shame in them that I could feel floating around in the air like dust motes, but I couldn't name. And, suddenly, it made me feel overwhelming tenderness for Auntie Margaret, and I put my arm around her waist and hugged her back.

The little supper went well and it was easy to clean up. But when I passed the living-room, the yearbook was gone.

That night, after I'd stretched, I went to put out clothes for the next day and saw some of Geoffrey's cast-off merchandise in my drawers. They made me smile, so I moved them up to the top of the pile.

When I came down to breakfast that Thursday, I was wearing the purple satin leotard with faded-on-one leg orange sweat shorts that read 'Dancer' in big white letters on the bum. Ethan choked on his coffee and, coughing, pointed to the stairs. So, I went back up and changed into the mustard leotard/skirt combo with one of the 90s patterned cropped t-shirts. But he didn't like that, either. So then I wore a plain black leotard in the old style—cap sleeves, scoop neck—and the leopard print velvet shorts.

Margaret was laughing so hard she'd started to cry and even the puppies had come in to see what was going on.

'Well?' I asked Uncle Ethan. 'Is *this* acceptable?'

'It's the best one out of the three,' he said. 'I don't know that I'd call it acceptable.'

I took that as a yes and settled down to my breakfast. He shook his head, and chuckled. 'I don't know what they're going to make of you down at the feed store. I'd better phone ahead to warn them.'

Margaret finally stopped laughing enough to reach down and bring up a box. I opened it and inside was a pair of brown leather, lace up work boots. 'The FedEx man brought them yesterday,' she said, 'but in all the excitement, I forgot. They don't come out of your pay. They'll protect your ankles and feet when you're doing all this work around the farm... and prancing around in cow pastures.'

I was only wearing trainer liners, so I ran upstairs and got some proper socks and came back down. It took me about ten seconds. Then I was putting on the new boots. They were a kind of tan colour and had a ridge that went right around the toe and metal hooks up the leg part. They had another tough layer of black leather to protect the ankle and another down the back for the Achilles tendon. They fit perfectly and they looked really, really cool.

I hugged Margaret and then hugged Uncle Ethan, too. I knew he had picked them out—they were the same kind he wore. He patted my back and handed me my wage envelope, saying gruffly, 'They've got steel toes.'

It was totally sweet of them both.

Geoffrey had interesting teaching techniques. That day, he was working on my turns.

'You keep falling off your pirouettes,' he said. 'Just a little, right at the end.'

'I know.' Trust me, I knew.

'Ooookay,' he said, with his head on one side. 'Try falling off more. Fall off on purpose.'

I did.

'Again.'

This went on for some time. Finally, I realized that I was never properly ready to stop, that I was always wanting to try and do one more, even though the music told me it was time to end. So, I had this little wobble, where I wanted to go but I needed to stop and so I fell off a little bit. A tiny bit. Honestly, most people would never even *see* that I fell off my pirouettes. Only madly picky ballet people could even notice. But if I told myself, 'This is the last one,' really hard in my head, I didn't fall off that tiny bit.

I explained it to Geoffrey and he said, 'You're really good at learning,' which is something *no* teacher had *ever* said to me before. He must have seen the look of shock on my face because he said, 'No, really. You take on challenges and work them through. You actually take it *in*.' He scribbled something down on a notebook he was holding that day.

I started to thank him, but then he said, 'Do another diagonal of pirouettes. Do eight, and let's see.' And put on the music.

And that's why I didn't hear Whitney and the Madisons come in. 'Oh. My. GOD!' Whitney said, when I'd come to my not-falling-off-even-a-tiny-bit stop. 'You really are a freaking ballet dancer!'

They did that American girl thing where they scream and run in and hug you and all talk at once. I looked at Geoffrey, because they were wearing street shoes into the studio and we still had ten minutes left of our session, but he looked happy with it all, so I just relaxed and let myself be hugged. I was starting to kind of get into American hugging.

Once they'd stopped squeaking, Madison B said, 'We just came in to get you to go for pizza with us. We haven't seen you all week,' then she looked at Geoffrey and said, 'Oh, I'm so sorry, Mr Mellon! We've totally interrupted your class.'

'You *always* interrupt my classes, Madison,' he said, smiling. 'It's nice to know some things don't change. I *am* still seeing you next year in ballroom, aren't I?'

Madison nodded vigorously. 'I've been practising,' she said. 'Wait until you see my cha-cha hips.'

Geoffrey winced. 'I'll wait,' he said, waving her away. And then to me, 'Why don't you take your bag and have another afternoon off?' He winked. 'After all,' he said. 'I've got a recommendation to write.'

I had no idea what he was talking about. But my legs were so sore and tired that sitting in the air conditioning and stuffing myself silly with salad and pizza sounded wonderful. So I tied on my new boots and went.

It wasn't until I was parking at the pizza place and saw the lime green bug with the lawn mower trailer that I remembered Brad would be there. Still, I told myself, everyone else would, too. Including, I was delighted to see, Pinky, who air kissed me and Madison B and then said Freddie was sorry not to come along, too. 'He couldn't think of a farm errand.' She shook her bright pink head. 'He just doesn't try hard enough.'

Then she clocked my outfit. 'Jules!' she said. 'You look fabulous! Is that what farm hands wear in England?'

'She's a ballet dancer,' Whitney said. 'She really is.'

'Really?' Pinky said and Carter said it at the same time. Brad was leaning against the booth with his full plate, waiting for us. He must have heard Whitney. The whole street must have heard Whitney. His face started a long, slow, satisfied kind of smile.

I turned away from him and nodded. I felt a bit embarrassed. 'I just started again,' I said, shrugging.

'She's really good,' Whitney said. 'Mr Mellon told my mom that only about one in a million dancers have the ability to be as good as Jules.'

I was busy putting salad on my plate and I dropped the tongs right into the coleslaw. 'Really?' I asked and my voice was so high it squeaked.

Whitney nodded solemnly. 'He told me my ankles were too fat and that I had no musicality,' she said. 'I'm glad I liked cheer better.'

'Oh, I had no musicality, too!' Madison B said. 'And he told me I was too floppy. He said my very bones lacked discipline.'

Carter said, 'Woah. Harsh.'

'He's famous for it,' Madison A said. 'I left when I was ten, but when Chastity said she wanted to go onto Intermediate, he laughed for five minutes and then said "no".' Madison A looked at us all in turn. 'Imagine,' she said. 'Just that one word—no.'

'Cold,' Carter agreed.

'My sister evidently had "asymmetrical shoulders and a total inability to remember steps",' Pinky said. 'I don't think he's taught an Intermediate class for twenty years. He turns everyone down.'

Part of me was horrified, but part of me really, really wanted to laugh. Geoffrey was a tough critic. And he thought I had what it takes. I had no idea what I'd put on my plate. I poured Ranch dressing over the lot and went back to the table. Pinky slid in beside me and Carter sat opposite me.

I was always hungry. It was all the dancing, of course, and all the farm work. At school, I might play sport twice a week and have a PE class and maybe go for a swim or play a game of tennis one or two evenings, but it never really made me properly work. Now that I was dancing again, I felt starved all the time.

I said something about it and Brad looked up and kind of smiled. He said, 'Mom says her food bill goes up fifty dollars a week when I'm in training for football.' He took a bite of pizza and kind of talked around it. 'What's your training regime like?'

I told him. I didn't tell him *where* I was doing my morning workout, I just told him about it and about afternoons with Geoffrey coaching me and how I was paying for it.

And that kind of opened the floodgates. Everyone asked me a lot of questions about ballet and it was funny and also really sweet. Carter asked me to explain what pointe work was and I showed him some videos on my phone, using the pizza place WiFi. He was horrified when I showed him images of dancers' feet.

'Ballerinas are *tough*,' he said. 'That's crazy.'

Whitney showed me a workout video that guaranteed you could get into Russian splits in two weeks and said she'd text me the link. That meant we had to exchange numbers and since my phone was out, I exchanged with everyone.

And that was actually nice, because they were really lovely

people. I know Whitney could be a bit… Whitney…but she was very kind with it, and always meant well.

Then Brad got his phone out of his pocket. I'd been giving out my number, over and over. And he just put it into his phone, without even asking. When he noticed me watching, he stopped. He said, 'Is it okay, Jules? Is it all right for me to have your phone number?'

The way he said it made it sound like I was making it into a big deal, like I was a drama queen. I said, 'Of course. I just wanted you to *ask* first.'

He rolled his eyes. 'I *did* ask, Jules,' he said. 'I just asked. Duh.'

'I meant that I wanted you to ask *before* you started putting it in your phone,' I tried to explain.

'Do you want me to delete it?' He looked like a hurt little boy again and I felt horrible, like I'd been kicking one of the puppies.

'No, of course not.'

'Because I thought we were friends again.' His eyes could open up and I swear you could see right into his heart through them. They did that now. But it felt like a kind of trick, like he only showed how vulnerable he was to *make* me be nicer to him. I got cross again.

'We *are* friends,' I said. 'Being friends has nothing to do with it, and you *know* that, Brad.'

I was suddenly aware that everyone else at the table had gone completely silent to watch us argue. I blushed up to the roots of my hair. Whitney looked at me for a long, long moment. Then she said, '*Anyway*, did anybody see that space cowboy movie?' Awkwardly, the table started to hum with conversation again.

I kept my eyes on my plate.

What was wrong with me? I wondered. I already had one horribly complicated relationship with a boy. I wasn't trying to start a collection.

I felt tired and full as I left the pizza place to drive back to the farm with a giant cup of diet vanilla root beer in the cupholder. The decent radio station always faded right before my left off Highway 69, so after I was safely across (it still made me sweat a little bit), I always turned off the crackly radio.

The cows in my studio pasture had come up to the front for a drink. It used to be a bit muddy around where they watered, but now even that was dry. It had been hot and sunny for days and days. We'd had a little rain over that one night, but it hadn't seemed to make any difference, and it was baking.

The grass was turning a yellowy brown and the leaves of the trees looked darker. The big blue bowl of sky seemed totally removed from us, nothing to do with helping us stay alive down here in the heavy heat. I'd noticed earlier in the week that the river was looking browner and getting lower. Now I could see that the ponds I passed were starting to shrink. There was dried, cracked mud all around their edges. Even the sunflowers seemed already shrivelled.

I had to wear my leather gloves to drive. They were

still stained, but not stiff anymore and it was better than trying to hold onto the hot metal steering wheel. Margaret had pinned a big beach towel to the truck's seat, because the plastic upholstery kept burning the backs of my legs.

As I pulled into the drive and shut off the engine, only Genius came out of the flap to investigate, and she didn't bark. It was too hot to bark. Even the chickens were resting in the shade, too hot to even scratch around. I patted Genius's head and noticed that I didn't have to bend down to do it any more. They were growing fast.

When I went through the mudroom, the house was quiet. Thing One and Thing Two softly stirred their tails, but didn't actually move to greet me, and Genius settled back down on her bed. The air conditioning felt wonderful on my skin.

It was so quiet that I thought Margaret and Ethan might be having a nap. They sometimes did, when it was this hot, in the middle of the day, and then they'd work later into the evening. I moved quickly and quietly through the kitchen and was actually on the stairs before I realised they were sitting around the computer on the dining-room table.

They only got their computer out for Margaret to do her genealogy work, or to Skype their kids. I thought it must be Skyping, because Ethan wasn't interested enough to look at Margaret's genealogy work. But there wasn't any sound coming out of the speakers, just some scratching and rustling. They were looking at it so intently, though, that I just went up the stairs. I was being quiet, not because I was sneaking around or wanted to listen to their conversation, but just because I didn't want to break their concentration by making noise.

I was on the third or fourth stair when I heard my mum's voice and, yes, I'll admit it. I sat right down to eavesdrop.

'Sorry,' Mum said and I could hear her sit down. 'We shouldn't be disturbed now. I do have a phone call I'm waiting on from Japan, and if that comes through, I'll have to take it. But that's it.'

'Where are you?' Margaret asked.

'I'm home.' Mum was flustered and hurried, so she must be in the middle of a big crisis. I hardly ever made her talk to me when she was in the middle of a big crisis. 'I mean, I'm in the London office.' For the first time, I wasn't irritated that she felt more at home at work than she did in our house. It might have been that I missed her so much I didn't care that she was like that. It might have been that I was learning more about letting the people you love just be themselves. Or it might have been what that man at church had said. Three thousand families she'd saved, he'd said. That was a lot of people.

I hadn't really been listening, and I'd missed some bits, but I certainly listened when I heard Mum say, '...so I've secured Jules an audition next week.'

'Next *week*?' Margaret said. 'I can't—'

'Now, I know,' my mother interrupted smoothly, 'that you guys can't take off at a moment's notice this time of year. So, I've arranged for one of my team, Bethany, to come and escort Jules to New York for the audition at the school and to bring her back. I thought Jules might want to stay a day or so in the city and see a show.'

Oh. My. God. I loved my mother *so much*. An audition at a New York ballet school??? *That's* what Geoffrey had been talking about. He was writing a recommendation *for me*. For me to go to a New York ballet school. I trapped a squeal deep in my throat and clapped both hands around my mouth, but I was still *breathing* excitedly and my heart was pounding like a big kettledrum.

Goodbye, dead chickens and cow poo. Hello, civilization.

'No.' Margaret's voice was flat and hard. 'No, Lisa Ann. No way.'

'Oh, come *on*, Margaret,' my mother said. 'It's a superb opportunity and—'

This time it was my aunt interrupting my mother. 'She's just settled in,' Margaret said. 'She's *just* started to make friends. She's just started to actually smile, to lose that whipped dog look she had. She's just starting to be confident enough to actually stand up for herself, to go after what *she* wants.'

Mum said, 'That's not fair, Margaret. Jules…Jules *is* her dancing. She danced before she could stand…she'd wave her little arms around to music. When she was four years old, she sat through an entire performance of Giselle with her little eyes *stuck* to the stage. I couldn't even get her to go for ice cream at the interval.'

Ethan broke in now. 'I know she's all about the dancing. But she started dancing again *here*. She's *safe* here. She's got folks looking out for her and she needs that, Lise. It's too soon to move her.'

Mum did her laugh that was more like a cough. 'If you think Jules is going to fall in love with farm life, you don't know her,' she said. 'Of course she'll make the best of things, but she will never be a Kansas farm girl.'

'You don't know *what* she'll be,' Margaret said. 'And I'll bet that just kills you.'

'There's no need to get nasty,' Mum said. There was a pause and I could hear all three of them breathing. They were—all three of them—upset, and so was I, sitting on the stairs. I could feel myself wanting to jump up and scream. I so wanted that audition. I wanted... I wanted to go to ballet school. If that made me a brat, then I was a brat, but I knew where I belonged, and it wasn't on that flipping farm.

'Look,' Mum said. 'I haven't signed any papers. If I send someone to get Jules, you'll have to let her go.'

'And what if she doesn't get in?' Margaret said. 'She didn't get in last time. What will you do then?' Mum was silent, and Margaret pushed her advantage. 'You cancelled your vacation in Tuscany.' Margaret said 'Tuscany' with the same ironic spin that Ethan had put on 'ballet studio'. 'What will you do with her, once you have her again? Will you look after her? Eat with her? Talk to her? Make sure she's not wearing anything inappropriate? Make sure she's got nice friends and things to do?' Margaret snorted. 'Like hell you will. You'll just leave her to rot in that big house and then get all surprised when she acts up to get your attention.'

It was harsh. It wasn't all true. But it kind of was, and I could hear Mum starting her deep breathing.

'You never had any follow through,' Margaret said. 'You always had these big ideas, but you never really managed the day-to-day work of doing them. I don't know how you've gotten so far in that job of yours...'

'That's *enough*, Margaret,' Ethan said. And then to Mum. 'I'm sorry, Lise. She gets carried away and just can't stop. She went too far. None of that last bit is true. Not one little bit.'

Now they were all breathing hard. After a moment, Margaret said, 'I'm sorry, Lise. I truly am.'

Mum said, 'If you bully my girl like you bullied me, I swear I will come there and tear you apart with my own bare hands.' Her voice was calm and cold.

'I won't let that happen,' Ethan said.

'I'm kind of counting on that, E,' Mum answered. There was the ding of her internal message service and she said, 'Oh, for the love of Mike. The Japan call. This isn't over.' And then there was the bloop of the end of the call and Margaret snapped down the laptop.

I tiptoed up the stairs and started to noisily run a bath.

'Jules?' Margaret called up. 'Is that you?'

I shouted down. 'You were on a call,' I said. 'I'm running a bath.'

'It was your mom,' Margaret said. 'She was just checking that you were all right.'

And I left it at that.

CHAPTER NINETEEN

I do my best thinking in the bathtub.

Before the bubbles had gone, I knew two things. One; I was not going to mention ballet school to Margaret or Ethan. Two; I needed to talk to Geoffrey. He knew more about it than I did, had known when I didn't...and more...he actually believed in me.

It was nearly four o'clock when I rang Geoffrey. I tried to hit the ten minutes after the Beginners Two tap class and before he left for his dinner break and, although I had to ring three times, I got him. I told him I needed to speak to him and he said to come straight away. And then I asked, so he rang the house phone and Margaret actually *told* me to go into the studio.

I went down with my hair wet in a t-shirt and my cut off jean shorts and sandals.

'Be back before sundown,' Ethan said. 'That's about eight forty-five. There's a storm due in tonight.'

'Eat something before you go?' Margaret asked, but I told her I'd been to the pizza buffet for lunch and she said, 'Oh.'

It was still well over a hundred degrees Fahrenheit, but I'd parked under a tree, so the truck wasn't boiling. I even tasted the diet vanilla root beer that I'd left in the truck by mistake and it wasn't too hot to drink. It tasted kind of nice, actually, though not as nice as it did cold and bubbly.

There was a *lot* of traffic on Highway 69 and I was

nearly shaking with fear by the time I finally made a safe turn. The whole chicken-insides thing came back to me, and the time I'd been waiting for the big truck to hit me, when I'd been parked on the wrong side of the road. But nothing happened. I just turned right and kept driving.

I passed the Tasty Queen and pulled over into one of the big car parks to text Robbie. 'Do you fancy a limeade tonight. It's on me. X Jules.' I'd just put the phone back in my bag when I got an answer. 'You bet, but I won't be there until 7. Hope that's OK. XX R'. I sent back, 'OK,' and signalled and waited another five hundred years before I pulled back into the traffic.

Geoffrey was waiting in the little reception, sitting on a chair and eating a taco salad with a plastic fork. I said, 'Oh, God, I'm so sorry if I kept you away from your dinner and you had to eat that.'

He said, 'Girl, please. I love these things.' And then, 'So? What's the emergency?' And I plunked down next to him and explained.

'That is just typical of Margaret Percy,' Geoffrey said. 'Ever since I came to this town, she's been ... irritating.'

'She's good to me,' I said. 'She just ...'

'Thinks she knows everything.' Geoffrey speared a big chunk of avocado and waved it around.

It was true. But I loved her anyway, even though she could be a bit of a bully. Even though she was ruining my life. She was only doing what she was doing because she loved me. And because she loved Mum. 'It's all messed up,' I said. I kind of folded myself up on the chair and rested my head on my knees. 'I don't want to wait a year,' I said. 'If I wait a year, they'll expect me to...'

'Have pointe work,' Geoffrey said. 'Fix your extension...a year is a long time with just me to coach you.'

I nodded miserably and then sat up again. 'Not that you haven't been great,' I said.

He waved it away. 'I was corps de ballet,' he said. 'In a second-rate company. Let's not kid ourselves, kid. I'm not what you need right now. And you're already a year behind.'

He stood up and put his edible salad bowl down on the counter with a slap, dancing a decision. 'Right,' he said. 'Let's do this.'

'Do what?' I wasn't about to fly off to New York City with Geoffrey.

'They take video submissions,' he said. 'I did your reference, so I have everything. I've got the email of the admissions officer. I've got your reference number. Your mom has already paid for your audition. All we have to do is film you.' He looked at his watch. 'And we've got a whole hour and a half to do it.'

He went into the back and shouted, 'Brush your hair,' and so I did. He came back with a funky little stand that turned out to be a tripod for his tablet. He went back again and gave me everything—black regulation leotard, pink tights, satin shoes.

I started taking off my sandals. 'I've got the RAD music here,' he said, holding his phone. 'Let me just go through what they want to see again ... Oh, and here.' He slid over a bit of white cardboard with pink thread wrapped around it and a needle through it. I pulled off my shorts and went to the back in just my leotard, emerging in full proper kit, just a few minutes later after frantically sewing on my shoe elastic. It felt ... normal.

He moved the chair and I sat down. He whipped my hair into a bun, gelling back the wisps and pinning it hard onto my head. He said, 'Cover,' and I put my face in my hands while he sprayed it.

'I just heard there might be a tornado tonight,' he said. 'That bun would survive it.'

It all took about ten minutes. He flicked on the studio lights, adjusted the dimmers a bit and put the tablet into place so it didn't show in any of the reflections.

'We don't have time to f ... mess about,' he said, 'because it's Salsa night.' He lowered his chin and thrust out one shoulder, dancing determination. 'We're going to hit them once and we're going to hit them hard.'

'I'm not warm,' I said.

'Do some sautés,' he said and I started bouncing.

It was madness. Thank God Geoffrey had run me through my Grade 5 stuff about five hundred times, because it was all the rehearsal I had. I had to do pliés, tendues, ronds de jambe, passés and adagio développé en croix, and balancés on one leg. I had to do the minute-long dance I'd done for my Grade 5 exam and Geoffrey made me do that twice, shouting, 'Hurt that leg if you have to, but get it higher.' It did hurt, a little, but it didn't actually do any damage and he looked happy with me.

He had printed off the email and was ticking things off on the list. Then he stopped and scratched his head. 'Original dance of the student's choosing,' he said, musingly.

I didn't have an original dance. I stood there and could see my shoulders slump down into defeat from about twenty-five different reflections.

'Under two minutes,' Geoffrey said. He kept repeating it. 'Original dance. Under two minutes,' and scratching his head. Then he stopped and looked at me. 'Right,' he said.

He ran over to the phone and found something on Spotify and blasted it on the Bluetooth speaker. 'Native American flute music,' he said. 'Do your coyote things.'

I kind of squeezed my head in my hands. It was all too much. Everything was just too, too much. Archie, getting expelled, Mum, the farm, the chickens, finding my father…and now this. The music was all over the place, big booming sounds that kept fading off and…

'Forget about the music,' Geoffrey said. 'It's just there to be there. The phrase keeps on repeating…'

'I can't,' I said. 'I just can't.' I was going to cry. I was going to fall completely apart. I was going to fail. Again. That cracked place, it was too big now. It was too big and I was too little and…

'Don't make me slap you,' Geoffrey said, marching across the room and getting in my face. 'You *so* can. I'm going to start the music again. Get into a position and then dance that flipping coyote. Do you hear me?'

He held my chin and looked me right in my eyes.

I heard him. I nodded.

He went back to the tablet and the phone and I saw myself tilt my head proudly and go into first position. My body looked like it knew what it was doing even when I didn't—that's what those years of study had done for me. I thought about all the hours my teachers had spent with me—Geoffrey and my poor old ballet mistress and all the others—how hard they'd worked to get me to this moment, where I could just move into first position and automatically look like a dancer. I was two years old when I took my first class. That's a lot of time in first position and a lot of people telling you to pull up your ribcage and slide down your shoulders.

Then I thought about my coyote, too, because he'd been my teacher when I didn't have one.

Just in that moment, I realised something. That crack in my middle, that's where all me as a dancer had come out. The potential had already been there, in my blood and bones, from Kris and the flapper and the ballroom dancer and the showgirl. My body was the right kind of body to dance ballet. And all my teachers had helped to make me ready. But I'd only actually become a dancer when my heart had cracked open and I'd begun to feel emotions so strongly. I didn't have to keep trying not to fall apart. I couldn't dance *without* falling apart...I'd *had* to fall apart to become a dancer. Falling apart was what my dancing *was*.

All I had to do was just go ahead and be open.

The music began and I heard the hidden rhythms inside it. My eyes snapped up to the camera in the tablet and I grew affronted, and circled away and grew affronted and circled away again, not sure of anyone. Not sure of anything. I found my mouse in the tall grass and pounced on it and carried it, so proud to feed myself. I came back through the tall grass and for a little while became the tall grass and let my love for Kansas and my longing for the days of the prairie come over me. And then I watched the camera just like the coyote watched me, and settled down, down, hiding but alert. And stopped right on the end of the musical phrase.

Geoffrey pushed the button on the tablet and did a little victory dance. 'Yes!' he said, punching the air. 'Yes, yes, yes!'

We watched them all back. There was nothing wrong with my barre work. My floor work was clean and my leg in the dance went up, for me, unbelievably high. I couldn't believe it. Maybe I hadn't pushed myself hard enough. Maybe none of us could push ourselves hard enough, which is why we needed teachers.

Then we watched the coyote dance. My transitions were rough, because I was making it up as I went along and hadn't rehearsed how to get from one movement to the next. But it was good. And I looked totally confident in it, because I had let myself go and that had let me actually be the coyote. I could practically see his ears on my head.

'Brilliant,' Geoffrey said. 'This will get you in or I'll eat my tap shoes.'

I'd dirtied the satins, but Geoffrey told me to keep everything and so I just slid my jean shorts back over my new uniform and pulled my sandals on over my tights. It was nearly seven o'clock and Geoffrey chatted as he uploaded the videos to the audition page.

'Once you get in,' he said. 'Margaret and Ethan will have to let you go. Just tell them that you'll come to the farm for breaks and summers.' He smiled widely. 'You can work here!' he said. 'And then when you're famous, I'll put up a big signed poster and people will drive out from Kansas City to get me to coach their little darlings. I'll make a fortune.'

I told him it was a good plan, but I felt cold inside, thinking how much I would miss Mum.

'And then you'll be ready to retire from dancing when I won't be able to totter on here any more,' he said. 'And you can pay me a huge fortune to take over my wildly-successful studio.'

He hugged me. 'At last,' he said, 'I have a retirement plan.'

I hugged him back, and it was so nice feeing another dancer's body, the muscle and bone and taut tone of it that for a moment I just enjoyed that. And then I thought how much I owed him. I didn't have any words for telling him how grateful I was. So I hugged him again.

'Margaret will kill you,' I warned him, finally pushing open the door. I held it as two women in big flouncy salsa skirts came in, chatting.

'I know,' Geoffrey called to me over their heads. 'That's the best part.'

CHAPTER TWENTY

I checked my phone on the way to my truck and found a text from an unknown number.

'Saw your truck—can we please talk. B'

Brad.

I texted back, 'Sorry. Can't tonight. Too busy.'

It was still light outside, but it was a little dimmer than I'd expected. That's because there were actual clouds in the sky. Not white fluffy lambs, but fully grown dark grey sheep. I hadn't seen proper clouds for ages. I got into the truck and was driving to Tasty Queen before I realized I hadn't needed my gloves and I wasn't boiling hot.

Robbie was already sitting on his tailgate. I pulled up and got my handbag and we went in to order. I had to admit, I really liked this making my own money and driving my own truck kind of thing. In England, I'd always had to depend on other people. I always had to ask and remind and beg and assume that things would be done for me. It was cool to work and get my own money given to me and make my own plans and get places on my own.

Robbie had a cherry limeade, of course, and I made him get a large. I got a large root beer float in a paper cup.

We just sat there and watched the clouds rolling in and didn't say anything, really, for a long time. It wasn't awkward, in spite of what we were going through. I felt like I was just kind of soaking up being with him.

Finally, Robbie said. 'Storm's supposed to be bad. I

got the house and yard ready, and Mom's coming home early.'

I said, 'I can't be out long, either.'

He looked at me for a minute. 'Did you want to tell me something?'

I told him about ballet school and then I told him why my hair was gelled up tight in a bun and what Geoffrey and I had done. I thought he'd be really pleased about me using the Native American flute music, but he shook his head. 'That's about as authentic as getting your Spirit Animal from an online quiz,' he said.

Then, I guess because my face must have shown my hurt feelings, he said, 'Sorry. You don't know anything about our culture. And the dance sounds pretty amazing. You'll have to show me sometime.'

Our culture. That made me feel a little breathless. When Robbie said 'Cherokee', he sometimes said it in another way and I knew he studied the language at school. There was all this *stuff* I didn't know about, things I could get wrong.

I didn't know what to say after that. I suppose that was why I told him what Geoffrey had said about Margaret. He kind of snorted and said, 'It was the same when I was going away to school. She kept telling my mom not to let me go, that I was needed at home...' he stared off at the sky. 'It made me feel bad. Then Mom told me that I was like a tool in a toolbox. That a sharper, cleaner, oiled tool was better than a rusty, blunt tool. She told me to go get as sharp and shiny as I could, if I wanted to help the family.'

'I'd like to meet your mother,' I said.

'Yeah,' he said. 'About that.' He looked at me. 'I shouldn't have told you anything about Kris. Evidently, Mom and Ethan and everyone had promised your mother not to say anything.'

So Kris was my father. It was official.

I looked out at the traffic and the clouds rolling in hard. I said, 'I'm glad you did. I like knowing. Even if I *don't* even know how to say Cherokee properly or what's authentic.'

Robbie put his arm around me and I moved over, and leaned my head on his shoulder. Just then, a gust of wind came and pushed Robbie's long hair all over his face and mine.

I rubbed my face and laughed as he twisted it and tucked it in the back of his t-shirt. 'Maybe you should get Geoffrey to do you a bun, too,' I said.

He didn't even smile. And that's when I realised that there was something on his mind—something *else* besides me not being authentic. I reached out and took his hand and we looked at each other for a moment. I don't know what he was seeing in my eyes, but I could see so much in his. I asked him what was wrong and his mouth curled into a reluctant smile.

'You already know me so well,' he said. He took a deep slug of limeade and wiped his mouth with the back of his hand. 'I'm not your uncle,' he said. 'Mom said we weren't close related and that I should stop worrying about it.'

I felt this big feeling that at the time I thought was about me and Robbie being okay to date. Looking back, though, I think it was more than that. I think I felt, right away, that Robbie was with me in my life forever, even though I didn't know exactly how.

He turned to me again. He said, 'But how can I stop thinking about who I am? If I'm not your uncle, then I can't be Kris's brother. That means I'm not my mother's son...' He looked up to the rolling grey clouds and back to me.

I got that 'it's all too much' feeling again in my head. And then I remembered the feel of Robbie's hair against my face. How it had felt almost exactly like my own hair. And how I was so comfortable with Robbie. I said, 'Maybe that's not what she meant. We must be closely related. We look so much alike.'

'I know,' he said. 'But lots of Cherokee guys at my school look like me. You're probably just in my clan.' He sighed. 'I can't date you if you're in my clan. It wouldn't feel right.'

He waved his hands in the air in frustration. 'I'm in trouble for telling you that Kris was your dad, but we're not close related? I'm not supposed to worry about it, but we're from the same clan, maybe? Am I even in the clan I think I'm in? She treats me like I'm a little kid.'

The pressure in my head felt bigger. The sky seemed to be pushing on it. The air tasted funny, too, metallic.

'I mean,' Robbie was saying. 'I've got every right...' he trailed off, looking behind me.

I turned to see Brad coming towards us with a face as thunderous as the sky. I hopped down to meet him.

'I thought you were busy? But you're hanging out at Tasty Queen?' he said, straight away.

He'd come right up to me, so close that I could see the little green flecks in his big blue eyes.

The air seemed to have turned green with pressure, as if the flecks in Brad's eyes had leaked into the sky.

Brad put his hands on my shoulders and I felt sparks where he touched me on my bare skin. What I felt for Robbie and what I felt for Brad were so different. But I always wanted to be with Robbie. I could *talk* to him. All Brad and I did was argue. Yet…yet I didn't want him to stop touching me. Robbie jumped down, as if he was going to make Brad go himself.

'I can't do this right now, Brad,' I said. 'We're talking about something important.'

Brad looked down into my face and I thought he was going to cry. His chin trembled. 'Something important,' he said sadly. His eyes fell open again and it bothered me. He might do it on purpose, but I really didn't like hurting him.

I said, 'I'm sorry. We'll talk, too. We really will. But not right now.'

If Robbie hadn't laughed, that probably would have been it. But Robbie did laugh, softly, just a little chuckle, and Brad got angry.

The cool breeze suddenly picked up speed as Brad's perfect face twisted. Very gently, he moved me to one side and then turned to Robbie and shoved his shoulder, hard. 'Why don't you shut up? In fact, why don't you do us all a favour and go back to the reservation?'

The shove dislodged Robbie's hair and it swirled up

again, in all directions, including over his face and in his eyes. I thought that Brad might hit Robbie when he couldn't see.

'Brad!' I took Brad's arm and tugged on it and he spun around to face me. 'Should I go back to the reservation, too?,' I asked. 'Because I'm Indian, too. If you're going to be like that, we don't have anything to talk about.'

That got his attention. He pointed at Robbie. 'Are you going out with him? Are you? Because I'll just leave you alone.'

I wanted Brad to go away. But I didn't want to lie to him. I didn't know *what* Robbie felt for me...or even what I felt for him. It was something big, but I couldn't say we were going out. I couldn't really say anything. We didn't know anything. There wasn't anything to say.

Robbie wasn't any help. He was looking at the sky.

'It's not that simple,' I said, and it sounded stupid, even to me.

Just then the biggest, fattest raindrops I've ever felt in my life suddenly splattered all over my arms and Robbie said calmly, 'We all need to go home. The storm's early. And it's bad.'

Brad turned to look up at the sky and Robbie motioned me to get into my truck. I didn't need telling twice, but Brad just stood there in the rain, with his arms crossed, blocking our way.

I got back out of my truck and ran to him. The rain was so loud that I had to get close to say, 'Don't be stupid. We'll talk about it later.'

When he heard me, he looked so lost and...desolated. I reached out, without meaning to, and put my arms around him. His body was warm and solid and I hugged him once, hard. He smiled crookedly and backed away to his car, shouting, 'I'll call you!'

It was like being in an ice-cold shower. My feet were already soaked, right through my tights. I ran back into my truck and put on my lights and my windscreen wipers. Behind me, Robbie flashed his lights goodbye and turned right. I had to turn left, across the traffic, and I was terrified.

The rain was incredible. I thought I knew just about everything anyone could know about rain, but I had never seen such huge drops so close together. My wipers were going crazy fast, but I could barely see. I just had to trust that anyone driving would have their lights on, because all I could see of the passing traffic was the blur of headlights. I had to go when I thought it was safe, hoping I was right. Even over all the noise of the rain and the wind, I could kind of *feel* my heartbeat pounding in my ears.

But I got safely across.

I had to do the same thing to get onto Deer Road and now I was terrified that someone wouldn't see my taillights and would run into the back of me while I waited for a break in the traffic.

But I made that one, too. Just as I got safely off Highway 69, two things happened. A faint siren noise sounded and my phone rang. It was the farm's number flashing up on the phone, so I stopped to answer it opposite the cow pasture where my coyote lived. Suddenly a huge, jagged finger of lightening jabbed down from the sky. It didn't hit the tree, and it didn't look like it had hit the pasture, but it came close. Even over the sound of the storm, I could hear the cows sort of scream. I wondered how the coyote was taking it…whether he had an actual den by the cottonwood tree or whether he was just hunched up under it, trying to keep dry and cowering with the force of the storm.

Margaret asked me where I was and told me to drive home slowly and safely but to come right now. Her voice was calm, but her tone was so urgent it made my throat dry. I could feel the truck rocking from huge gusts of wind and the rain started to come down even harder. Little bits of ice were mixed in with it and they started to gather on my wipers and the bottom of the windscreen. I was absolutely freezing, even with the windows tightly shut. It was so terribly dark that I missed our driveway and had to find reverse. My hands were wet with sweaty palms and it was hard to get the truck in gear so that I could go back and try to find the driveway again.

When I finally made it up the drive, I didn't bother to take the truck around by the garage, I just put the brake on where it was and ran inside. The door banged open and then nearly slammed shut right onto me. I jumped out of the way just in time. But the screen door was open, banging against the porch wall, so I had to pull the big wooden door open again and slide my arm out to catch the screen and shut it properly. The big door pushed and pushed on my arm, the whole time, and nearly caught my fingers when I'd finally done it.

Margaret had said, 'Oh, thank God,' from the kitchen when I'd come in. Now she carried in a box of candles and some matches from the kitchen. 'Go get into something comfy and warm.'

'Can I have a bath?' I asked, rubbing my arm. I wanted to get the gel and spray out of my hair.

'Not now. Come down as soon as you can... bring shoes and a jacket.'

I ran up and stripped off my wet things and shoved on sweat pants and an old baggy t-shirt. I didn't even put on pants or a bra. I left everything on the floor and ran back down with my boots in my hand just as Ethan came into the mudroom, shaking off bits of ice. Genius was with him. Things One and Two peered out of their beds.

'I don't know how she did it,' Ethan said. 'I haven't even trained her on left and right yet. But she got those sheep in like a pro. I didn't have to do a thing.' He bent down and gave Genius a cuddle, kissing her on the top of her head. 'You really are a Genius,' he told her. She leant into him, gazing up in total adoration.

I felt useless, standing like an idiot in the kitchen, while Margaret ran around getting water bottles and other things, so I stepped over the baby gate, put down my boots and took up one of the dog towels. I rubbed Genius down while Ethan got out of his coat and boots. I kept telling her what a good girl she was and she licked my face.

Just then, the whole house felt as if all the air had been

sucked out of it. It rattled and kind of bent together, as if the walls were trying to touch. It didn't really move, I don't think, but that's what it felt like. 'Cross vent!' Ethan called to Margaret.

He stepped over the baby gate and hustled to the front window while Margaret went to the ones over the kitchen sink. They were shut tight to keep the air conditioning in, so my aunt and uncle had to lift up the sashes and then these other things that were called 'storm windows'. I went to help Margaret on the storm window bit. Opening them immediately made the house feel more stable, but it let in the rain and the sound of the storm.

I'd forgotten to get any socks and my feet were freezing, but the idea of going back upstairs on my own just...I decided I'd rather freeze.

I'd been in some gales in England, but it was the most violent storm I'd ever known. Everything was being shaken and rain and sleet hammered at the deck and on the roofs. The wind rattled everything—gates, flaps, doors, windows, roofs. 'Here's where we find out how well the solar panels are screwed down,' Ethan said grimly. He put a towel down on the wooden floor to absorb the rain pouring through the gap in the living room window—it was blowing the rain the whole way across the porch and straight in.

Then Margaret turned on the television and we all went to it. The screen was filled with a big map of Kansas with a huge bright orange blob over our part. There were some pink blobs inside it. 'That's the storm,' Margaret said, pointing to the orange. 'And those are tornadoes,' pointing to the pink. 'There's the one they say is headed down this way.'

Ethan hustled out of the room and came back holding a flashlight. He opened the cupboard under the stairs. 'Right,' he said. 'I think we should...'

Suddenly, the world went black. Outside, the rain had stopped, but the wind blew even harder, as if the storm knew we had just lost our electricity and wanted to take advantage of it.

Ethan showed a clean circle of light at the door of the cupboard and in we went. I'd opened that cupboard before and wondered why they used it just to store old sofa cushions and blankets. Now I understood. Margaret ran out for a moment and then all the puppies tumbled in, too. There was a radio on a little shelf. When Ethan turned it on, a man's voice told us where the tornado was. Margaret lit a candle in a special windproof candleholder and Ethan switched off his torch. Understanding that they were saving the torch batteries in case we needed them again made me feel terrified.

We all listened to the towns and direction of travel of the tornado, which were in this man's very clear, very even and emotionless voice. I barely knew anything about where I was living, but even I could tell the largest tornado was headed towards the farm.

I'd seen some television programmes in England where people went looking for tornadoes so that they could film them and study them. It always looked kind of cool, rushing around and being close to the big funnel clouds. But I can tell you, I had absolutely zero interest in going outside and having a look.

Thing Two crept up and put his head on my lap and I absentmindedly stroked his ears. He was shaking with fear and I was shaking, too, with cold and fear and what I think now was a bit of shock from everything that had happened that night. Margaret passed me a fleece blanket that I wrapped around my feet and me and Thing Two and it didn't quite fit. I curled down around Thing Two on the cushions to cover us, just as a sound like a huge heavy goods train rattled through the air above us.

I closed my eyes.

I woke up far too early because I needed the loo. I was still sleepy, but my back hurt a bit, too. I wondered why my bed was so lumpy.

I didn't recognize the cupboard at all when I finally managed to open my eyes and I had a long, strange moment of a kind of panicky thinking before I finally remembered where I was. By then I'd gone all the way down the list of my life; home, school, holidays, friends, Kansas, the farm. The farm. The storm! I'd been under an actual tornado!

It was oddly bright. The lights were back on. I crawled out and stretched my back. Margaret had left the dining room light on and a note on the table. 'J: You looked too peaceful to wake up. Storm is over, no big damage except to the tunnel. Thank God we didn't buy the shade sheet. Love, M.'

I went up to the loo as quietly as I could. One of the dogs woke and started to whine for attention, but I whispered, 'Be quiet,' and it was.

Afterwards, I looked in the mirror. My hair was still firmly in Geoffrey's bun. It really had lasted through a freaking tornado. I'd have to tell him. The pins were killing my head, though.

My sweat shorts and t-shirt smelled horrible, from my fear, sweat and something Thing Two had rolled in and the dust under the stairs. I stripped them off and dropped them on top of my wet things from the night before. I'd have to deal with all of that today.

I looked out my window as I started to pull my hairpins out. It was just starting to get light and there was a faint, low mist. When my head was hardware-free, I took a moment to open the window and push up the storm window. The air was as clean and sweet-smelling as I had thought it would be, but I felt cold standing around naked. I grabbed my handbag and jumped into bed to start to brushing the product out of my hair, and then I got out my phone because brushing product out of hair is boring. I was planning to Google about the tornado before I saw that I had forty-three missed calls from an unknown number.

Brad. He'd also sent me five texts, asking me to ring him. None of them had been spelled correctly. For a moment, I put my phone back down.

Half my hair was gel and spray free. Before I started on the other half, though, I sent a quick text back. 'Are you awake?'

'Nice to know you're alive,' came back. And then my phone rang. I'd had it nearly a month, but Margaret and Ethan didn't know about it yet. The ringtone was loud and obviously more complicated than the clam phone's. It seemed to ring through the whole house. I pounced on it and held the big rectangle of glass and metal to my ear.

'Jules?' Brad's voice was perfect, too. It was warm and if it was a colour, it would be brown. If it was a fabric, it would be velvet.

'Hi,' was all I said.

'Hey.' He yawned. 'You guys okay? I heard it went right over your place.'

'They think everything's fine,' I said. 'It was pretty scary, though.'

'I'll bet.' There was a pause. I put him on speaker and started brushing the other side of my hair.

'So, what's with you and Robbie Slater?'

Really? I thought. Seriously? I said, 'It's none of your business, Brad.'

'Oh,' he said, 'But I think it is. I don't want my girl going out with another guy.'

'I'm not your girl,' I hit a big chunk of lacquer in my hair and tugged through it mercilessly. It hurt.

'Well, you're going to be. One day. When you're ready.' His voice was lazy and sweet and... totally infuriating.

'I think I might have something to say about that,' I said tartly.

It just made him laugh. 'What are you wearing?' he asked.

I blushed and pulled the bedcovers up tighter around me, as if he could actually see. 'I'm going to put the phone down,' I warned.

He laughed again. 'Don't do that. I'm sorry I made you mad. I always make you mad.'

'You don't know anything about me,' I said. 'All we do is argue.'

'I know that you look up when you're thinking. I know that you've opened up, just like a flower, since you've been here. I know that you're always afraid your feet will get hurt. I know that you've got no idea how beautiful you are and that you don't care, either.' He was a little breathless, after all that.

I was a little breathless, too.

'Brad,' I said. 'I don't know...*what* Robbie is to me... yet.'

'He doesn't care about you like I do.'

I looked around my room, at the white floorboards and the pile of wet and smelly clothes and the hairpins on my dresser. How had this happened to me, so quickly? How could Brad have made this into some big romantic drama in, I looked at my phone, three minutes and fifteen seconds?

'I can't do this,' I said quietly, and then repeated it, louder. 'I can't do this,' I said. 'I don't have time for some big romantic doodah.'

'Doodah?' Brad laughed again. 'Did you just say you didn't have time for a romantic *doodah*?'

'Whatever.' I brushed my hair furiously. 'You tell me a better word and I'll use that, instead.'

'Look,' Brad said. 'I don't think you understand. I could have any girl in school. I've chosen *you*.'

I nearly threw my brush across the room. I sat up and looked at myself in the wardrobe mirror. Was I beautiful? Did I care? And what did any of it have to do with *Brad*?

'No, *you* look, Brad. Girls aren't there to be *chosen*.'

'I *know* that.'

'Chosen!' I repeated the word with scorn.

'Doodah!' he said, with even more scorn.

'I'm going to ring off now,' I said. 'I don't think this conversation is going anywhere.'

'Don't you hang up on me, Jules. Don't you dare.'

How, I wondered, had this happened to me? How had some random boy acquired the ability to make me so incredibly angry? Had *I* given him that power over me? And could I take it back now?

'This is pointless, Brad.' My finger hovered over the red button. 'This conversation is going nowhere. All of our conversations go nowhere.'

Brad's voice came out of the speaker, crystal clear.

'If you hang up on me, I'll shoot your coyote.'

Through my mind went all those videos of people killing coyotes...those horrible videos of how to skin them, trap them, lure them. I thought about my coyote...how thin he'd looked, how much he'd grown to trust me...

My cracked part ached. I couldn't swallow down pain anymore. I no longer had a place to swallow it *to*. I said, 'You dare hurt my coyote, and...'

I could hear Brad getting up. He said, 'It's early. By

the time the sun's up, I can be at that pasture. I can get the rifle. I can get the ammo. I'll be doing the Buchwalds a favour.'

I tried to keep my voice steady. 'Think about what you're saying, Brad. You're threatening me so that I'll talk to you. Is that how it's going to be? This big relationship we're going to have? Are you going to *hurt* me whenever I don't do what you want?'

But he didn't even listen or think about it. All he said was, 'Don't hang up on me, Jules. Don't hang up on me, or I swear, I'll do it. And no one will blame me.'

There was only one thing I could do. He'd left me no choice. I pushed the red button and hung up on Brad.

For a moment, I stared at my phone, as if it had turned into a rattlesnake. As if it rang again, I would die. And then I jumped up and looked out the window. It was getting light *now*.

I pulled on clothes—underwear, a t-shirt, shorts, socks for my boots—and swirled my hair up into a quick messy bun. I couldn't call the police...it was legal to kill coyotes. It was legal for fifteen-year-old boys to own rifles. It was legal for them to drive around with guns in their cars. Everything Brad had threatened to do was completely legal.

If I woke up Margaret and Ethan, it was going to take forever to explain. My coyote might be dead by the time I got them to do anything...if they even actually decided to interfere...They thought I was a little crazy. Maybe they'd *prefer* it if Brad shot the coyote.

No. I was going to have to go myself, *now*.

I shivered from the cool air coming through the window. I didn't have time to change into anything warmer, so I pulled on my brown cashmere cardigan. I put on my boots in the mudroom, explained to the puppies that they had to wait some more, and left. Just as I shut the door, I heard Margaret call, 'Jules? Is that you?'

But I jumped into my truck and drove.

Everything was perfect that morning. The air was still and the sky was the same blue bowl it had been almost every day. I looked for damage from the big storm, but I couldn't see much. A cottonwood tree I drove past every day had lost a branch and there were leaves all over the road...not just from it, but from every tree for miles around, but you couldn't actually *tell* from looking at the trees that they had lost leaves. Even the sunflowers had survived.

I was so relieved not to see Brad's lime green bug when I pulled up and parked that it made me feel nearly faint in my head. I took my phone out of my bag. What should I do?

What would it mean if I called him? Would it mean that I'd given in, that all he had to do for the rest of my life was threaten me and I'd do what he wanted? Or maybe he'd gone back to sleep and forgotten all about it. If I rang, it would wake him up and remind him...

Maybe I *should* tell Margaret and Ethan about it, now, over the phone. But they'd have to tell Wayne and he...

He probably already *knew*, I thought. I remembered when Margaret wanted bullets and Ethan had the key. Brad probably had to tell his dad to get the rifle...and Wayne was all about shooting coyotes. He wasn't going to stop Brad. He might even *help* him.

There were so many ways I could actually make things worse.

I'd...I'd just have to tell my coyote to leave. It was time for him to leave, anyway. He needed to be with a pack. He'd probably hunted out his territory.

I pulled on my work gloves—you could hardly see the bloodstains anymore on the rough brown leather—and got out of the truck. And then I thought, What if Brad tries to call *me*? What if he's calmed down, but me not answering makes him cross again? I pulled my phone out of my bag—I'd got used to it, but there was no doubt about it, it was huge.

It wouldn't fit inside my glove and I didn't have a pocket, so I tucked it into the hollow of my left hip, in the waistband of my shorts and down into the waistband of my underwear, like I normally did with my ballet shoes. At first I noticed that it was a lot thicker and heavier than my ballet shoes. And then I just forgot about it.

The cows were still bunched up by the water trough and the fence. When I came through the fence, the big, red mama cow came over and complained vigorously. I told her I knew and that I was sorry, but that the storm hadn't actually been my fault. I don't think she believed me. She flounced off back to the herd like she just couldn't bear to hear any more of my useless excuses. Her calves looked at me with disdain.

On the ridge I searched for my coyote's ears in the tall grass, but he wasn't there yet, so I walked on down to my platform, as if it was going to be a normal morning.

The mirror had blown over again in the storm and the glass was shattered...little pieces of blue sky were all over the wooden floor. I found the ironing board on the ground off the other side with a bent and twisted leg. I just left it.

The whole morning had an enormous feeling of everything ending. A big, heavy sadness kind of leaked out of me and I just let it. It was all those feelings I'd been swallowing down, ever since I heard what Robbie had to say...every since Archie fell...ever since I didn't get into ballet school...ever since I found out that some people had fathers...ever since I was little and I'd wake up and run into my mother's room only to find she'd already gone to work.

I'd been unhappy for a long, long time. The sky held ending and I leaked sadness and together we just sat together until the sky held my sadness, too.

If I didn't make it into that school in New York, I didn't know what I'd do.

But then, just for a moment, I leaned against the platform and looked up at that big blue sky. It was, I thought, the same crazy idea I'd had the day I found my ballet shoes at Walmart. If there really was something up there...or I guess...and I stopped looking up and started looking around me...*out* there...somehow, it would be good if it helped right now. I thought that and then I thought it again, harder, with my eyes squeezed shut.

When I opened my eyes again, two ears were clearly visible in the long grass.

I walked in front of the platform. I hoped this was going to work. We might not have much time. I tried to stop my jangling nerves with my breath, and it worked—a bit. And then I sat down on a rock and waited.

It took what seemed like hours, but was probably less than five minutes. Then a nose pushed out of the grass and my coyote was standing about two metres away from me.

The first thing that struck me, and I know it wasn't nice to notice, was that I could totally understand Brad's father, about the pelt not being great in summer. His eyes and nose and everything looked fairly healthy, but his coat was thin and patchy from the heat and the thick fur was kind of peeling away off his shoulders and flanks. Anyway, his face and his ears were still beautiful, as was the long, strong line of his body, his elegant legs and his fat, bushy tail.

We looked at each other for a moment, and then he sat down himself, curling his tail neatly around his feet and turning his head on one side as if to say, 'Okay, I'm here. What did you want?'

Mischief sparkled in his golden eyes. He looked at me like he was interested in me, but also like, under different circumstances, he might be glad to eat part of me. I supposed that was what it was like to be a coyote. You were always looking for your next meal, and you never counted anything... or anyone... completely off the menu.

'You have to go,' I said. 'You can't stay here.'

I stood up and made a shooing motion and he backed away, a bit, just into the long grass where he looked at me with his affronted ears.

So I tried to tell him. I danced Brad, his big muscles and body. I danced a gun and danced being shot in the chest.

Now the coyote was interested and not affronted anymore. But he wasn't going anywhere. He didn't get it.

I went into the tall grass myself. It was strange in there. My body seemed to disappear from the waist down. I did the Brad dance again and again mimed shooting and being shot and waved him away.

All he did was back a tiny bit further away into the long grass.

It was *so* frustrating. And then I remembered when he had been trying to warn me about the rattlesnake. He'd been frustrated, too. And that gave me an idea.

I moved deeper into the tall grass and started to dance his rattlesnake warning.

'Jules?' It was Brad's voice, shouting into the field. 'I see your truck. Come out right now.'

I motioned with my head and interrupted the rattle-snake dance to dance Brad again, his bigness, his anger.

'Don't be stupid, Jules.' That seemed a bit rich, coming from Brad, the illiterate texter. 'I'm not doing this because you hung up on me. I'm going to put that coyote away before he hurts you or someone else.'

I did some of the rattlesnake movement again, bending down to face the coyote in the tall grass. It was like we were in a tunnel together. I couldn't see anything but him. Warning! I danced. Warning! I did some more of Brad and a rifle and some more of the rattlesnake dance.

He was getting it. He bent his own head and his elegant furry eyebrows drew together as he concentrated hard.

I arched my back and leapt at the air snake again and...something hard punched me in my side. I only heard the shot afterwards.

I had been looking at the coyote's face. His golden eyes widened with alarm before he turned and ran.

I fell hard. My side hurt. A lot. I put down my hand to feel it and I couldn't touch my skin for some reason. Something was in the way. Still, my leather glove came back into sight with brand-new bright red blood on the fingertips.

CHAPTER TWENTY-ONE

I must have blacked out for a few seconds, because the next thing I knew, Brad was kneeling over me. He'd taken off his t-shirt and was pressing it into my side, which really, really hurt. He was also shouting into the phone in his other hand. 'I shot her!' he shouted. 'I didn't mean to, but I did.'

The other voice squawked a bit and he said, 'That's right. Just off the Deer Road turning. Right hand side. In a cow pasture.'

He rang off and dropped the phone to put his other hand on the t-shirt as well.

That's when he noticed I was awake. 'God, Jules,' he said. 'I'm so sorry. I thought you were the coyote.'

His perfect face was screwed up with worry and horror. I didn't know what I wanted to say. I didn't feel like I could say anything, anyway. And I didn't need to, because Brad kept talking. 'And I don't know why I even wanted to shoot your coyote,' he said. 'I always have to have my own way. Mom says if I don't learn to back down, I'm going to end up in jail. It's a big family joke. But it's true, isn't it? I'm going to end up in jail.' He closed his eyes for a moment and then opened them again to check my side.

'It's not bleeding as fast,' he said. 'I think you're going to be all right. But I'm sorry, Jules. I really, really am.'

And then I had something to say. I said what Ethan had told me, 'It was an expensive lesson. Learn it.' Brad solemnly nodded.

I could already hear sirens in the distance, coming closer.

I must have gone back to sleep in the ambulance. I woke up in a hospital bed.

It was a different world—quiet and white and clean. I was wearing a hospital gown and had a drip in my arm. When I looked down at my side, there was a large bandage where the pain had been. There was still a shadow of pain there, but really, I couldn't feel much. I could tell, by the heavy way my head felt on my neck, that I'd been given drugs.

The room was small, with a high window, out of which I could just barely see a part of the big blue sky. My mouth felt dry and I was hungry and I didn't know what time it was. I tried to sit up and realized how weak and sore I felt. But it was one of those electric beds, so I pushed a button to see what happened.

It was the wrong button, so what happened was a nurse appeared.

'Are you trying to sit up?' She sounded like she didn't approve. Still, she helped me to do it. I told her I was hungry and thirsty, but she said I couldn't have anything. There was part of a bullet in me, she said, although most of it had gone into my phone. A surgeon was on his way to get it out.

I remembered tucking the phone into the waistband of my shorts and underwear and kind of smiled. That big old brick.

'Does my aunt know I'm here?'

She nodded. 'You had some pain medication in the ambulance,' she said. 'And you didn't react well to it. You were unconscious for a while and then you've been just asleep. For hours.' She was making notes on a little tablet she'd carried in with her. 'Margaret and Ethan had to go down to the police station, but they'll be back.'

The police station? 'Will Brad really go to jail?' I asked. 'He didn't mean to shoot me.'

The nurse made a noise through her nose, kind of a ladylike snort. 'He's a spoiled brat. I hope they throw the book at him.' She snapped the lid of her tablet case down briskly. 'Okay,' she said. 'I've let the doctor know you're awake. It's that,' she pointed, 'button for the bed and here is the tv remote. Do you need the bathroom?'

When I said no, she was gone.

I was fumbling with the remote when Robbie Slater slid around the doorframe. 'Hey,' he said.

I just looked at him. He said, 'Brad has issues.'

It hurt so much to laugh that it made me stop. I said, 'You think?' and Robbie grinned.

He looked too big and too colourful for my tiny white world. He was wearing work boots and jeans and a red t-shirt with a faded American flag graphic. His hair was brushed and neatly tied back off his face with a bandana. On any other guy, a bandana hairband would look a bit... not right. But on Robbie, it looked amazing.

He crossed the room and I put out my hand to be held.

His was warm and rough and he smelled of grass and sky and summer. He said, 'How bad is it?' and I tried to shrug, winced and answered.

'I don't know,' I said. I thought for a moment. 'Not very bad, I don't think, or the staff would be more panicky and hurrying. They're just, like, Oh, we'll have to get the bullet out pretty soon... when we can be bothered.'

'I heard the phone I gave you saved your life.' Robbie grinned. 'I reckon that's worth two dozen large cherry limeades.'

I dropped his hand and tried to sit up again, gave up, and made myself more upright with the electric bed. When it finally whirred me into place, I said, 'Everybody always knows everything in this town. How did you already find out about my phone?'

He looked at me. 'Already?' he said. 'It's after six o'clock, Jules. It's been over twelve hours.' He nodded towards the door. 'You've got about ten bunches of flowers out at the nurses' station.'

He looked... he looked very Native American at that moment, with his dark hair and red bandana. And so, I got this idea. 'Robbie?' I asked.

He leaned over the bed. 'Still here,' he said.

'Are you good at tracking things? Like animals?'

He smiled. 'Jules,' he said, 'You're going to have to stop with the racist stuff. No, I don't know how to track.' I felt embarrassed. But he was grinning, and he went on, 'You want to know what happened to your coyote, don't you?'

I nodded. Yes. That's what I wanted.

He said, 'I'll see what I can do.'

I heard footsteps coming fast and then Margaret and Ethan were in the room. Margaret ran to me and kind of clucked over me, patting me everywhere and asking if I was hurting and if I was okay and not listening to my answers and hugging me and asking me again and not listening again.

I had never seen her so flustered.

'I'm fine,' I said. 'The nurse said there's a bit of the bullet left in me, but that my phone got most of it.'

Margaret then flung herself into Robbie's arms. He kind of staggered back as he caught her. I met Ethan's eyes and he half shook his head. He loved her, but he thought she was awfully funny sometimes.

'Oh, Robbie,' Margaret cried. 'If you hadn't given her that phone, she would have *died*. There were frangible bullets in that rifle. She would have been ripped to shreds.'

I felt a sudden cold wind blow through my side. No wonder it had felt like everything was ending this morning. It nearly had.

I was too tired to sit up any more. I pushed the button and the bed whined its way to let me lay down.

Margaret was still talking, '...interfering in your life, when your mom *told* me boarding school was the best thing for you. And I've looked up the school and I *know* how good it is. But I just didn't want you to go...not for your mom or your family, but for *me*, I guess. Because you remind me so much of Kris.'

'Margaret,' Ethan said, and Margaret put her hand to her mouth. 'I shouldn't have said that,' she said. 'But it's true. And I'm sorry, Robbie. And thank you so, so much for all you've done for Jules.'

Robbie was totally embarrassed. 'It's okay,' he said, awkwardly patting Margaret's shoulder. 'But I've got to go. I think Jules is tired.'

As she turned back to me, Robbie gave me a little look, and wiggled his eyebrows significantly, to make sure I hadn't missed Margaret's slip. Another clue! In spite of being totally wiped out, and hurting, and dealing with Margaret's emotional outpouring, I couldn't help but grin.

He left, but then two seconds later I heard him come back. Ethan and Margaret were standing by my bed, so I had to kind of look around them to see what he wanted, or what he'd forgotten.

But it wasn't Robbie. It was Mum.

She smelled exactly like she always did. She felt amazing, too, that wonderful combination of softness and firmness that was especially Mum.

She sat down on the visitor's chair and pushed her sunglasses up on top of her head. 'First things first. I've flown down with one of the best sports surgeons in New York. He's looked at your x-rays and he's going to do the procedure. He says if the bullet hasn't moved, and if it's where he thinks it is, you'll be able to start working out again in a fortnight.'

That was my mum. Straight to the point and moving heaven and earth to make things happen.

Margaret was sniffling in Ethan's arms. Ethan asked, 'How did you just happen to find the best sports surgeon in New York?' His lip did that twitch thing it often did when he talked to me.

'I was in the Hamptons,' Mum said coolly, 'Which brings me to another point.' She waited for a moment and then said, 'Margaret, could you please come out of your husband's armpit? I need to talk to you.'

My aunt was clearly still feeling the effects of her emotions. She could barely look at my mother. She said, 'Lisa Ann, I am *so* sorry. I thought I had Jules under control and...'

Mum interrupted. 'It's hard to keep Jules under control.' She said, 'I don't know where she gets all her energy, but she's got more than a normal human being. We mere mortals can't be expected to keep up.'

Margaret sighed and nodded her head and my mother continued. 'Which is why it's a good thing that she's been offered a place at the School of Ballet, New York City.'

Relief washed over me in such a deep and total wave that I thought I might drown in it and go back to sleep for another twelve hours. Every tiny bit of me felt floppy and relaxed.

And then I thought, 'Oh, no! I've been shot!' and then I remembered that Mum, my brilliant mum, had organized a super surgeon and that in a fortnight I could be working out again and went all floppy again.

I heard Margaret and Ethan and my mother talking about the schedule at the school and agreeing it would wear me out so that I couldn't get into trouble. 'But of course, we've got the problem of what Jules will do in breaks and summer,' Mum said. 'And I listened to what you had to say on our Skype call, you two, I really did. So, if it's okay with Jules, I think she should come back to the farm for those.'

Then I saw something I'd never seen before. Margaret kind of hurled herself at Mum and Mum stood up and grabbed Margaret and they hugged so, so tightly. They made little half-sentences to each other that Ethan and I couldn't really follow and both of them got a bit teary. It seemed to go on forever.

Nobody seemed to need me right then. So I went back to sleep.

I had my surgery that night and went home to the farm the next day. All the flowers made the house look really nice. Which was a good thing, because everybody—it felt like the entire town of Fort Scott—came to visit. Whitney came with her mother, but Madison B came with Pinky and Freddie. Later, Chastity and Madison A came together with Carter. Carter had asked me if I hated Brad and I knew he was there only to ask that... that Brad had sent him.

The last time I'd seen Brad, he had been crying and trying to save my life in the dirt and dust of the pasture. Of course I didn't hate him.

I was laying on the sofa with Thing Two curled up beside me. I reached out my hand and Carter took it. 'Tell Brad,' I said, 'That we'll talk. Later. Maybe a lot later.' And Carter squeezed my hand and thanked me.

I lay there on the sofa every day and people kept coming.

People from the lumberyard and the feed store and the tractor shop and the roadside stand came to see me. The man who nearly hit me when I was on the wrong side of the road came by. Geoffrey came three times.

Everyone brought food—casseroles and loaves of homemade bread, mixed salads and cookies. Mum told me that it was traditional, that they did it so the people with the trouble wouldn't have to cook and would know the community supported them. In England, everyone but the actual family would have given the troubled family space. I guess there, under that big blue sky, space wasn't really an issue.

The owner of the Tasty Queen even packed a root beer float in a frosty glass into a cooler stuffed with ice, covered the top of it in cling film and drove it all the way out to the farm. It had melted just the right amount by the time they gave it to me and it was totally delicious.

I don't think I'd ever felt more appreciated. It was like going to your own funeral or something. Everyone kept saying nice things about me to Mum. It was horribly embarrassing, of course, but it was also really nice.

CHAPTER TWENTY-TWO

It was nice having Mum there, too. Her computer and phone came to live on the end of the dining table. One day I woke up to her speaking urgently in Russian, even before Ethan had made the house smell of coffee. The dogs actually got to know the FedEx driver and stopped barking when he delivered her endless documents.

On the second or third day, in between visits and farm work, we had a big dining table meeting, to work out how Mum and Margaret and Ethan were going to care for me. Mum had originally gone to the Hamptons to talk to Gloria's new employers, who were looking after their children on their own for the summer while Gloria minded the pets in their uptown apartment. The employers had *already* decided to let me stay with Gloria for the rest of the summer, so I could take a couple of masterclasses. When Mum found out I'd been shot, she had just met a sports surgeon at a dinner party at their house. Evidently everybody dropped everything to help—the surgeon interrupted his holiday to fly down with Mum and do the surgery, Gloria's employers insisted I move into their apartment straight away, so that I could go to the sports rehabilitation clinic.

Mum also insisted that I go to see a counsellor that Gloria had found for me. She said I'd been through too much to deal with it all on my own any longer. I started to argue, but both Margaret and Ethan were nodding energetically, so I didn't bother. I still sometimes saw Archie's face. I hadn't told anybody about that. Maybe, I thought, I should.

At the end of August, I'd move into the dormitory at school before Gloria's employers came home to the city—there was just one weekend's difference—and Mum said she'd booked the two of us into a spa she knew about on Long Island for that weekend. When Margaret said it sounded nice, Mum changed the booking to three and my aunt turned pink with pleasure. 'I shouldn't,' she kept saying, 'but I will.'

Mum said she'd visit as often as she could and was going to take all next year's holidays at the farm…she said she'd actually *take* her holidays.

Margaret and Ethan and I looked at each other. We'd believe that when we saw it. Part of me was kind of horrified that I'd have to come back to the farm and deal with the poo and the dirt and the bugs and everything. But part of me felt deeply satisfied about it. I'd wear my big lovely boots some more and Ethan said he'd keep my truck running.

When I said that I was a bit homesick for England, Mum put her hand on my arm and made me look into her eyes. 'You can't have everything,' she said. And then she looked at Ethan. She said, 'Nobody gets *everything*.'

There was this moment when Margaret and I kind of looked at the floor and those two had something private happen between them. But then my mum said, 'Anyway, I'm sure we can work in a week or two in London. Somewhere.'

And Margaret looked right at me and rolled her eyes and I suppose we had a private moment of our very own.

After the meeting, I collapsed back on the sofa, while everyone else got ready for more visitors. I was kind of ready to feel something strong about not moving back to England. But...I didn't. I just...didn't.

I didn't feel any of that, 'Who am I really,' stuff anymore, even though I was *still* kind of exiled and I *still* wasn't one hundred percent sure who my father had been. I played with Thing Two's silky ears while I thought about it. In the end, I decided that who I *was* was a dancer. That Mum was right when she said that I *am* my dancing. As long as I had that, and a family to love me and look after me, I knew enough...I *was* enough.

Thing Two was glued to my side and only left for meals and the morning walk. He had to be scolded to go out and get some fresh air and then, as soon as Margaret's back was turned, he'd sneak in the mudroom flap, hop over the baby gate and lean on my legs some more. The visiting nurse called him 'the patient's representative'.

Ethan kind of grunted when he noticed. 'At least he's good for something,' he said.

Brad's father Wayne came, but he didn't come into the house. He and Ethan just talked outside, walking around the barns and tractors in a big circle. Brad was going to have to go to a hearing. He would probably, Wayne told Ethan, have to go to counselling and do community service. But it might be worse. He might have to go to a juvenile detention centre.

I'd told the police that Brad hadn't meant to shoot me. I'd also had to tell them that the bruises on my arm weren't from Brad and explain about the storm door in the tornado. 'It was the door,' I kept saying and they kept asking if Brad had been shutting my arm in a door. It took forever to get all that straightened out.

However, then they'd asked if Brad had known I was in the pasture. I had to say yes. That was the charge...he'd put me, a minor, into a situation where I could be harmed by a firearm. It didn't evidently matter that he was a minor, too. He'd still broken the law.

I thought about it, lying on the sofa with Thing Two. Brad was like I had been. He couldn't keep going like he'd been going, just like I couldn't. He had to change, too. He really *needed* to change. But it would be harsh. I couldn't help but feel sorry for him. Still, I guessed we all had to have our runt pigs, the things that hurt so badly that they cracked us open.

The man that owned the cow pasture visited, too. He said he'd killed the rattlesnake if I ever wanted to go back and gave me official permission to dance on the old foundation. But without the coyote, there wasn't any point. And I felt bad about the rattlesnake. I started to tell him that I was sorry about the mirror glass and the ironing board and stuff, but Margaret kind of coughed and changed the subject. She told me later she'd already cleared all of that away.

Robbie visited, too. Twice.

The first time, he showed me photographs on his phone.

One of his farm work clients helped him and they'd camped out overnight, following the trail until they saw my coyote.

I saw photos of my coyote's pawprint in the mud around a pond where he'd stopped to drink and photos of where he'd made a little nest in the grass as he'd travelled. I saw photos of rabbit bones and a rather gross gnawed head. I saw photos of his poo, with rabbit fur stuck in it. And I also saw *him*, my coyote, in a group of eight or ten coyotes, including young pups. There was one of him dozing next to another coyote and one of him play-fighting with the puppies. He was over twenty miles away from the cow pasture where he used to live. Now he lived on the edges of the state park. He wasn't safe, Robbie said, but he was about as safe as a coyote could get. It would be a long walk to shoot any of them and most hunters wouldn't think a few pelts were worth it.

It was hard to hand the phone back to Robbie. I didn't have a phone for him to send the photos to, since mine had been blown up by the bullet. Mum had told me my old British phone wouldn't work here, but that I could buy another one in New York. I watched her looking at the photos with her head so close to Robbie's, trying to see if her face showed another clue, but her phone rang and she went back to her makeshift office.

A moment later, she came back with the phone. 'It's Archie.'

Everyone else kind of melted away. Only Thing Two and I were left. I took a deep breath and held the phone to my ear.

'Hey,' I said. 'Sorry I almost killed you.'

I could hear him breathe in. 'I heard you got shot,' he said. 'Couldn't have happened to a nicer person.'

British banter. God. I missed it. I felt tears come to my eyes. I said, 'Yeah, well. I guess it was my charming manner.' There was a television wherever Archie was. I could hear the sound BBC News makes right before the headlines start. I could hear someone calling to someone else.

I listened to England and to Archie breathing. Finally I said, 'Are you okay?'

'Yeah,' Archie said.

'I mean, really,' I said.

'Everything hurts like mad,' he said. 'And I'm going to be spending my summer doing physio. And I think I can kiss a career in rugby goodbye. But yeah, I'm okay, really.' There was a pause. 'How about you?'

'I'm fine,' I said. 'I just have to wait for another ten days and I can start ballet training again.' There was another silence. I don't know why I told him, but I said, 'I keep seeing your face, while you were sliding.'

'What?'

'When I'm trying to go to sleep. When I get upset. About fifty times a day. I remember that night and I see your face.'

He made a kind of 'huh' sound, and then he said, 'Well, it's an adorable face. If you've got to see something.'

And we kind of laughed a little.

'I really am seriously sorry,' I said.

'You had to have things your way,' he said. 'It was easier

to do what you said. You would have just pushed and pushed and pushed at me. I should have said no...but I...I didn't want the hassle.' Archie sounded tired. I looked at the clock. It was only about seven o'clock back home. He must still be feeling ill. He was probably still taking pain medication.

And then what he'd said hit me. I'd pushed and pushed at him. I always had to have my own way.

I sounded...just like Brad. Tears leaked out of my eyes and ran down the back of my throat, as well. 'Oh, Archie,' I said, sadly. 'I'm sorry...about all of it.'

'I miss you, anyway,' Archie said. 'We all do. New York should be good.' He cleared his throat. 'I, uh, won't be going up the Empire State Building.'

We listened to each other again. We'd spent, one way or another, an awful lot of time just sitting next to each other. So I suppose, we were just doing that again. 'Give my love to everyone,' I said. 'I'll have a phone soon. I'll be in touch.' I clicked off.

My nose was running, too. Mum brought me some kitchen roll and Thing Two licked my neck clean.

I'd been such a jerk. My cracked-open bit burned with it. I just lay there and looked at the living-room ceiling and let it burn. It reminded me of the tornado. You had to get somewhere safe and then just wait for it to blow over you. There was nothing else to do.

At dinner that night, Mum said that Archie's mother had

talked to her about the Christmas shopping trip and all of us getting together. Mum said that Sophia and Izzy's mums were thinking about coming, too. Max was meant to go skiing, but Judith said she had a feeling he'd insist on coming, as well.

Margaret didn't even bother to roll her eyes. She just looked at me and I could tell exactly what she thought about teenagers flying across the Atlantic to do their holiday shopping.

When Mum was tucking me into bed, I asked her why she and Margaret were so different. Margaret didn't like the idea of too much travelling and travelling was pretty much all Mum actually *did*. Mum said that Margaret had always been tied to the farm and she'd ended up thinking everyone should be tied somewhere.

And then I asked why Margaret was in the same senior year as her and Mum turned her big blue eyes on me calmly. She said, 'How did you find out about that?'

I got really interested in smoothing out my bedclothes for a moment. 'I can't remember.' There was no way I was going to tell Mum I'd snooped in the yearbook.

'Anyway,' I said into the long silence while my mother looked at the top of my head and I avoided her eye. 'Why was it?'

Mum sighed. When I dared to look, she was staring off towards the wall, as if she could push a window through time and see into the past. 'When your grandfather died,' she said. 'I was fourteen and Margaret was sixteen. Karen was only eight and Jan was ten...'

And then she told me. Margaret had given up school to look after her sisters. She spent three of her teenage years working on the farm and taking care of the other girls. 'I didn't really appreciate it,' Mum said. 'I didn't give her the respect she should have had.' She rolled her eyes. 'And Margaret was pretty mean to me.'

There were about ten million other questions I wanted to ask. Why would you break up with Ethan to go out with Kris? Did Margaret steal your boyfriend? Do you know who Robbie really is? I wasn't going to ask any of it right then. But there was no way I was going to wait until I was eighteen.

Before I left, Robbie came back. He told me he'd got up extra early two mornings before and had hiked back out to the pawprint. He'd pushed a pastry cutter into the earth around the print and had mixed up plaster in a plastic bag and poured it in. Then the evening before last, he'd hiked back out to prise up the plaster with his knife. He unwrapped a red bandana and showed me the rounded bumps of my coyote's paw pad in a perfect circle of white plaster.

I had never touched the coyote, but now I could. I ran my fingers over all the little bumps and hollows of the rough surface of his little paw pad. I could put my finger where the fluffy bits of his fur came through in between his toes. I could even feel his claws, though Robbie told me they were so fragile that the plaster on them probably wouldn't last too long.

Robbie had worked hard to make it—he'd wanted me to always have my coyote with me, even when I was on my way to New York, even before I could get the pictures he'd promised to send me on my new phone.

I hugged him so hard the glue pulled on my wound. I didn't care if he was my brother or my uncle or what he was. He was my Robbie. That's what he was. And I loved him.

I loved it all. All the nice people from town. My new friends. My truck and my aunt and uncle. But I was also happy to be back in touch with Archie. And I was utterly thrilled to be spending the rest of the summer in New York City with Gloria. I'd really missed her.

And civilization.

I thought about it as Mum drove us back to the airport in her rented SUV. Her phone was off and she was listening to a BBC-like radio station that I'd never heard before. She said it was National Public Radio. They were talking about how all matter is made out of recycled atomic particles from the Big Bang. They'd been talking about it for a half an hour and it seemed like they were ready to keep going until the next Big Bang.

I looked out at the land. There were farms and little towns. I saw cow-calf operations, noticed that the wheat crops weren't quite as ripe as we went north, watched a few hay harvests and tried to see what kind of grass they were growing. I looked at the water levels in the creeks and lakes. I imagined how it must have looked when it was all like Margaret and Ethan's favourite hayfield and there were no fences and you could see from one end of the world to the other as you walked through an endless field of flowers.

Just a month or so ago, it had seemed like nothing. And now I felt like I could see just a little of it, and that after next summer, I'd be able to see even more. I felt like it all belonged to me and I belonged to it, too.

My coyote and I had both found new homes. He'd found a new family and I supposed I'd found the family that I'd had all along.

As the tyres and the people on the radio murmured through the miles, I thought about the people on Margaret's dining-room wall. I thought about people in Fort Scott, in London and at school, and about Gloria, and the people I would get to know in New York. I thought about how we were all caught up in a giant dance of each other's lives, meeting and parting endless times.

We were, all of us, just moving our bodies around, moving and moving, because we were alive, because we could. We were using atoms that had belonged to other things, other people, other animals . . . even stars. We were using DNA from our ancestors to put the atoms into place, but we weren't really solid. We were really mostly open bits, just like the sky. We kept endlessly leaking things and taking things into ourselves and moving around. The whole planet was dancing—a dance that never ended.

I thought all that out in my head. Then I turned to my mother, to tell her what I'd been thinking.

And she shut off the radio and listened to me.

Acknowledgements

Many thanks to Clare Whitston, Liz Cross and to Elv Moody for her inspiration and patience. OUP are the best publishers ever, ever, ever. Every bit of their process is done with love and care.

Thank you, too, to Sophie Gorell-Barnes and everyone at MBA Literary Agency. And to my friend and speaking agent, Karen Cooper, I send my utter admiration and thanks. I would never be able to visit so many schools without her help.

Bath Spa University and the Royal Literary Fund supported me with writer-friendly work throughout the writing of this novel and I am very grateful. I am also grateful for the fellowship and stimulation of colleagues at Bath Spa and the Journalism department of Cardiff University.

My writing group are...well...brilliant. Tanya Appatu, Victoria Finlay, Emma Geen, Susan Jordan, Sophie McGovern, Peter Reason and Jane Shemilt.

My amazing husband and daughter, Andy and Olivia Wadsworth, don't just make my writing possible, they make my *life* possible. My mother, Katy Beard, has always allowed me to run free and have adventures, bless her.

My extended family are remarkable people. They've provided the setting and inspiration for this story and are a never-ending source of inspiration, love, help and humour. I might not be here today without them...and

I certainly would not be writing books. Some of them are: Kim, Hope, Barbara, Bryan, Jan, Dan, Mike, Peggy, Shon, Jackie, Jess, Bridget, Brandan, Margie, and Christine...there are literally dozens more and they know I love them all. I also have an adopted extended family: the Strongs; Joan, David, Annemarie as well as Sue and Tom Yates.

And my friends are...well, pretty wonderful. They put up with my poor communication skills, my frequent extended absences and my popping up and demanding them at inconvenient intervals. Shout out especially to Alison, Sam and Deidre.

To dog-walkers Roger, Jess and Karen and to my cleaning whiz Jean, I owe hours and hours of writing time. Thanks for not telling anyone when I'm still in my dressing-gown in the afternoons or about the state of my bedroom.

And then there's my readers...thank you. Thank you all very much.

About the author

© Olivia Wadsworth

Mimi Thebo was born in America – her cousin's farm is the setting for this story. Her books have been translated into nine languages, signed for deaf children and adapted for a BAFTA award-winning film.

Ready for more great stories? Try one of these ...

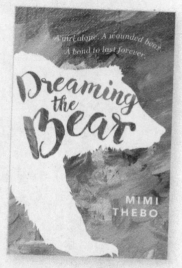